Midsummer magic

JULIA WILLIAMS

A V O N

This novel is entirely a work of fiction.
The names, characters and incidents portrayed in it are
the work of the author's imagination. Any resemblance to
actual persons, living or dead, events or localities is
entirely coincidental.

AVON
A division of HarperCollins*Publishers*
77–85 Fulham Palace Road,
London W6 8JB

www.harpercollins.co.uk

A Paperback Original 2013

1

Copyright © Julia Williams 2013

Julia Williams asserts the moral right to
be identified as the author of this work

A catalogue record for this book is
available from the British Library

ISBN-13: 9781847563576

Set in Minion Pro by Palimpsest Book Production Limited
Falkirk, Stirlingshire

Printed and bound in Great Britain by
Clays Ltd, St Ives plc

MIX
Paper from
responsible sources
FSC™ C007454

FSC™ is a non-profit international organisation established to promote
the responsible management of the world's forests. Products carrying the
FSC label are independently certified to assure consumers that they come
from forests that are managed to meet the social, economic and
ecological needs of present and future generations,
and other controlled sources.

Find out more about HarperCollins and the environment at
www.harpercollins.co.uk/green

For Dot with love and gratitude

Prologue

'Thou speakest aright:
I am that merry wanderer of the night.
I jest to Oberon and make him smile'
　　　A Midsummer Night's Dream: Act II, Scene 1

'"Lord what fools these mortals be . . ." *You could say*
that's my mantra. It's easy to hypnotise the gullible, but
I've managed to hypnotise sceptics too. I like to think
Shakespeare knew a thing or two about hypnotism.'
　　　Freddie Puck interviewed in The *Sun*, June 1982

1982: Tatiana

'You're late,' Freddie Puck was standing languidly by the stage door, as Tatiana came flying down the street straight from dinner with her agent, Susan Peasebottom, where she'd both eaten and drunk more then she should have. He was smoking a cigarette, and as usual, looked calm and in control. She hated the way he always did that; she always felt ill at ease around Freddie, as if he knew a secret about her that she did not. But then that was part of what he did, play mind games on people to screw them up.

'You're lucky I'm here at all,' she muttered. After the offer Susan had put to her this evening, she had been very tempted not to turn up.

Freddie looked her up and down quizzically – honestly, sometimes she felt like she was just a lump of meat to him.

'You done something to your hair?'

Tatiana blushed. She wasn't sure about her new haircut, a drastic departure from the Farrah look she'd been sporting for the last couple of years. Her hairdresser, Julie, had produced an article from an American mag which pronounced that long flickbacks were out, short was in, and hair for some reason should be red. So Tatiana had been persuaded to have it dyed, trimmed and hacked, so now she had a longish piece at the back, but the hair at the top was cut short and swept back in waves – or it had done when she'd come out of the salon this afternoon. After a couple of hours in a smoky dive with Susan Peasebottom, followed by an undignified race up the road, Tatiana felt sure her hair wasn't quite the crowning glory the article had promised.

'Yes,' she mumbled, almost wishing he hadn't noticed.

'Nice,' said Freddie, nonchalantly flicking out his ash as she walked past him into the theatre, and as usual she had no way of knowing whether he really meant it, or whether he was just kidding her.

'Tati, darling, love the hair!' Damn. Bron came out of his dressing room (it still irked her that he had his own dressing room, while she had to share) and gave her a hug. 'How was dinner?'

'Great,' said Tati, hoping he hadn't noticed the slight flinch as he touched her. It was still the same between them. It was. She kept telling herself that. She had to believe it.

'Any news?' he said lightly. She'd let slip there might be something, now she wished she hadn't. She wanted time to work out what she was going to do.

'There might be a part in a soap coming up,' she said.

'A soap?' Bron's face was almost comic in his dismay. 'You can't do a soap, darling, Tati, you can't. It's selling out.'

The frustration spilled out of her.

'And this? This isn't selling out?' she said. 'Freddie bloody Puck's promises won't pay the rent.'

'He's in talks with a TV production company,' said Bron, 'it's only a matter of time . . .'

Tati put her hands up, 'I don't want to hear it,' she said. 'Freddie's always in sodding talks with a TV company. This is *real*, Bron. I want you to be happy for me.'

Bron slumped, and gave her the sad look she'd seen too

much of late. 'But what about us?' he said. 'What about our plans?'

'I know, we'll have our own theatre company,' she said. She'd heard it too many times before. 'Perhaps I had plans too, but we all know what happened to *them*.'

She couldn't disguise the bitterness in her voice.

'Tati,' said Bron, there were tears in his eyes, 'You know I'm sorry –'

'Don't.' Tati looked at him sadly. 'It's too late for all that. I have to think about the future now.'

'We both do,' said Bron, reaching out and holding her hands. 'Come on, Tati, we're still young, I still want to do Shakespeare with you. One day . . .'

'Maybe I can't wait for one day anymore.'

She'd said it. Words that she'd never wanted to say, and when she saw how Bron slumped even more, she wished them back. 'Look,' she said, letting go of his hands gently, 'I'm late, we've got a show to do. We'll talk about this later.'

Giving him a swift kiss and a hug, she left him in the corridor and went to get ready, her thoughts churning. Susan's offer was tempting, but was it the right thing to do?

As usual, it was squashed in the girls' dressing room. Bron didn't have this problem in his single dressing room, thought Tatiana bitterly as she found her dressing table in the corner. Naturally the *male* star of the show couldn't slum it like she did. She was so mixed up. She loved Bron, she really did, but she hated this, and it wasn't fair. Someone had laughingly written 'Star' in lipstick on her mirror. Ha, bloody ha. The joke was certainly on her, she thought sourly as she sat herself down, and with the practice of an old hand started to apply her stage make-up.

The room was hot and crowded, and full of the noise of

women's chatter. Like so many cheeping hens, Tatiana thought bitchily. She was more of a man's woman. Women and their idle talk bored her. Which didn't make for popularity among her peer group, but Tatiana didn't really care. This batch of hens was even duller than most, so she didn't feel she was missing out. They were the backstage chorus dancing to Freddie Puck's tune, as all of them were on this *Illusions* tour. As she was. As Bron was.

She sighed and looked at herself in the mirror. Pushing twenty-five and was this all there was to offer? She thought again about the deal on the table, and felt her stomach churn. It was all very well for Bron to tell her to be patient, that Freddie's incessant talks with production companies about a TV series of *Illusions* would eventually come to fruition, but she couldn't see it herself.

Tatiana scrutinised her face. Still pretty, she judged – pretty enough to do what she had to do in Bron's show, at any rate. But for how long? This was a cruel business for a woman. Twenty-five wasn't far from thirty. Then what would happen to her? When she and Bron had started out, he'd promised her an equal part in the act; equal shares in the profits, and then, when they could afford it, their own theatre company, Shakespeare, *proper* acting. So how come it was still her looking decorative and pretty, Bron taking all the credit, the gasps and plaudits from the crowd, as he performed yet another incredible trick? If she hadn't been so damned in thrall to Bron . . .

They'd met as extras in rep, doing Shakespeare in dreary towns to uninterested punters. It had been a far cry from her drama school ambition to play Juliet at Stratford, and the only bright spot had been Bron, with his lean handsome look and sardonic manner. They had laughed their way through most of the misery of the tour, and he'd taught her

6

card tricks and outlined his twin obsessions of magic and owning his own theatre company. When, after the tour was over, he rang her to say he and his friend Freddie had got a gig doing a magic show in Brighton, it had seemed like a lifeline. Regular money, regular work. After months of scrabbling to pay the rent, it was an easy option. It had always been meant to be temporary – Bron was never going to give up on his theatre plans, but as time went on, they seemed to recede into the distance. And now Tati often found herself wondering if he still wanted it as much as he said he did.

Tatiana formed a cupid's bow, and painted her lips bright red in a fury. With her green and blue sparkly eye shadow, over-blushed cheeks, and the new haircut (which despite her best efforts didn't look anything like the photo Julie had shown her), she looked like a painted doll. Which is all she was. Being pretty and decorative was all she was good for. Unless . . .

Unless she took the offer. She hadn't been quite straight with Bron. It wasn't just any old soap: she'd been offered the leading role in a new soap opera the Beeb had just commissioned. Susan thought she should; couldn't understand her hesitation. 'You don't want to be doing this forever do you?' she'd said with uncharacteristic honesty. Tatiana knew she was right. So why was she still hesitating? Misguided loyalty to Bron was what Susan had called it. But, Bron and her . . . a future without him was unthinkable, even after what had happened. She pulled on her spandex bodysuit, wincing as she realised how tight it was getting. She still hadn't managed to shed all her excess weight. Even Bron had noticed and Freddie had made sarky comments too. All the time she was getting older and fatter and there were any amount of silly hens in this hen coop desperate to take her place.

So why don't you let them?

As Tatiana stood waiting in the wings for the fanfare which heralded her arrival on stage, the thought came to her more strongly than ever. As she let Bron tie her up, throw knives at her, try to cut her in two, and pull hankies out of her ear, while she span and danced like a pretty doll around him, with the same fixed grin on her face, she felt her strongest urge yet to leave. What was there for her here now? She and Bron were growing apart, she could feel it. She knew Bron was hurting too, but what had happened was forming an insurmountable barrier between them. And Freddie was too much of an influence not to suggest she was replaced when she got too fat, too wrinkly, too old.

At the climax of Bron's act, he produced doves out of a hat, which flew onto Tatiana. As she paraded round the stage (hating what she did with a passion) the bird that had landed on her head shat on her.

In that instant her decision was made. Susan was right. She could do much better than this.

'Sorry babes, about Henrietta,' Bron said as they came off the stage. Bron had the absurd habit of naming all his birds. 'Hope your new hairdo can stand it.' He laughed, and Freddie, who was standing with him, laughed too. Tati was enraged, it was as if their earlier conversation had never taken place.

'My hair, yes,' said Tatiana. 'Me, no.'

'Sorry?' Bron looked confused.

'That's it,' she said. 'It's the last straw. Tomorrow I sign up for *Sail for the Sun*. I'm going to be on the TV.'

'What about the act?' said Bron, aghast.

'What about it?' said Tatiana. 'You don't need me. You just need a pretty face. Well Auberon Fanshawe, I'm tired of being your Debbie McGee. I'm better than that.'

8

With that, she turned and left the theatre, without even taking her make-up off.

She'd done it. She was free. And a shining future beckoned.

Halloween

'Combining your moving-in party with a Halloween one was a brilliant idea,' declared Diana. She looked gorgeous as ever, in a little black dress which accentuated her curves, her auburn hair piled high on her head, with some fetching curls escaping, as she bustled round Josie's kitchen. From the lounge – which they'd spent the afternoon decorating with wispy bits of cobweb, spiders dangling from the ceiling, flashing skull-shaped lights and pumpkin-shaped candles – came a loud set of expletives, as Harry tried to plug in various bits of electrical equipment to make a sound system any nightclub would have been proud of, but which Josie was somewhat doubtful was needed in a small London flat on a Saturday night.

'I seem to remember it was more your idea,' laughed Josie, as she got out plastic cups and put them on the kitchen drainer with the copious amounts of wine and beer that Harry had cheerily brought back from Sainsburys. 'Josie, it's so fab that you and Harry are moving in together, why don't you have a party?' she mimicked. 'Josie, Halloween's coming up, you can combine them, wouldn't that be *amazing*!'

'Well if I left it up to you, you'd have just snuck in here like a pair of sneak thieves, as if you were embarrassed about the whole thing, rather than celebrating the wonderfulness of you two becoming a proper partnership,' declared Diana. 'Honestly, I don't know what you'd do without me.'

'Er, get on with my life without being bossed about?' said Josie, and ducked as Diana chucked some peanuts in her direction.

'I can only hope Harry's more domesticated than you are,' said Diana. 'I don't know how you'll manage to keep this place clean without my help.'

Until recently Diana had been renting Josie's spare room, but when it became clear that Harry was becoming a permanent fixture, she'd tactfully moved out to live with friends down the road. 'Three is definitely a crowd,' she'd said, 'and I don't fancy being a gooseberry to you two lovebirds.'

'I miss this,' said Josie, 'are you sure you're okay about leaving?'

Di had been incredibly positive and supportive since Josie had first broached the awkward subject of Harry moving in, but Josie knew how good she was at covering up her emotions. Di didn't have a huge social network, didn't get on immensely well with her family, and for all her playing the 'I love being single' card, Josie had the sneaking suspicion that she was secretly yearning to settle down herself.

'Of course I am,' said Diana, 'I mean, it is bloody annoying being best friends with someone as pretty, rich and successful as you are, who's managed to nab a gorgeous man to boot, but I'll survive.'

'Oh, Diana, now I feel terrible,' said Josie, giving her friend a hug.

'It was a *joke*, Josie,' said Diana affectionately. 'You are so gullible.'

'Still,' said Josie wistfully, 'it's not going to be the same now, is it?'

Josie had met Di five years earlier, through a mutual friend, Carrie, who worked with Josie and had been to school with Di. They both quickly decided they didn't like Carrie as much as they did each other. They'd started meeting once a week for drinks, and soon it had turned into regular weekends on the pull – Diana's confidence taking Josie places she would never have been alone. Without Diana pushing her, Josie doubted she would have followed up Harry's tentative calls when they'd first met up again. It was no good, happy as she was, Josie was going to miss sparky, lively Diana, who called a spade a spade and always let you know when you were in the wrong, but was also an incredibly loyal, fun friend.

'No, it won't,' said Diana, 'but it will be different. And that's good too.'

She was being so positive about it, Josie hoped she wasn't protesting too much.

'And you really don't mind?'

'Don't be daft, of course I don't,' said Diana, 'I'm happy for you. You and Harry are made for each other. Now what else do we need to do? How's the punch?'

Josie looked at the punch into which Harry had cheerfully flung a bottle of vodka, copious amounts of red wine, and not nearly enough orange juice, in Josie's opinion. It seemed to be a bit lacking in the fruit department, and they'd run out of oranges. 'What do you think about this punch? Does it need more fruit?'

'Haven't you got any more apples?' said Diana. 'It's Halloween, you have to have apples. It's the law.'

'I think I might still have some left in the cupboard,' said Josie.

She rummaged around, and then produced a couple of rather wrinkled-looking apples.

'Great,' said Diana, 'here, let me peel them.'

'Why?' said Josie.

'Because . . .' said Diana. 'It's Halloween and you need to see the name of the man you're going to marry . . . which will begin with H, obviously.'

Despite her straight talking and often cynical nature, Diana was extremely superstitious, always walking round a ladder, and freaking out if a black cat strolled across her path.

She grabbed one of the apples from Josie and peeled it with a flourish.

'Now,' she instructed, 'you have to fling it over your shoulder, and it should fall in the shape of the letter that begins the name of your future husband.'

'What are you talking about?' said Josie.

'Famous Halloween tradition, young maids did it all the time in olden days, don't you know *anything*?' Diana was a force to be reckoned with so, feeling incredibly foolish, Josie threw the apple peel over her shoulder. It landed with a plop on the floor, and despite herself Josie turned round to see what the result was.

'Knew it was stupid,' she said, 'look, it's formed the letter A. I don't know anyone whose name begins with A, apart from Harry's mate Ant, and I'm hardly going to marry him.'

'Oh,' said Diana, looking a bit despondent. 'I can't believe it hasn't worked.'

'Come on, Di, you can't believe all that mumbo jumbo,' said Josie, laughing. She could never get over how gullible Di could be.

'Well, you never know, Halloween is a strange time of year,' said Diana. 'I just think there are things out there we know nothing about.'

'Go on then, you have a go,' said Josie indulgently.

Diana peeled the other apple and with a great sense of drama, slowly threw it behind her shoulder. This time the apple peel landed with a more definite thud, and split into three pieces which, if you were being very imaginative, may just have formed the letter H.

'Well that's not right, either,' said Diana, 'the only H I know is Harry.'

'There you go,' said Josie, 'I knew it was daft. Besides, I'm not marrying Harry just yet. Without your help I'd never have persuaded him to move in here. I might just get him convinced about marrying me in the next decade.'

'Get me convinced of what?' Harry came into the kitchen holding a pair of leads and looking a bit bemused. Josie's heart did the little leap it always did when she saw him. Lovely dependable Harry, with his brilliant blue eyes, curly black hair and cute smile. It made her feel warm all over thinking they were now a proper item again. They had first met at university, although Josie might never have paid much attention to the quiet studious boy on her course if he hadn't tagged along on a group weekend away at her parents' home in Cornwall. When he was the only person who was prepared to go and watch Shakespeare with her on a rainy summer's night at the local open air theatre she knew he was special. And for a while there it looked like they might go the distance, then time and space and work intervened and somehow they lost touch. It still seemed such luck not only to have met Harry again at Amy's wedding, but for him to have still remembered, and (apparently) thought about her, just as she'd thought about him over the years. In one way their relationship had been a whirlwind, they'd only been 'together' properly for a few months, but in other ways it felt like she was coming home. Harry in her mind had always been the one who got away.

'I think I'm going to have to head out to B&Q to find another lead,' he said, 'there's a connection I'm missing.'

'Nothing,' said Josie, digging Diana in the ribs and glaring at her to stop her spilling the beans. But as usual it did no good.

'Josie's been doing an old Halloween trick of seeing the name of the man she'll marry,' said Diana. 'She threw a piece of apple peel over her shoulder, and look, it fell down in the shape of the letter H. I wonder what that could mean?'

Josie felt herself blush deeply. Marriage was something she wanted with Harry, of course it was, but given how fast they'd moved so far, she thought marriage might be rushing things a bit. She wanted him to ask her in his own way, at the right time.

Harry peered at the floor, 'Are you sure that's an H?' he said. 'What about that one?'

'Oh, that was my turn,' lied Diana glibly. 'I got an A.'

'Ah, shame Ant's still in Oz, otherwise I'd introduce you,' said Harry with a grin.

'Ant? You want to inflict Ant on my best friend?' said Josie as she swept the peel away. 'It's all foolish nonsense anyway. As if an apple peel can tell you who you're going to marry.'

'As if indeed,' said Harry, but he looked thoughtful as he picked up the car keys and left the room.

'There, he's going to ask you now,' Diana teased her, 'sure as eggs is eggs. Did you see the look on his face?'

'Don't you *ever* stop interfering?' said Josie, blushing. 'He'll ask me if and when he's good and ready.'

'Well, there's no harm in pushing him along a bit,' said Diana. 'You know you two are made for each other. You just need a little help from Cupid's arrow, that's all.'

*　　*　　*

'What was all that about?' Harry muttered to himself as he got in the car and drove the short distance to B&Q. One of the most restful things about being with Josie was that she had never ever mentioned the 'M' word. Not that Harry was against the idea, but things had already moved faster then he'd anticipated, and he wasn't in a hurry to get married. Indeed, his best friend, Ant, had laughed like a drain when he found out that Harry was even contemplating moving in with Josie.

'You are joking?' he'd said over the phone, when Harry had tracked him down to a bar in Australia to tell him the good news. 'Before you know it, you'll have his 'n' hers slippers and she'll be walking you down the aisle. And then it will be only a matter of time before she starts mentioning babies, and your life will effectively be over. Don't do it, mate. You'll really live to regret it.'

Knowing that he really wouldn't regret it, or at least regret taking the first step of sharing a home with Josie, allowed Harry to pass off Ant's teasing in a good-humoured fashion. 'You're only saying that because you're a jealous saddo who doesn't have a clue how to attract, let alone keep a beautiful woman,' he joshed back. 'Women, beware, Ant's here.'

Ant had always had plenty of women, but no one serious, apart from one mysterious relationship after uni, which he rarely mentioned, but had clearly left a scar.

'Your funeral, mate,' said Ant. 'Don't say I didn't warn you.'

Ant, who was currently taking the gap year he'd been threatening ever since before he and Harry had been students, had sent him a very rude Facebook message when he found out that Harry actually had gone the whole hog and was going 'all domesticated', as he put it.

Harry didn't happen to think Ant was right. Sure, when they were young guns straight out of college there had been a certain cachet in seeing who got the most women – getting any women at all had been Harry's main aim when he'd arrived at university, in the autumn of the millennium – but once Harry met Josie again at a mutual friend's wedding, nights on the pull had definitely lost their charm. It hadn't taken long for Harry to realise he'd fallen swiftly, deeply, irrevocably in love. He and Josie had got together at the end of university, and he'd always regretted letting her get away. He'd never been quite sure how it had happened, but he and Josie had been together such a briefly short time, and once they went to work – him to a small local newspaper in Newcastle, her to be a marketing assistant in a factory in Swindon – things had fizzled out. He had always thought he should have fought harder to keep her. So now they had found each other again, nothing was going to keep them apart. However much Ant might bitch about it, no amount of teasing would change his mind.

But . . . marriage? Harry thought about it as he scanned the electrical shelves in B&Q for the right scart lead, wishing, not for the first time, that manufacturers would just make a universal lead which adapted to fit every bit of electronic equipment it seemed necessary for a modern man to have in his possession. Were he and Josie ready for that? He had to admit to a certain amount of relief and pleasure when they'd made the decision to move in together. No longer the need to be out there in the savage forest of dating; time to hang up his spurs, sit by the fire, and sip wine with his one true love. Simples, as the meerkats would say, but true.

Eventually buying two leads, certain that one of them would fit, Harry made his way back home, where he found

Josie and Diana already giggly, having tried out his punch to 'see that it was strong enough', according to Diana, although Josie was worried it had too much vodka. 'Nonsense!' said Diana, 'you can never have too much vodka!' and promptly poured the remaining half of the bottle Harry had resisted pouring in before. Diana was a whirlwind. One he quite liked, he thought, but so different from Josie, Harry sometimes wondered how they could be friends. She was vivacious, lively, pretty and incredibly flirty: like a female version of Ant, a good-time girl out on the pull. She often gave off a tough vibe, but underneath it all Harry suspected she hid a vulnerability she wasn't prepared to let most people see. And she liked him and seemed genuinely happy for them both. Harry had a huge soft spot for her.

Josie poured some more orange juice into the punch, while Diana answered the door to their first guests. Once Harry had sorted out the music, the next few hours went by in a blur of congratulations, drinking and laughter. By midnight, Harry was feeling distinctly the worse for wear, and sitting happily ensconced on the sofa, watching Josie dance to the dulcet tones of Lady Gaga. He could sit and watch her dance for hours, she moved so gracefully, it was mesmerising. He was so lucky to have her. Josie was so beautiful, and kind, and wonderful. And she was his . . . sometimes he couldn't quite believe it.

Maybe it *was* time to make things more permanent between them.

Someone had put something slower on, and a few of their friends were cosying up together – Diana, he noticed with amusement, was smooching with Josie's boss – 'Come on, lover boy,' Josie came swaying towards him, as drunk, he realised, as he was, 'time to dance.'

'Always time to dance with you,' he smiled, and pulled her close. She leant against his shoulder, and he felt her softness, and smelt her perfume. He was suddenly overcome with a dizzying sense of what could only be described as joy. He wanted to hold her and keep her and never let her go. 'You are so perfect,' he said, kissing her softly on the lips, 'how did I get this lucky?'

Josie blushed, and said, 'I'm the lucky one,' as she kissed him back, and he was overcome with a happiness he could never remember feeling before. With her small trim figure, her gorgeous fair pre-Raphaelite curls, and her stunning blue eyes, Josie was perfect in every way. She was kind, sweet, funny, loyal and he already knew he wanted to spend the rest of his life with her. So why not make it formal? What was wrong with marriage, after all? A perfectly sensible institution which had been round for centuries.

'Josie,' he said, feeling his heart hammering with happiness, 'will you marry me?'

'Oh my God, Oh my God!' An overexcited and slightly pissed Josie dragged Diana away from a rather interesting situation with Josie's to-die-for good-looking boss, Philip (trust Josie to nab a lovely guy *and* have a good-looking boss) into the kitchen. 'It worked, I can't believe it, but it worked.'

'What worked?' Josie wasn't the only one who'd drunk too much, Diana realised, as the walls came crashing in on her suddenly. 'What are you talking about?'

'Your Halloween thing,' said Josie, 'you know, the apple peel.'

Diana dragged herself away from the delicious prospect of a night in a penthouse with Philip, to focus on a faint memory of the early evening. 'But you got an A!'

'No I didn't,' said Josie, 'I got an H, remember? Ta-da!'

She waved her ring finger in front of Diana's bleary eyes. There was a platinum-looking ring on it.

'What? He didn't?'

'Yup, Harry just proposed!' said Josie triumphantly. 'Of course we need to get a proper ring, but this will do for now.'

On closer inspection, Diana realised Josie was wearing the ring pull from a Coke can on her finger.

'That's, that's – words fail me,' Diana suddenly felt the urgent need to sit down, and slumped against the wall and slid down it. She wanted to say something more effusive, but somehow the words wouldn't come.

'I know,' said Josie, sliding down to join her, 'and it's all down to you. You *are* going to be my bridesmaid, aren't you?'

Diana screamed in delight.

'You're getting married!' she whooped, 'and I'm going to be bridesmaid. That is fabulous!' *Fabulous*. That was the word she'd been searching for.

'I know!' said Josie, 'isn't it great?'

Diana suddenly felt a sudden, sober chill. It was great, of course it was great, but drunken misery set in, 'What about u-u-uss?' she wailed. 'You're going off to get married and you'll be shacked up and happy and I'll be on my own and single for ever!'

Great sloppy tears were running down her cheeks. Damn, that punch had been a serious mistake.

'Oh, Di, don't say that,' said Josie, clutching her in panic, 'you're my best friend, I couldn't live without you.'

She was crying too.

'You couldn't?' Diana paused and blew her nose, not very

attractively. She hoped Philip didn't choose that particular moment to look for her.

'Of course not,' said Josie, sobbing nearly as loudly as Di was, 'you're always going to be my best friend. What would I do without you?'

'But it's not going to be the sa-aa-me,' hiccoughed Diana.

'It will, it will,' said Josie, 'pinkie promise.'

She linked her little finger in Diana's, setting off a fresh round of wailing, 'Oh, that's so lovely,' she wept, 'I love you so much.'

'And I love you too,' howled Josie, hugging her tightly.

'But you love Harry more,' said Diana.

'I do,' said Josie, her eyes shining through her tears, 'I really do.'

Diana looked around her, suddenly surprised that they were sitting on the floor.

'Then what are we doing sitting here?' she said. '*You're* getting married. That is *so* fantastic. C'me on, let's dance!'

She staggered up, dragging Josie after her, and went to find Harry who was sitting looking slightly dazed in the corner, 'Woohoo, you two getting married, that is so brilliant! Listen up, everyone, Harry and Josie have just got engaged!'

'This calls for champagne!' someone shouted.

'We don't have any,' laughed Josie, 'we'll have to make do with vodka.'

'Vodka it is!' said Diana. She busied herself filling people's glasses, and then declared a toast, 'To Harry and Josie!' she said. 'Harry and Josie!' everyone said, raising their glasses and cheering, and the next half hour disappeared in a flurry of congratulations and back slapping. It was only as the party began to die to down that Diana remembered Philip.

She looked round for him and couldn't see him anywhere. Sneaky bastard. A bleep from her phone confirmed it. *Sorry, had to dash. Catch you soon?* This year, next year, sometime, never. She looked over at Josie caught in a romantic clinch with her future husband, and tried not to feel that she was getting left behind.

In a bar in Australia, Anthony Lambert, known to his friends as Ant, opened his laptop and checked his emails. He'd sent a rude message to his best friend, Harry, the previous day in response to the dire (in Ant's mind at least) news that he was settling down and moving in with his girlfriend, Josie, after a ridiculously whirlwind romance lasting a few short months. Ant had been horrified, not least because at twenty-eight the notion of settling down seemed as far removed as it had when he'd first met Harry at uni ten years ago, but also because Harry had already dated Josie back then, and they'd lost touch. If she was so great, why hadn't they stuck together before? Hmm? Ant's motto was always look forward, never look back. He felt sure that Harry was making a big mistake, and had told him so in so many words. Well. Very few words actually. It had been more along the lines of *What are you doing you stupid bastard? I thought Josie was all in the past?*

It seemed Harry had been remarkably swift in his reply. Their correspondence while Ant had been away had been in the main, short and sweet, and they'd often been known to go weeks without hearing from one another. It was only the imperative need to tell his best friend not make a complete dickhead of himself which had impelled Ant to write yesterday.

From: Harry@gmail.com
To: Antonhistravels@gmail.com

Hi mate,
1 I hope you're sitting down . . .

2 And I hope you are in a bar . . .

3 And I also hope you have a drink in your hand . . .

What the . . .? Ant had a sip of his beer, and scrolled down to the bottom of the email where he read words which caused him to nearly spill his drink. He had to reread in case he'd got it wrong, but no, there it was in black and white.

I know you're not going to like this, mate, but it's my life.
So . . . the big news is Josie and I are getting married. Next year, September, we think.
I know, I know. It's sudden. And I'm going to have to put off travelling for a bit. But . . . I let her get away once. I'm not going to make that mistake again. Try to be happy for us.
Harry.
P.S. We'd like you to be best man.

Best man. Harry wanted him to be best man? Could it get any worse?

'Fuck me sideways,' said Ant out loud. 'I think it's time I went home.'

Part One

There May I Marry Thee

'Four days will quickly steep themselves in night
Four nights will quickly dream away the time . . .'
        A Midsummer Night's Dream: Act I, Scene 1

'Magic tricks are all about dissembling. Distract the
punter with your voice, or a bit of stage business, and
they miss the actual trick itself. It's easy when you know
how.'

Freddie Puck: *The Art of Illusion*

Chapter One

'Is that the lot?' said Harry as he paused to take a breather. Though early in the morning, the June sun was already hot and he was already working up a sweat. He looked on in horror as Josie, still somehow looking cool and collected in a strappy summer dress and sandals, came down the flat steps, with the second large holdall she had apparently packed for a simple weekend away. 'How long are we planning to be away again?'

'This one isn't mine, it's Di's,' said Josie. Di had come to stay the night before, terrified of oversleeping on her own. 'And before you start bitching about how Diana always takes advantage of me, she's bringing her bigger one.'

'She's got a bigger bag than *this*?' Harry said as he took the bag from Josie, and tried to squeeze a space for it in the not-too-huge boot of his Honda Civic. A car that, not unnaturally, Ant had sneered at very loudly, as being 'a girl's car.' Sometimes Harry wished Ant would keep his opinions to himself. But there was no chance of that. Ant, back from his travels, was louder and more opinionated than ever since his time away. It hadn't taken him long to be employed by a flash advertising company ('Recession, what recession?' he'd queried) with more cash than sense and was driving down alone in his brand new top of the range Merc. He

27

was planning to meet them at a motorway service station en route, as, hilariously for Ant who was always overconfident, he appeared to have had an attack of nerves at the thought of arriving before them and meeting Josie's parents on his own.

'I don't think I'm going to be able to fit this all in,' said Harry, looking despairing as Diana, her ginger curls escaping from a straggly bun, tottered down the steps in high wedges, skinny jeans which accentuated every curve and a skimpy top which left nothing to the imagination, dragging an even bigger and more cumbersome bag behind her.

'Di, you're going to have to have your bag in the back with you,' said Josie when she realised that there really was no more room in the boot. 'Either that, or we'll ring Ant up to see if he can take you in his car.'

'No, it's okay,' said Diana as she squashed herself into the back, complete with the offending bag. 'Ant's an unusual name.'

'It's short for Anthony,' said Harry, 'though sometimes he goes by the name of Tony.'

'I knew a Tony once, he was a total wanker. What's yours like?'

'A total wanker,' said Josie, and Harry dug her in the ribs. 'Well, he is,' she protested, 'as far as women are concerned. He's charming and witty and funny of course, but I wouldn't trust him as far as I can throw him.'

'He's not that bad,' protested Harry half-heartedly as he started up the car.

'He so is,' said Josie. 'Don't you remember Suzie at uni? Poor cow was so in love with Ant, and I lost count of the number of girls he cheated on her with. And still she came back for more.'

'I'd forgotten about her,' said Harry.

'Then there was the time we were out for my birthday and he started the evening with one girl and went home with another.'

'Oh, God, and the time we met him at the cinema and he pretended not to see us because he was with the wife of the local landlord,' said Harry. 'I'd forgotten all that. But you never know. Maybe he's changed since he's been away.'

'I doubt it,' said Josie. 'He hasn't stopped sulking since you asked him to be best man. Anyone would think you were committing suicide the way he goes on about the fact that you're getting married.'

'Well, to Ant, marriage *is* a form of suicide,' said Harry, as he turned left out of their road and headed for the main road which led to the motorway. 'I can't see him ever getting hitched. He'll be trying to pull birds when he's old and grey.'

'Birds,' groaned Diana. 'Does he really use the word birds?'

'Afraid so,' said Josie, 'but it's all right, he doesn't bite, honest.'

'To be fair to him,' said Harry, 'I think there was someone after uni he was quite serious about, and she ditched him. He's always been really cagey about it, but I think she really hurt him.'

'Well then, maybe it's time he got over it,' said Diana.

'Perhaps you can help,' said Josie slyly.

'Don't look at me,' said Di firmly, 'he really doesn't sound like my type.'

Within half an hour they were on the motorway and heading down to Cornwall, to Josie's parents, where Josie's mum was indulging in a spot of pre-wedding hysteria. After much dithering, Harry and Josie had only recently fixed the date for next June. They'd talked vaguely about September when they first got engaged, but it turned out getting married was like planning a military operation and no one in their right minds would attempt to organise a wedding in such a short space of time. Harry, who'd been hoping for something small and quiet, was beginning to realise his wishes were unlikely to be met. Josie's mum, Nicola, had firmly taken charge since Christmas, and now most of their spare time seemed to be taken up with wedding plans. Harry was beginning to find it a little wearing.

Nicola had insisted on having a long weekend with Josie, Harry, the best man (Ant, naturally) and bridesmaid (Diana, of course), to plan things. Quite why he and Ant were needed was a mystery to Harry. So far his input into preparations was to have been told things, like what he had to wear (morning suit, top hat, and pink ties – Josie was very insistent on the pink) – who he was inviting ('we get twenty-five friends each and twenty-five family, or in my case, forty family and twenty friends, as I have more family'), and where the event was going to take place ('St Cuthbert's of course,' Josie's mum opined, 'it's where we got married, and Josie was christened, and Reverend Paul has known her since she was little, so it's perfect').

Just recently, the tone of the long phone conversations Josie was having with her mum seemed to have ratcheted up a notch. Having read in a magazine that it was all the rage to have live entertainment in the evening, Josie had got a bee in her bonnet about having not only fireworks, but possibly hiring jugglers and magicians for the night. Harry's protests about the money had been ignored – he was beginning to appreciate his fiancée had a steely side of which he'd been hitherto unaware – 'Dad won't mind,' Josie had assured him, which was true. Josie's dad Peter doted on his daughter and would spend any amount of money to keep her happy.

But Harry minded. Peter was always polite to him, but he had the distinct impression that his future father-in-law was disappointed that his daughter had come home not with a City magnate, but a lowly paid journalist without much ambition. Harry would much rather have had a smaller affair, to which he and Josie could contribute financially, without him feeling so indebted to Josie's parents. Harry still felt his career had time to get going. He'd always wanted to get into travel journalism, and had been planning to join Ant out in Australia when he met up with Josie again. Since then, everything had happened so fast that Harry had laid aside his ambitions to see something of the world. And when he'd tried to talk about it to Josie, she'd laughed and said, 'There'll be plenty of time for that later.' But the further the wedding preparations went on, the more he could feel that particular ambition receding, particularly as he had the sneaking suspicion that Nicola was already laying plans for them to move down to the neighbouring village as soon as they were able. She was a very forceful woman, and sometimes, he worried what Josie might be like in middle age – whether behind that mild-mannered image was a female tiger, just waiting to pounce on him. Harry sighed; he was beginning to wonder if he'd rushed into this marriage thing. He felt he was on a roller coaster and couldn't get off.

'Why the heavy sigh?' said Josie. 'Is anything wrong?'

The lightness of her touch on his arm, and her quick and ready sympathy were enough to bring him to his senses. He was marrying Josie, who was gorgeous, and everything he wanted in a woman. Of course it would be all right.

31

'Nothing,' he said. 'Nothing at all. In fact, nothing could be more right.'

Diana was regretting the amount of packing she'd done for a weekend away. But she was nervous. She'd only met Josie's parents once or twice when they'd come up to London to see Josie and they were so posh, they'd turned her into a gibbering wreck. She wasn't often ashamed of her council house upbringing, but a few days with Josie's mum and dad had managed to make her feel inadequate. Josie hid her privileged upbringing well, and because she was so kind, went out of her way to put people at ease, so most people who met her in London would have had no idea of the luxury awaiting her at home. Of course, she took that for granted too, and was often puzzled when Diana mentioned that she couldn't afford something, giving a delicate little frown and a perplexed smile. With anyone else, Diana might have felt envious, particularly since she'd bagged such a great prize in Harry, but Josie was such a joy to be around, envy just seemed like the wrong emotion.

Harry was the kind of man any girl would be happy to have. Lovely, solid dependable Harry – a bit dull maybe for her tastes, but Diana had a soft spot for him. He was always kind and welcoming to her; she could do worse than have a Harry of her own. But men like Harry never came Diana's way, which was partly her own fault of course. Diana had had to fight to get where she was – opposing her parents' plans for her to go into law, to take advantage of the opportunities they never had, and choosing travel as a career instead (and the way that was going at the moment, she was going to have to admit to her dad soon it might have been a big mistake) – and learning the hard way that people let you down, especially in love. Josie had never had those kinds of experiences. Things had a habit of going her way, and sometimes that was an annoying trait in a best friend. But Josie was the kind of person it was impossible not to love, so Diana put such thoughts behind her as unworthy. She was the unkind one, Josie was not, and didn't deserve anyone to be bitter and nasty about her.

'So where are we meeting this friend of yours?' Diana said, from her uncomfortable position in the back of the car, squashed up as she was against her big suitcase. She knew taking it had been a mistake, but she'd wanted to make sure she had something to wear for any occasion.

'There's a service station not far from Honiton,' said Josie, 'we thought we'd catch up with him there.'

'And how soon will we be there?' said Diana, looking at her watch. They seemed to have been in the car for hours, and she felt hot, cramped and awkward. Diana didn't drive herself. Although she'd miraculously passed her test, after having a car in the first few months she'd lived in London she'd decided the stress of driving the mean city streets was far too much to be going along with. Besides, after three prangs in as many weeks, she couldn't afford the insurance any more. As a result, most of her travelling was done by train, and she really hadn't a clue how long this journey would take.

'Not for another half an hour at least,' said Josie. 'Honestly, it's like having a small child in the back. That's the fourth time you've asked since we set off.'

'Well, you two are like my surrogate mum and dad,' grinned Diana. 'Okay, I'm going to have a kip. Wake me when we get there.'

Josie was a bundle of nerves. It was only the second time she and Harry had visited her parents since their engagement, and this time she was bringing Diana and Ant. Her mother could be a terrible snob, and Josie knew that while she was too polite to say so, she thoroughly disapproved of Diana, whom she thought rather common. What she was going to make of Ant, the Lord only knew. Josie just hoped he could manage to keep his mouth shut and behave himself. Knowing Ant, that was highly unlikely.

She was also nervous about how Harry was going to get on with her parents. They seemed to like him, but she suspected they were slightly disappointed in her choice. They'd wanted her to marry someone in the City, not an impoverished journalist – her dad's clumsy jokes about them starving in garrets making it clear what he really thought. It didn't matter either that Josie had a good career in marketing and was earning enough for both of them, and that more importantly she loved Harry to pieces and had never been happier than the last few months when they'd been living together; her parents were desperately old-fashioned about life. As soon as Josie was married, she would be expected to stay at home and raise a family, which was why marrying someone rich was so important.

They couldn't see that that was what appealed to Josie about Harry. That he wasn't rich, didn't set much store by all of that. He was kind and compassionate, and the loveliest person Josie knew. They'd originally met and had a brief fling on their English course at university years before, but the physical distance between them afterwards had meant they'd drifted away from one another. Meeting Harry again at Amy's wedding, after years of dating unsuitable and complicated men and seeing how straightforward and uncomplicated he was, had made him instantly attractive. The fact that he didn't earn much money didn't matter. She earned enough for the pair of them.

It was a pity Mum and Dad didn't see it like that. No doubt Dad at least, would be more impressed with Ant. He had the flash job and car, and was annoyingly good at charming the birds off the trees. Josie hoped Dad wouldn't compare Harry unfavourably to his friend.

'You all right, hon?' she said to Harry, squeezing his knee hard. He was very quiet, and she had a feeling he was even more nervous than she was. It was going to be a long weekend.

'Yeah, fine,' he said. 'Just hope I can get through the weekend without making too much of an idiot of myself.'

'You'll be fine,' Josie assured him, 'Mum and Dad love you.' She crossed her fingers behind her back while she said this. Perhaps if she wanted it to be true enough, it would be . . .

She looked at her watch, they'd been on the road for nearly three hours and they weren't too far from Honiton now. Josie turned back to Diana who was snoring in the back.

'Wakey, wakey, sleepyhead. We're nearly there. Time to meet up with the man of your dreams.'

'Wha-a?' Diana jerked herself awake.

'Just saying, we're nearly at Honiton. And finally you get to meet Ant. It could be a match made in heaven.'

'From everything you've said, I doubt it,' snorted Diana.

'You never know,' said Josie, 'he might surprise you.'

'Hmm, we'll see,' said Diana, but Josie was amused to see she'd got out her compact and was anxiously checking to see her make-up hadn't smudged.

'The best man and bridesmaid have to get together,' declared Josie. 'It's the law.'

'In your dreams, pal,' said Diana, chucking an empty crisp packet at her friend. 'I'm happily single, and however good-looking the best man is, that's how I plan to stay.'

Ant sat leaning on his convertible, sipping a coffee, and smoking a cigarette. The sun was very bright and the sky a clear blue, so the sunglasses he had put on, part affectation, part a means of deflecting the hangover from the night before, had turned out useful. His head was pounding and he could have done with a couple of hours more kip. God, he wished he hadn't been persuaded to go to Cornwall for the weekend to meet Harry's new in-laws. He wasn't quite sure how he'd even agreed to do it, but Harry was his best mate. And despite being certain that he was making a huge mistake, Ant felt duty bound to support him, and even he had to concede, certain as he was that it would all go pear-shaped, Josie was pretty gorgeous and a lovely person to boot. If Harry hadn't got in there first . . . In fact, thinking about it, how had Harry got in there first? From memory it was Ant who had introduced them at some party or other. And then she'd invited them all down to her place one summer. Ant felt sure he'd gone down with the express intention of nabbing Josie, but it hadn't happened. Unbelievable that Josie could have possibly chosen dull old Harry over him.

He looked at his watch. Harry had thought they'd be arriving around midday, but there was no sign of them, yet. Ant had been at a sales conference in Salisbury (hence the hangover) and come straight on from there. He checked his BlackBerry and dealt with a few outstanding work issues, before ringing up Harry to see where he'd got to.

'Harry, where are you, mate? I'm feeling like a right idiot standing here in this car park on my own.'

'It's Josie,' said a crisp clear voice on the other end. Josie's

36

voice sparkled like a babbling brook, he'd forgotten what a lovely sound it was. 'And we'll be with you in about five minutes. Don't be so impatient.'

Delicious. Josie even sounded lovely when she was telling him off. Harry was a lucky man. No doubt about that.

Five minutes later, true to Josie's word, Harry's poxy little Honda Civic drove into the car park. It really was a girl's car.

Putting out his cigarette, Ant unrolled himself from his position and strode over to say hello.

'Harry, great to see you, mate!' he said giving him a thump on the back and feeling absurdly affectionate towards his oldest friend.

'You, too!' said Harry punching him in the ribs.

'Josie, you look lovely as ever,' he said, giving her a hug and a huge kiss on the lips.

'Flatterer,' said Josie, neatly escaping from his grasp.

'And who have we here?' Ant noted with pleasure a very fetching pair of legs encased in a pair of skinny jeans, emerging from the back of the Civic.

'Ant, meet my friend, Diana,' said Josie with a smile. 'Diana, this is Ant.'

Ant nearly dropped his coffee in shock, as he followed the legs up (via the jeans and busty top) to a ginger (she said auburn) head of hair and pretty face, with those emerald-green eyes he remembered with clarity even though they'd last met eight years ago.

'You!' they said simultaneously.

Chapter Two

Diana was shaking as she got back into the car. She'd have recognised him anywhere, the arrogant tilt of his chin, the fair hair swept back off his face, revealing deep brown eyes that had once been tender, but then cruel. *Teflon Tone*? Harry's mysterious best friend Ant and best-man-to-be. Teflon Tone? How could they be the same person? How was that even possible? Since Josie and Harry had been together, Ant had been mentioned frequently, but he had only recently returned from his travels. Of late, she'd seen less of Josie then she would have liked, so she'd been aware that Ant was back on the scene, but had never met him. She couldn't believe this was happening to her. Teflon Tone. The guy who'd ruined her life. And she had to spend a whole weekend with him.

'So what's the deal with you and Ant, then?' Josie turned round in the car to face her friend. 'How do you know each other?'

'We don't,' mumbled Diana. 'Not anymore.'

'Come on,' teased Josie, 'I saw that reaction. There must be a story there.'

'Well, there isn't,' said Diana shortly. 'Can we just drop it now, please.'

'Oh,' said Josie, in surprise. 'Okay.'

She settled back into the front and started making small talk with Harry, while Diana stared out of the window and remembered . . .

She'd been twenty-two when she met Tony eight years earlier, and happily whiling away a winter working as a chalet rep in Switzerland. At a loose end after university, Ant had taken a temporary job working for her firm, while he worked out what to do with his life. She'd noticed him the first time he'd walked into the bar, it was impossible not to: good-looking, tall, fair, charming as he was. Her instant reaction had been that he wasn't for her, particularly as he seemed such a flirt, but there'd been something about him from the start. And then she'd fallen in so deep, she couldn't get out easily, and it was too late to escape the broken heart that had ensued. Eight years she'd spent trying to forget him. Eight years, and now she had to spend the whole weekend with him.

Diana sighed. That was the past, this was the present. She was here for Josie and Harry, she'd just have to try and ignore Tony/Ant/whatever his name was. Because this was Josie and Harry's weekend and she didn't want to ruin it for them.

Diana had envied their relationship from the start. A couple truly suited to one another, truly at ease, truly in love. She could never imagine that happening to her. She was far too difficult and spiky, as all the boyfriends she'd ever had had told her. There were reasons for that of course. Having once given her heart irrevocably, and been hurt so badly she thought she might never recover, Diana had sworn never to let herself be so vulnerable again. So she cultivated her tough exterior, sought out short-term relationships she knew would go nowhere, and resolved to stay single and in control for the rest of her life.

Which was all very well, but the downside was she was sometimes lonely. A fact she barely ever admitted to herself, let alone anyone else. Particularly since Josie and Harry had been living together. Diana had little in common with her new flatmates, who were friends of friends, and when not working late, spent most evenings alone watching crap TV. Recently the offers from men seemed to be less forthcoming than in the past. Josie had once told her that she scared them off. The trouble with cultivating an image of invulnerability of course, meaning that people thought it was true. If only they knew . . .

Diana wished in a way she could be more like Josie, who was most definitely not spiky. Everyone loved Josie. It was impossible not to. Josie was kind and open and friendly, all the things Diana found it hard to be. It wasn't that she didn't have friends, but people didn't love her the way they loved Josie. Not at work, where her ambitious nature had given her a reputation for ruthlessness, nor in her social life, where she'd ended up dropping most of her girlfriends once they were shacked up. Apart from Josie. But that was because Josie was exceptionally kind. As was Harry. Diana felt sure he didn't quite get his fiancée's sarcastic; difficult friend, and put up with her for Josie's sake.

While Josie, Josie was kind and tolerant of their differences. And one of her special gifts was bringing people together in difficult social situations. When she realised the extent to which her best friend and Harry's actually did know each other, she'd talked of other things, and Tone had followed Di's line of *we've met but we barely know each other* with barely concealed relief.

Another memory resurfaced, searing Diana with a pain she'd forgotten she was capable of. Tone promising her the earth then abandoning her in her hour of need. No one had ever let her down that badly, and she'd sworn never would again.

Oh, God. Teflon Tone. Best Man. And she was Chief Bridesmaid. This was going to end up being the wedding from hell.

Ant sped along the motorway in a state of – what? Fury? That wasn't quite the word. But agitation, certainly. Bloody hell. Fancy quiet little Josie having made friends with Dynamite Di. How the hell had that happened? How the hell had he not known? He'd only been out of the country for two years, and it seemed like everything had turned upside down in his absence. Bad enough that Harry had had to go sentimental on him, and decided to get married. But to have Dynamite Di as a bridesmaid? That was adding insult to injury. *And* he had to spend a weekend with her, being polite? Bloody Hell. Bloody Bloody Hell.

Mind you, there had been a time when he couldn't get enough of her. Diana still remained one of the sexiest women he'd ever encountered, and he'd fallen for her in a way he'd never fallen for anyone before or since. But then it had disintegrated into a mess of bitterness and accusation. And the last time they'd met, she'd unceremoniously tipped a pint of beer over his head and called him a bastard of the finest order, in front of everyone they knew. He found out why much too late, and by then she wouldn't see him, wouldn't hear his side of the story. Ant couldn't bear to admit to anyone how heartbroken he'd been about everything that had happened – only briefly telling Harry the details – so he'd buried those feelings deep, and sworn never to let a woman get that close again. He'd certainly never imagined meeting Diana again. And now here she was, larger than life, looking just as gorgeous as ever. And they had a whole weekend to get through.

He'd been thinking about it so much, Ant nearly missed the turning to Tresgothen, the village where Josie's parents lived. He vaguely remembered the pretty little lane, with high hedges and scary bends, as he drove down it. Some time ago – a lifetime it seemed now – when they were still students, Josie had invited them all down here for a long weekend, and they'd had a fine boozy time of it, as he recalled. Josie's parents had been away so they had the place to themselves, which at the time had been amazing. Josie's parents were hugely wealthy and their house had been the height of luxury, even then. He'd brought a girl – he couldn't remember who now – Kim? Kelly? He could barely recall her, but had vague and rather erotic memories of skinny dipping with her at midnight.

The place was bigger than he remembered: a beautiful oak-beamed house on three floors with pitched roofs and ivy growing up the side. To be this rich, Ant thought, as the car crunched across the enormous gravel drive, *that* really would be something. Josie, Harry and Diana were already getting out of Harry's car, to be greeted by Josie's mum, a tiny, older version of Josie, dressed in a cream linen dress and flat sandals.

'Welcome, welcome,' she said. 'I see you've brought the lovely weather with you. I've put you in the annexe, as I thought you'd be more comfortable there.'

The annexe? Ant followed them in awe, for once silenced. The house had six bedrooms as he recalled it, and now they'd built an annexe? Maybe Harry had a point about this getting married lark. As an only child, Josie presumably stood to inherit the lot.

'The annexe is for our guests,' Josie's mum was saying cheerfully, as she took them into the enormous hall, which had expensive looking rugs on the parquet flooring and a wide-panelled oak staircase. It was light and airy, a welcoming, rather than an intimidating space, the kind of hall Ant would like to have some day. 'It's so much nicer for people to have their privacy.'

Of course, thought Ant. The way she said it, was like this was normal. Ant immediately decided whatever else he did with his life, he wanted to end up with a property portfolio like Josie's parents.

'More like for Dad to have his,' laughed Josie.

'Did someone take my name in vain?'

Josie's dad, an ambling six-foot academic-looking type, wandered in from an enormous room on the side, which looked like a lounge.

'Dad!' Josie shrieked and threw her arms around him.

'Lovely to see you too, darling. Harry, good to see you again.'

He shook hands with Harry, who looked unaccountably nervous. Ant dimly recalled Harry saying how terrifying he found his future father-in-law.

'Diana, always a pleasure,' he continued, 'and you must be the elusive Ant. Peter Hampton at your service.' He looked him up and down appraisingly, with sharp blue eyes, which reminded him suddenly of Josie. For an instant, Ant felt sorry for Harry; great to be marrying into the money certainly, but despite the scatty professor persona Ant had a feeling Peter was a hard man to impress.

'At your service,' said Ant, then felt ridiculous. What a stupid thing to have said.

'Are we eating outside, darling?' said Peter, 'as it's such a beautiful day?'

'I thought we would,' said Nicola. 'We don't often get the opportunity, and it's so lovely that you could all be here.'

43

She beamed cheerfully at them, and Ant tried to smile back, but suddenly he felt quite claustrophobic. He wasn't good at families, this felt all too domestic and cosy for him. Surely it was time for the pub soon? Otherwise it was going to be a very long weekend . . .

'You know there's a local plan to revive the theatre, don't you?' Nicola said, ushering Harry and Josie straight into the dining room as soon as they'd deposited their bags, while she left Peter sorting out drinks for Ant and Diana on the patio. Harry looked after them longingly, even more so when he saw to his horror a huge array of wedding catalogues lying open on the magnificent mahogany dining table.

'I hadn't, no,' said Josie.

'Well, they might be hiring it out for weddings,' said Nicola.

Hang on a minute. Harry was confused. The last conversation they'd had, Nicola had been insisting on a church wedding.

'That would be awesome!' said Josie, 'could we get a marquee up there?'

'Well, I've been looking into it,' Nicola said. 'It's worth a thought.'

'Don't you think it would be nicer to have a marquee at home?' asked Harry, but he knew the answer straight away.

'No!' Josie and Nicola said simultaneously.

'I think it would be amazing to have our wedding on the cliff edge looking out to sea,' said Josie. 'It would be different, stand out; be a wedding like no other. No one would ever forget it.'

Why did their wedding have to stand out? Harry wondered. He didn't care if anyone else forgot it, he knew he never would.

'And what about getting married in St Cuthbert's?' he continued, though he knew it was futile. The idea of that had been filling him with dread, but now he clung onto it longingly, 'I thought that's what you wanted.'

'I did,' said Josie, 'but the open-air theatre would make such a great setting for the wedding. So romantic. You can't have forgotten our first date there?'

Of course he hadn't. The first time he'd ever been to this house, years ago, with a group of their university friends, he'd found himself suddenly alone with Josie, the only one wanting to go out to the theatre for the night. It had rained, and they'd huddled together in their plastic macs under an umbrella, watching a magical version of *A Midsummer Night's Dream*. It had been a wonderful, incredible evening and he'd fallen head over heels in love. Though they'd drifted apart after uni, Harry had never forgotten either that night, or Josie. He still couldn't believe his luck in finding her again.

'Of course not,' he said taking her hand. 'It was one of the most amazing nights of my life.'

'Aah,' said Nicola fondly, 'what a romantic.'

'Of course he is,' said Josie, 'that's why I'm marrying him.'

Harry blushed. He never quite knew what to do when Josie was so public about her feelings for him.

'Stop it,' scolded Nicola, 'you're shaming the poor boy. Now, what do you think about these bouquets . . .'

'Oh, Mum, they're gorgeous,' Josie was peering at pictures of pale pink roses entwined with white carnations and wound in unknown greenery. There were pages and pages of pictures of bouquets that all looked the same to Harry. He endured five minutes of Josie rhapsodising about flowers and then, deciding his presence wasn't necessary, beat a retreat into the garden, hoping he wasn't going to face a grilling from Peter about his latest prospects.

Diana had disappeared to take a nap, claiming a headache in a very pointed manner, evidently her desire not to spend time with Ant overcoming her normal politeness in front of Josie's parents. What was going on there? They clearly knew one another, but were being icily polite to the point of freezing. And Ant was pretending to barely know Diana, which was clearly not true. Harry wondered which of Ant's many conquests Di must have been. It was always hard to keep track with Ant, but for the life of him he couldn't recall Ant mentioning her before. He wondered if she was the one who'd broken Ant's heart. It would explain an awful lot. Resolving to ask him at the first opportunity, Harry went into the garden where he found Ant animatedly talking business with Peter.

'So what do you think about us losing our triple A rating then?' Ant was saying as he approached. 'The country's being run by idiots.'

'You're not wrong there,' said Peter. 'This bunch is no better than the last lot. I worry about the future for you kids, I really do.'

'It could be worse, at least we're not Italy,' said Ant, provoking a hearty laugh from Peter which made Harry feel like punching a wall. He'd never made Peter laugh like that once, not in all the months he'd been coming here.

In truth, while Harry had grown very fond of Nicola, Peter terrified him. A self-made millionaire who'd used Nicola's money to make one fortune in the dot com bubble, which had enabled him not only to buy this house, but a pied-à-terre in London, a villa in Spain, and another fortune in the technological boom of more recent times. And he appeared to be recessionproof, living evidence that money made more money.

Harry, who came from a more modest background and

was quite happy to be earning what he regarded as a reasonable income in a job he enjoyed, was totally baffled when Peter started on about stocks and shares, and even more so when Ant joined in. How the hell did Ant even know all this stuff? It wasn't even as if he was any good at maths.

Gloomily, Harry sat between them as Ant quizzed Peter ever more heavily about the future of the economy, then Josie and Nicola joined them and went into frenzies about menus, venues, and other things which he felt were insignificant. When he'd impulsively asked Josie to marry him last October, he hadn't foreseen this. There seemed to be no end to the minutiae that had to be planned for a wedding. All he wanted to do was go into a wood somewhere and plight his troth with his lady love, like in some kind of mediaeval knight's tale. He loved Josie, she loved him. All the rest was frippery. But she clearly didn't see it like that . . .

Chapter Three

'You'll never guess who's staying in the village?' Nicola said gleefully as they sat down to a huge lunch on the vast patio by the pool. Josie had tried to stop her, told her they'd be just as happy to head to the pub for lunch (she could see Harry and Ant were already getting twitchy), but her mother was unstoppable. Nicola was the perfect matriarch. She'd been made to mother a huge family, and it had been a source of unending disappointment to her that she had only been able to have one child. She made up for it by feeding anyone who came within a mile of the house. Josie felt sure Nicola kidnapped people from the highways and byways when she wasn't there.

'It makes me feel useful,' her mother had once confided in her daughter. Josie tried not to feel irritated that her mother could only see one way of being useful, and bit her lip so as not to retort, well go and do something *properly* useful if you feel at a loose end. It exasperated her that her mother seemed to be so happy with so little, having given up on any career aspirations long before Josie was born. Her own father had been wealthy in his own right and Nicola had never been expected to work. When she met Peter who even then was on the up, she devoted herself to being a full-time wife and mother. She wouldn't even work with Dad, saying the figures were beyond her. It was exasperating. But it wasn't in Josie's nature to quarrel, and she didn't want to hurt her mum's feelings, so she said nothing.

'No, who?' said Josie, laughing as her dad rolled his eyes.

'Only Tatiana Okeby,' said Nicola triumphantly.

She was met with a stunning silence and blank looks.

'Er. Tatiana who?' said Diana.

'Tatiana Okeby. You must know her. *Sail for the Sun*?'

'Nope, not ringing any bells,' said Harry.

'Sandy Kane, tart with a heart. Who went through abortion, rape, several husbands, and sailed off into the sunset, never to be seen again? How can you not remember *Sail for the Sun*?'

'Might be a bit before our time, Mum,' said Josie.

'What, none of you ever saw *Sail for the Sun*?' Nicola looked baffled. 'I could have sworn we watched it together, Josie.'

'Did we? I don't remember. When?'

'Let me see . . . It must have been around 1983, I suppose,' said Nicola. 'Tatiana Okeby was tipped to appear as Auberon Fanshawe's assistant on Freddie Puck's *Illusions* show, but she quit to play Cassandra instead. She and Auberon used to have a bit of a thing.'

'Now, *Illusions* I do remember,' said Harry. 'It was awesome.'

'Do you remember the trick they did with the lighted candle?' said Ant. 'You know the one where Auberon's assistant lit the candle and he made it disappear. I still can't work out how they did that.'

'Oh, I remember that! It was brilliant!' Di burst in, then reddened when she realised she'd agreed with something Ant had said.

'Well, that aside,' said Nicola, 'I'm very excited. Tatiana

Okeby's staying in that new place with the yurts near the open-air theatre, and the rumour is she's going to be playing Titania in this summer's production of *A Midsummer Night's Dream*. I was telling Josie earlier, the theatre has been a bit down in the doldrums in the last few years, and they're thinking of hiring it out for weddings.'

'What, you two getting married in a theatre?' said Diana, 'what about a church wedding?'

'That's so passé,' said Josie, nonchalantly. 'I want our wedding to be different. To be the one everyone will be talking about for years to come. I think the theatre's the perfect venue. And in the evening it will be brilliant for entertainment: jugglers, acrobats, magicians, that kind of thing. Won't it, Harry?'

Harry didn't appear to be paying any attention, and she had to kick him under the table before he mumbled, 'Oh, yes, great,' rather unconvincingly.

'Wow,' Diana seemed slightly stunned. 'Sounds amazing.'

Josie checked to make sure Di wasn't being sarcastic, but she seemed genuine.

'Anyway,' Nicola continued, 'if we could get someone of Tatiana Okeby's calibre playing at the theatre, it could help put us back on the map.'

'Now, that I would like to see,' said Josie. 'The open-air theatre is so special. Isn't it, Harry?'

'Oh, er, yes,' said Harry, looking a little guilty. He'd been deep in conversation with Ant about the many and varied delights of *Illusions,* and Josie wasn't entirely sure he'd heard her. She wondered whether it had been a good idea to bring Ant along this weekend. Especially as there was clearly something weird going on with him and Di. She'd been dying to find out what was going on there, but hadn't had a moment alone with Diana since they'd arrived.

She hoped whatever it was wouldn't spoil the atmosphere of the weekend, especially as she didn't trust Ant not to make trouble. He'd never been a good influence on Harry in her eyes, and so far this weekend seemed intent on dragging him away from anything to do with the wedding. She'd already caught them muttering about going for a pint. The only reason she'd let Harry bring him along was because he'd been so worried about spending the weekend with her parents, and she'd wanted Harry to have some moral support. There was a point to Di coming. They were going searching for hers and Di's dresses tomorrow, and although the boys were getting fitted for their suits, Ant didn't really need to be here. She hoped he wasn't going to ruin everything . . .

'Does anyone fancy a walk?' Diana said after lunch. She was getting fed up with Ant, who kept sending her significant looks across the table. The last thing she wanted to do was to have deep meaningful chats with him. What was done was done. She'd long ago consigned him to her past, and wasn't at all interested in having him in her future. She was hoping that he'd be more interested in going to the pub, then she and Josie could at least have a girlie chat. It felt like ages since they'd had any time on their own together, and Diana missed her friend more than she'd thought she would.

'I'd rather have a pint,' said Ant. Good. True to form.

'A walk would be great,' said Josie. 'We can get up to the Faerie Ring from the footpath at the end of the lane, walk along the cliff edge and then make our way down to the village, and have a pint in the Lover's Rest. It'll only take us an hour or so. And it's a glorious day.'

Diana frantically tried to signal to Josie that this wasn't her intention, but Josie was looking fixedly at Harry, as if to say, *Don't you dare think about going straight to the pub.* Harry clearly understood the look, because he responded with, 'A walk sounds like a brilliant idea.'

Great. Now Ant would feel obliged to come.

'I suppose we could stretch our legs,' said Ant. 'So what's this Faerie Ring place then?'

'They're a bunch of Standing Stones on the cliff,' explained Josie. 'Local legend says magic happens there on Midsummer's Eve.'

'Don't tell me, young lovers plight their troth while fairies dance around them,' snorted Ant.

'Something like that,' admitted Josie. 'All nonsense of course.'

'How about it, Di,' Ant said slyly. 'Fancy finding yourself a red-hot lover on the cliffs at midnight?'

'I think the key word that is wrong in that sentence is lover,' said Diana sarcastically. 'And until you can find me a red-hot lover worthy of me, I can safely say the answer is no.'

'As if I'd be interested in you,' said Ant. 'You clearly still have no sense of humour.'

'Not for puerile infants, no,' said Diana. She was furious. A couple of hours in Ant's company was all it had taken her to remind him what a prick he was.

'Woah! Children!' said Josie. 'What is it with you two?'

'Nothing!' said Diana and Ant, simultaneously glaring at one another.

'Okay point taken,' said Josie throwing her hands up, and tactfully changing the subject, to Diana's relief. She sighed deeply. She couldn't wait for the weekend to be over.

But, as they set off down the lane that led past Josie's house to the footpath that took them up to the cliffs, Diana felt a bit better. The hedgerows were alive with birdsong, and the air heavy with scent from the riot of wildflowers that lined the path: the pinks and whites of scarlet pimpernels and red campions jostled with blue mallow and purple speedwell and other flowers Di couldn't identify. There was barely a cloud in the azure sky, and the sun was so warm, they soon discarded cardigans and jumpers. She breathed a deep sigh of contentment. It was great to be away from London for once and the tension that she'd left behind at work.

'This way,' said Josie, confidently leading them over a stile which led onto a sandy cliff path, where the foliage gave way to yellow gorse, green bracken and pink heathers, and tall cow parsley bowed down in the breeze. It was a steepish climb, but with the wind on her face and the sun on her skin, Diana was beginning to enjoy herself – until she caught sight of Ant whispering to Harry, and glancing in her direction. She felt sure it was about her, and her stomach plummeted. How utterly miserable. To think she not only had to spend a whole weekend with him but also a whole wedding, when she'd be forced to be nice to him. Diana couldn't think of anything worse.

'So what's the deal with you and Di, then?' Harry said as he and Ant forged their way up the cliff path. After the little display of histrionics between them, he and Josie had decided it would be better for now if they kept their warring friends apart.

'Dynamite Di?' said Ant, looking back down the path at her, affecting nonchalance. 'Oh, nothing.'

'Didn't look like nothing to me,' said Harry. 'You reacted like a scalded cat when you saw her.'

Ant stopped to take a breather and stared back at the lane, Josie's house reflecting the sunshine in the distance.

'We knew each other a long time ago. Had a bit of a thing. Didn't work out.'

'Which is why you're so down on her,' snorted Harry, not believing a word of it, and feeling more convinced than ever, she was the one. He paused too and took a sip of the water he had thought to bring in his small backpack. It was hot work climbing the path. Last time he'd done this walk it had been in the winter and much easier.

'I'm not down on her,' protested Ant. 'You've seen the way she is with me. She's a cow of the highest order. Can't think why someone as nice as Josie could be mates with someone as chippy as Di.'

'Oh, Di's okay,' said Harry, 'and she's been a good friend to Josie; really helped her through some tough times. So do me a favour, mate, and be nice to her. Just for the weekend. If not for me, do it for Josie.'

'All right,' said Ant. 'Anything you say.'

The sun was out and the walk was invigorating. Soon they'd reached the top of the cliffs, and could look out to sea. To their left, the green of the cliffs fell away to the sea, and the path led down towards the dip where the Standing Stones stood, hidden from sight from this angle. To their right, a path led to down to a little cove in the distance. Boats on their way back to Tresgothen bobbed on the turquoise-green sea below, and seagulls keened in the sea breeze. The sparkling blue-green waves, dancing in the sunshine, looked really inviting. Harry had the mad impulse to throw himself off the edge. Here, out in the fresh air on such a glorious sunny day, Harry had a sudden urge to get away from everything, to be free. He'd had the feeling for a while now: that life was becoming more constricted, constrained, even. Particularly since Ant had been back, and Harry had listened to his travelling tales with increasing envy. The lure of going abroad was rearing its head again. And today, the thought of diving out, getting *away*, suddenly seemed irresistible. Particularly when they reached the famed Faerie Ring, which stood in a dip, a slight way from the cliff.

Approaching them, Harry, who wasn't often given to fanciful notions, felt a shiver go down his spine. The stones were so old, and weathered; had stood here for generations, through wind and shine. It wasn't hard to think somehow there was something deeply magical here.

'Well, go on then,' said Di, pushing Josie at Harry. 'Time to plight your troth. It will bring you luck at your wedding.'

'Don't be daft,' said Josie, 'it's only a silly superstition. And you have to do it at midnight on Midsummer's Eve. Plus, you need love-in-idleness.'

'What's that?' asked Ant.

'A flower; a sort of wild pansy,' said Josie. 'The legend goes that if your true love picks love-in-idleness at midsummer, your love will be eternal.'

'Oh, that is so romantic,' Di clapped her hands together with glee. 'I do love all these old tales.'

Harry could see they were both angling for him to say something, but he laughed it off and said, 'I wouldn't know a wild pansy from a geranium,' till Di said lightly, 'See, there are some growing here, by this stone.'

At that moment, he could have cheerfully strangled her. It had been the same, the day he'd proposed. That had been Di's doing too. Would he even have thought about marriage without Di's interference? Sometimes he wondered. To Josie's evident dismay, he laughed it off, saying, 'We've got two days to Midsummer's Eve, I'd hate to get it wrong, and anyway, as Josie says, it's all nonsense.' He tried to ignore her hurt look as he strode through the Standing Stones and made his way to the path that led back to the town. It was just a silly local legend. She must see that. So why did he feel so guilty?

Ant's bad mood had dissipated as the afternoon wore on. True, he still had to spend the weekend with Di, but despite moaning about it, he did enjoy a blow in the country, something he didn't get to do very often now he was working back in the big smoke. The sun was shining, it was a beautiful summer's day, and it was hard to stay cross for long. Besides, Peter had given him a great tip for an investment. He'd checked it out and it seemed sound. He was still reeling from the thrill of having had a chat with *the* Peter Hampton. It was the stuff that dreams were made of.

As they left the Standing Stones, Ant sidled up to Di. He was beginning to enjoy this weekend and he didn't want her sour looks ruining things.

'Look, Di, I know this isn't ideal, us both being here –'

'I should say so,' snorted Di.

'But let's just get on with it, for Harry and Josie's sake. We don't want to ruin things for them, do we?'

'No, that would be too dreadful,' Diana sounded as sarcastic as ever. Ant felt doubtful his approach was working.

He tried again, 'I know you think I'm a dick.'

'Because you are,' said Diana.

He'd said it partly in jest, and was surprised by the power she still had to hurt him. For a moment, he really wanted her not to think badly of him, wanted her to think of him the way she used to, but he tamped the thought down. No point going there; that door was long since bolted.

'And I think you're a cow,' continued Ant, putting more venom into his words than he'd intended, wanting to hurt her the way she'd hurt him. She looked cross at that, but couldn't really say anything, given that she'd just insulted him, 'but we can at least be polite to one another, can't we?'

'I suppose,' Diana said grudgingly. 'But don't think you're going to use that famous charm to worm your way back into my affections. I never make the same mistake twice.'

'Understood,' said Ant, raising his hand. 'Wouldn't dream of it.' He resisted the impulse to say *you should be so lucky*.

'Good,' said Di.

'Good,' agreed Ant, wondering if he could risk shaking on it, but decided it was best not to. There being very little else to say, they sped up to catch up with the other two, and Ant naturally fell back into conversation with Harry, while Diane and Josie resumed their chat about . . . whatever girls chat about. Even after all these years of bedding and chasing them, Ant wasn't entirely sure what that was.

1983: Tatiana

Tatiana heard the phone go as she knelt on the floor, checking and rechecking the contents of her suitcase: passport, plane tickets, clothes, bikinis, sunglasses, suntan lotion – not that she'd get much time to sunbathe probably. By all accounts the workload on *Sail for the Sun* was phenomenal, but you never knew.

The phone was still ringing as she finally zipped up her suitcase, and placed her tickets and passport in her handbag, but she decided to ignore it. It would only be Bron, begging her to come back. God knows why he'd suddenly turned so needy after all these years. Who'd have thought?

Walking out on a five-year relationship hadn't been quite as easy as she'd imagined. Bron had half his stuff at her flat for a start, and she wasn't quite angry enough to dump it all out in the corridor for him to collect. So instead she'd endured several excruciating visits, when he'd begged her to change her mind.

'I know the last few months haven't been easy,' he'd said.

'Who for, you? Don't make me laugh.' Fear that she might crumble made her cruel. She knew he'd been hurting too, but she pushed the thought to one side. She needed this. She needed to get away, if she had any hope of surviving.

'No, you,' he mumbled, his face creased with guilt and

pain. He stood underneath the hall light looking forlorn, a little boy lost – a familiar tug pulled at her heart but she ignored it. 'Of course, for you, they've been tough. And I haven't helped, I know.'

'No, you haven't,' said Tati, then, briskly changing the subject, 'We seem to have two copies of *Rumours*, do you want one?'

She went into overdrive, tidying, cleaning, sorting, organising. Anything to stop herself from actually talking to him. All those months, and all she'd wanted was for Bron to listen, to hold her, to share it with her. And now he was ready to, and it was too late. If she let him pull her back now, she'd be lost again, and this opportunity would be gone.

'Can't I at least hope?' Bron had pleaded on his last visit, the one where she'd eventually banned him from seeing her again.

'You can hope,' she said, hardening her heart, 'but it probably won't do you any good.'

Hearing the catch in his voice as he left made her stronger once more, particularly when she could see tears in his eyes. It meant she was able to resist the heart-melting hug he gave her as he left. She'd cried a river over him, time for him to cry one over her.

Tatiana had spent so long in thrall to Bron it was quite satisfying to discover that while she could manage perfectly well without him (she ignored the painful little twist of her heart that still persisted whenever she thought of him), Bron was finding it difficult to do without her. Well, he'd have to manage, wouldn't he? Her contract on *Sail for the Sun* was only three months, to be extended if her character proved popular. When she came back, Bron might be suitably sorry. *Then* she could think perhaps about having him back.

The beeping of a horn outside signalled the arrival of her taxi, while the beep from the answerphone told her that Bron had left his latest message. Well, he could wait. She'd wasted enough time on Bron. Time to seize her future. Time for Tatiana Okeby to have her day in the sun. Taking one last look at the small flat where she and Bron had shared so many happy times (she felt that familiar twist again, and reminded herself they'd had their fair share of bitter times too), she picked up her suitcase, strode through the door, and locked it for the last time. She was on her way. The future was bright and shining and golden.

As she got into the taxi and sped off, the phone in her flat rang again.

'Tati – I know you're there. Pick up, please. I've got some great news. *Illusions* is going to be on TV. And we can have equal shares this time. I promise. Tati? Are you there? Tati?'

Chapter Four

The pub was heaving, when they got to it. It was a lovely whitewashed old building with a thatched roof, wisteria growing up the sides, and hanging baskets tumbling down with bright red geraniums, blue and purple lobelia and yellow petunias. There was a pretty beer garden overlooking the harbour, and Diana was hugely relieved when the boys elbowed their way to the bar, and Josie suggested going outside. They managed to squeeze into a wobbly wooden table in the farthest corner of the beer garden, by a low granite wall, with a great view of the harbour. The sea was a turquoise green, and the sun was bright and warm. There was the constant humming of sails as the summer breeze danced its way through the myriad of boats bobbing in the harbour. On any other day it would have been perfect. But Ant's presence had unsettled Diana more than she would have liked to admit. Dammit. How bloody typical of her pathetic little life, that Harry's best mate should turn out to be Tony. The only man she'd ever let close enough to break her heart . . .

Christmas 2005 had found a twenty-two-year-old Diana working a season in the Alps as a chalet girl. She'd loved it. She was out of England, and therefore away from the ever-present sense of her father's disappointment that she hadn't made more of herself, and her mother's rueful comments about 'If only I'd had the opportunities you've had'; Diana's decision to not go to uni and saddle herself with a load of debt having gone down badly with her parents.

But she was good at what she did. She enjoyed the challenge of organising skiing parties, plus she loved the outdoor life, and the partying hard aspect of the job. Life was for living, and the young Diana had wanted to seize it with both hands. She was earning good money, and unlike her peers, independent of her parents. She couldn't see what their problem was.

She'd been having a ball, and then Anthony sodding Lambert had walked into her life and ruined it all. He'd knocked her sideways from the minute they met. For a while there, she – cynical, hard-bitten Di, who was never going to let a man near enough to break her heart – had even considered he might be the one person to make her change her mind about settling down. Which just goes to show how wrong you can be . . .

'So go on then,' Josie cut bluntly into Diana's reverie. 'What's the story with you and Ant?'

'There is no story with me and Ant,' said Diana. 'We worked together once. It was years ago.'

'Yeah, right,' Josie said. 'Which is why you both looked as though you'd seen a ghost when you met.'

Diana had been dreading Josie's interrogation since the morning. Josie had clearly given her some leeway about Ant, and not asked too many questions so far. Besides, she was happy to chat for England about what kind of flowers she was having, and Diana had kept her talking for as long as she was able. But it was clear Josie wasn't prepared to be fobbed off anymore.

'It was just a shock to see him,' mumbled Diana. 'It was years ago.'

'Spill,' said Josie, looking accusatory.

'There is nothing *to* spill,' protested Diana. 'I worked with him one Christmas when I was doing the ski chalet thing. I barely know him. There is nothing to tell.'

'Oh my God!' Recognition suddenly dawned on Josie's face. 'Ant's Teflon Tone, isn't he?'

Diana felt the bottom fall out of her world. She really didn't want to have this conversation.

'No,' she said unconvincingly.

'You don't fool me,' continued Josie mercilessly. 'Ant, Teflon Tone. No way.'

'Yes, way,' said Diana, realising there was no point denying it any longer. 'Now can you see why I'm so freaked?'

'He's the one who —?'

'Yes,' said Diana. 'That's him. The bastard of all bastards.'

'Oh bloody hell,' said Josie. 'If I'd had any idea, I'd have told Harry not to have him as best man, and I *certainly* wouldn't have invited him for the weekend. God, Di, I'm so sorry. I'll tell Harry he has to get another best man. It's not as if Ant's even that interested in the job.'

'Not your fault. You weren't to know,' said Diana. 'Just my godawful luck, as usual. Besides, whatever's happened between Tony and me, it's nothing to do with you two. Harry has to choose his own best man. I'll cope.'

Josie sat looking thoughtful.

'I still can't get over Ant being Teflon Tone. What on earth possessed you? Or was he different when he was out there? At uni he always had a terrible reputation with women.'

'Youth, stupidity, vodka?' said Di. There'd been more to it than that of course. But she couldn't bear to let her friend know quite how foolish she'd been. She'd heard

Josie rant often enough about the idiocy of women who'd fallen for Ant's charms and didn't want to admit quite how easily she had done the same. It had all seemed so different back then . . .

'Anyway, it was ages ago. All forgotten now.' Diana looked round, desperate to change the subject; when talking to Josie about Tony in the past, she'd always played up the bad stuff, never mentioned any of the good, but there had been a reason why she was in love. 'Where are the boys with those drinks? The bar isn't that packed.'

'Oh,' said Josie. 'Look. Seems like we've got more than one local celebrity.'

Di looked to where Josie was pointing, to see Harry and Ant standing on the patio, deep in conversation with none other than Freddie Puck, the famous TV illusionist.

'So go on,' Ant was saying, clearly puppishly in awe of his childhood hero. 'Spill the beans. How does the candle trick work? Is it sleight of hand, a false candle, what?'

'You should know by now that I never speak of how the show works,' said Freddie with a mischievous smile. 'Shh, it will spoil the magic.'

'He said it!' Ant roared in delight.

'Shh, it will spoil the magic,' had been Freddie Puck's catchphrase back in the day, solemnly chanted in playgrounds up and down the country every Monday morning after the show was aired the previous Saturday.

'Yes, brilliant,' said Harry, feeling somewhat embarrassed by his friend. He was beginning to wonder if he'd made a big mistake bringing Ant with him this weekend. He'd forgotten in the two years that Ant had been away, just how loud, how forward, how full of hot air, how *thrusting*, his best friend could be. They'd been mates a long, long time, and Harry had always felt slightly overshadowed by his

64

funnier, more confident, better-looking friend. And today, as Ant grew more expansive, Harry felt himself shrivel a bit, partly from embarrassment (Ant *would* insist on talking to Freddie Puck), partly from an old and familiar feeling that in Ant's presence no one was interested in what he had to say. Luckily Freddie seemed to have an ego to match Ant's and was revelling in the attention.

'I'll just get the drinks to the girls, shall I?' Harry muttered as Ant went into an interminable discussion about how he'd watched *Illusions* week after week, and tried to work out how they did the tricks. Freddie just smiled enigmatically as Ant came up with ever more outlandish theories about how they were done.

Sensing they didn't really need him, Harry took the tray of drinks over to the girls.

'Sorry about that,' he said, sliding gratefully into his seat. 'Ant would insist on holding court with Freddie Puck. Honestly, he's incorrigible.'

'That's one word for him,' Diana said pointedly.

'Look, Di,' Harry felt even more embarrassed, 'I'm sorry. I had no idea that you and Ant knew each other. I'd never have brought him if I'd known.'

'It's okay,' said Diana, with a grateful smile. It almost made her look vulnerable, and he noticed with slight surprise how pretty she was. 'Past history. Done and dealt with a long time ago. Now let's get onto something far more interesting. Like you two getting hitched.'

Harry tried to smile with enthusiasm. He wasn't sure he wanted to talk about the wedding either. For reasons he felt uncomfortable dwelling on , the thought of the wedding was making him feel more and more uneasy. But he'd do anything to avoid a row, so he smiled again and said, 'Yes, it's going to be great, isn't it?'

'I know,' said Josie grabbing his hand. 'We're so excited, aren't we, Harry?'

'Yes,' said Harry, with more enthusiasm than he felt. 'We can't wait.'

He felt mean then. He squeezed Josie's hand and kissed her on the lips. Of course she was excited. They were getting married; they were going to spend the rest of their lives together. The thought of spending the rest of his life with Josie made him tingle all over. She was so gorgeous and she was his; he was very, very fortunate.

Diana was looking at her texts, and frowning.

'Shit, first signal I've managed to get all day, and apparently I need to ring work. Will you excuse me for a moment? You two can keep wedding planning in peace.'

'Wonderful,' said Harry, trying very hard to feel it *was* wonderful.

The afternoon was turning out better than expected. Ant still hadn't come to join them, as soon after Harry had sat down with Josie and Di, Freddie had been joined by none other than Auberon Fanshawe, the star turn in the *Illusions* show. While Freddie's act had been all about the art of illusion and the power of the mind, Auberon Fanshawe had been everyone's favourite TV magician. They'd made a formidable duo, and a formidable fortune in the process. Ant looked like all his Christmases had come at once, sitting between them; a small puppy trying to please two masters.

'Look at that,' Diana smirked, having sat back down after being unable to get a signal. 'It makes a change to see Tony, I mean Ant, looking overawed. That is something positive to take from this weekend, at any rate.'

Josie laughed. 'I know what you mean,' she said, 'Ant is

always so much in control. Hilarious. Anyway, back to the wedding; let's talk table plans . . .'

Josie was feeling a little out of sorts, and she couldn't work out why. The sun was still really warm, and the beer she was drinking was making her feel ever so light-headed. She didn't often drink in the day. It was pleasant sitting basking in the sun, and watching the seagulls whirl above the cliffs, and dive down to catch fish. Part of her wished she could stay here always. She missed Cornwall when she was up in London. It should have been a perfect afternoon, but somehow she felt that Diana and even Harry just weren't as interested in talking about wedding plans as she was. Diana kept drifting off, looking across at the bay, and acting as if she hadn't heard what Josie was talking about, while Harry . . . Well. Sometimes she wondered why he'd asked her to marry him. He couldn't have appeared less interested if he'd tried.

Josie wasn't the sort of person to get irate, or worked up about things; she normally hated taking charge, and being confrontational, but this was her's and Harry's wedding and she just wanted it to be special. So she decided that she would have to take charge for once, and be more forthright.

'Look, Harry,' she said, as she caught him drifting off again, 'this is important. We can't just sit your Auntie Vi with Dad's sister. It won't work. Lulu is a huge snob and an alcoholic to boot. She'll be vile to Vi, I just know it.'

'I can't believe we're even talking about the tables,' said Harry. 'The wedding's next *year*. Auntie Vi might not come.'

'Fail to prepare, prepare to fail,' said Josie. 'I do not want my wedding to turn into an episode of *My Big Fat Gypsy Wedding*, with brawls at the top table.'

'Come on, it can't be as bad as all that,' laughed Diana, 'weddings aren't normally that exciting, except in films.'

'And we'll have to keep Ant away from pretty much everyone. He's bound to upset somebody.'

'Now that, I can agree on,' said Di.

'Oh come on, Josie,' said Harry. 'I think you're being unfair now. And you're worrying about nothing. Why would anyone want to fight at our wedding?'

'I just want things to be perfect,' said Josie, wishing he'd understand.

'I know,' said Harry, 'and they will, I promise. But the most important thing is we're getting married, and nothing else matters.'

He grabbed her hand, and squeezed it tight, then gave her that little grin she found endearing, and she was instantly mollified. Harry was right; she was getting hung up on detail. Everything would be fine.

'Excuse me while I barf,' said Diana, with characteristic sarcasm. 'I think I'll just leave you two lovebirds to it.'

'Di,' said Josie, stricken. She hadn't meant to make her friend feel left out, but she knew sometimes she felt she and Harry were in their own little bubble and the rest of the world was excluded.

'It's all right,' said Diana, 'I really need to get hold of work. I might get a signal on top of the cliffs. And I fancy watching the sunset anyway. I'll wander back up to the Stones, and see you back at home. At least it means I get to avoid Tony for a bit longer. Result.'

'If you're sure,' said Josie.

'Absolutely,' said Di firmly. 'So lose the stricken face. You and Harry can have some time to yourselves. I'm sure you need it.'

And with that, she was gone.

'Okay,' said Josie, 'time to talk about flowers . . .'

'Josie,' said Harry with a groan, 'do we have to?'

'Yes,' she said firmly, 'we absolutely do. Now shut up and listen.'

'I love it when you come over all dominant,' said Harry, giving her a grin that made her go shivery all over.

'Oh, do shut up,' said Josie, throwing a beer mat at him, but she felt better. Organising weddings was hard work, it was bound to make them tense with each other sometimes. So long as Harry always looked at her like that, they'd never have anything to worry about. 'And concentrate, we have a lot to organise.'

Ant was having a whale of a time. Freddie Puck was fascinating company and Auberon Fanshawe a master of the discreet, or not-so-discreet, celeb story. Ant couldn't believe his luck. Fancy meeting his boyhood heroes. No one, but no one would ever know how much time the young Ant had spent alone in his parents' shed with a box of matches and a firelighter, trying out Auberon's 'How Do You Light The Burnt Match?' trick. It was his little secret, but for the first time in his life he felt able to share it. They would understand. Freddie and Auberon were both good sports too, happy to have their photos taken with him, joking that their pictures would no doubt be all over Twitter and Facebook in an instant. Discreetly, when he thought they weren't looking, Ant had done exactly that. He felt a little foolish when they caught him out, but it wasn't every day you met your heroes . . .

'So what's your next project going to be?' Ant asked.

'Hush, hush, my boy,' Auberon tapped his nose. 'Early doors and all that. Let's say my agent is in some . . . interesting discussions. And I have a few irons in the fire production-wise. I'm more in the production side of things now, with Freddie here.'

Freddie gave Auberon a sly look.

'You could always sign up for *A Dream*. I hear an old friend of ours is playing Titania soon.'

Auberon blushed, and looked flustered. 'I don't think so,' he said.

'What about you, Freddie? Any chance we'll be seeing *Illusions* back on our screens?' asked Ant.

'Possibly,' said Freddie, 'but actually, I'm down here researching a new project.'

'Which is?'

'Going to different locations in the UK, and trying to work out if the local myths have any grain of truth in them.'

'Such as?'

'Well, here it's the Standing Stones,' said Freddie. 'Locally people claim to plight their troth at midnight, and fall in love for ever. I'm going to see whether by suggestion and hypnosis, we can actually make two people fall in love with one another.'

'Right,' said Ant. 'Now *that's* something I'd like to see. Because I don't believe it can be done. Take me for instance. I'm not in the slightest bit suggestible.'

'Really?' said Freddie. 'In my experience most people are a bit suggestible.'

'Well, if you could say, make me fall in love with – *that* woman,' said Ant, 'then maybe I'd believe you.' He pointed in the direction of Diana, then realised Diana had disappeared and he was pointing at Josie.

'What, that pretty little girl?' said Freddie. 'Easy peasy.'

'No, not her,' Ant looked round wildly for Diana. 'She's marrying my best friend. The other one – she was here a minute ago, tall, large, redheaded, loud, thoroughly obnoxious. She must be round here somewhere. I can honestly tell you she is the last person on earth I would want to be with, and vice versa. If you could make *her* fall in love with me, then maybe I'd believe you.'

'Are you a betting man?' said Freddie with a smirk.

'Okay,' said Ant. 'Tenner says it can't be done.'

'Twenty, that it can,' said Freddie.

He extended his hand to Ant.

'You have a deal, my friend.'

Chapter Five

'Well, that was exciting,' said Ant, finally making his way over to where Harry and Josie were sitting. Auberon and Freddie, no doubt glad to be free of their most enthusiastic fan, had settled down with their drinks in the far corner. Harry felt guiltily relieved. Maybe Josie would calm down on the wedding chat for a bit. He had tried to be as fascinated about flowers as she was, but he found he just couldn't do it. All he really wanted was to spend time alone with Josie and not have to mention weddings for a week.

'You've come to join us at last,' said Harry, 'and save me from this endless talk of weddings.'

He'd intended it as a joke, but a trace of irritation had entered his voice, and he could see from Josie's slight wince it wasn't lost on her. He immediately felt guilty again. He didn't want to upset Josie.

'What happened to Dynamite?' said Ant as he sat down.

'Gone for a walk to the Standing Stones,' said Harry.

'And don't call her that,' said Josie.

'Talking about the Standing Stones,' said Ant – before he was interrupted by a dramatic figure striding into the beer garden, followed by a retinue of apologetic-looking people clearly trying to calm her down.

'Who does he think he is?' she was saying angrily, 'coming here, spoiling my moment.'

'Don't worry about him, darling,' said a rather androgynous creature dressed in the tightest chinos that Harry had ever seen, and a long flowing top. Harry would have hazarded a guess at the figure being male, if it weren't for the long painted nails, and the high heels. He/she appeared to be following the woman, a blowsy-looking blonde dressed in tight leather clothes thirty years too young for her and dripping in gold, touching up her make-up at every opportunity. 'Don't frown, darling. You've only just had the Botox done.'

'Which means I can't frown, Gray,' snapped the woman.

'Is that?' asked Harry.

'Tatiana Okeby, yes,' said Josie, 'I remember her now. She and Auberon Fanshawe were all over the papers at one time. But, God, she's gone to seed.'

'Put your claws away,' said Ant. 'I think she's rather magnificent.'

Harry couldn't see it himself, she was a bit bold and brassy for his tastes, but she certainly had . . . something. The whole beer garden had stopped to listen to her, enthralled by the situation unfolding before them.

'Tatiana, my darling, what a lovely surprise,' Auberon Fanshawe drawled. He and Freddie had been sitting quietly in the far corner. Harry could see that Freddie was sniggering into his pint glass, clearly enjoying the drama.

'Surprise, my arse,' said Tatiana. 'You planned this, didn't you? You and Freddie. Just couldn't wait to spike my guns, could you?'

'What do you mean?' said Auberon, wide-eyed and innocent. 'Freddie and I are here quite by chance. Freddie's researching a new TV programme. We're staying at Tresgothen Manor.'

'How very convenient,' said Tatiana. 'That you just happen to turn up in the same village, where I've been staying already, negotiating to play Titania in *A Dream*. I've been in talks with Mike Slowbotham about it for days. You'd better not screw this up for me.'

'As if I would, Tati, as if I would. I'm sure the world is waiting with bated breath for your Titania.'

'Don't you dare,' she glared at him angrily. 'And don't call me Tati.' But she seemed mollified enough to calm down. Suddenly aware of her audience, she smiled graciously around her at the holidaymakers packing out the pub.

Before long someone had plucked up courage to ask for her autograph, and she smilingly obliged, as if the previous scene had never occurred. Soon she was surrounded by an adoring crowd and the chatter had returned to normal.

'Well, that was entertaining,' said Ant. 'What a woman. Never a dull moment.'

Josie laughed and took Harry's hand. 'At least we're not like that,' she said.

'I should hope not!,' said Harry, squeezing her hand tight. She smiled and squeezed his hand back.

'I do love you, Harry,' she said, leaning in to kiss him.

'Give me a break,' groaned Ant, and Harry threw a beermat at him.

'Sorry, mate, I am not going to pretend not to be in love, just to please you,' said Harry, kissing Josie full on the lips.

'Oh, Harry,' sighed Josie, blushing in a manner which was both sexy and endearing, and Harry felt a burst of happiness.

Josie was no diva, thank God. She was lovely and down to earth and straightforward. It was true at the moment she was going overboard on the wedding thing but it was a big deal for her, even if he'd rather have kept things simpler. But the bottom line was they loved each other very much. And that was the most important thing.

Josie walked back from the pub alone. After their all too brief moment of solidarity following Tatiana Okeby's outburst, when she and Harry had started to actually relax and enjoy some banter about the wedding instead of rub each other up the wrong way, Ant had come along and spoiled it all. Within minutes Harry had become absorbed in a deep conversation about rugby. As Josie had no interest whatsoever in the subject, this was tedious to say the least. She resented the way Ant seemed to expect to have Harry's attention by virtue of being his best friend. *But I'm his fiancée, I get preference*, she wanted to scream, even knowing it was childish. In the end, feeling like a spare part as Ant was extolling the virtues of some rugby prop she'd never heard of, she kissed Harry on the cheek, got up and left, telling him not to be too long.

'I promise I won't,' he said, squeezing her hand and mouthing *sorry* at her, which made her feel a little better. Ant could be overwhelming. It wasn't easy for Harry, she could see that.

The sun was low in the sky, and a warm breeze played through her long fair curls as she left the pub and walked through the rambling network of streets that made up Tresgothen. The shops were busy, tourists spilling out onto the streets, mingling among locals eating ice creams, and bearing gifts from the Piskie Shop, which prided itself on selling the widest variety of piskies this side of the Tamar. As Josie made her way up the steep winding hill home, past the little grey and white houses nestling in the hillside, she felt a wonderful sense of peace. Josie loved it down here; the colour of the sky, the sound of the sea, the call of the gulls, the briny tang in the air. While she enjoyed her life in London, Cornwall was in her blood, and she missed Tresgothen. The pace of life was slower, calmer, and *it's 200 miles away from Ant*, she caught herself thinking. She felt uneasy that he was here. Josie remembered that long-ago summer, when she'd invited a crowd from uni to stay. She'd actually been interested in Ant, she recalled, blushing. She remembered the way he'd looked at her, remembered the way he'd been back then: exciting, alluring . . . dangerous. But as soon as they'd arrived he'd been all over some girl, Kerry, was it? Josie had forgotten now. And then, Harry had been there, quiet, sweet Harry, the only person who'd been prepared to come out to see Shakespeare at the theatre with her. Harry. Her lovely Harry. How glad she was she'd found him again. She couldn't wait for them to be married.

Although . . . Harry didn't seem quite as enthusiastic as he had done. Josie blamed Ant, who kept making snide remarks about wearing a ball and chain. Di had told her not to be so stupid when she'd voiced her fears earlier in the day, but Josie was worried. Harry just didn't seem the same since they'd got here. She wasn't sure if it was just nerves. There was a strange feeling in the air. It was unsettling and Josie couldn't put her finger on it . . .

'How was the pub?' Josie's mum came to greet her. So warm, so reassuring. Some things never changed, and knowing Mum was always there was one of them.

'Great fun, the boys are staying a bit longer,' said Josie. 'We saw Tatiana Okeby –'

'– Who had a fight with Auberon Fanshawe,' continued Nicola. 'I know.'

'Who told you?' said Josie, laughing. She'd forgotten how swiftly news travelled in Tresgothen.

'Well, Mrs Allison was just coming out of the butchers,

when she met Jenny Osgood, who'd been walking past the beer garden and heard the whole thing.'

'More like snooping past the beer garden,' said Josie. Jenny Osgood was a well-known local gossip.

'So what happened, then?' Mum was all agog. 'Those two have history, you know.'

'We gathered,' said Josie. 'She accused him of following her down here. It wasn't pretty.'

'I bet,' said Josie's mum. 'The most exciting thing to happen in Tresgothen for years, and I missed it.'

'Oh, and she's apparently talking to Mike Slowbotham about being in *A Midsummer Night's Dream*,' said Josie. 'I didn't think he was anything to do with the theatre.'

'Oh, it's his new thing,' snorted Josie's mum. 'Somehow he's got on the board of directors who are behind the renovation project. He's got a bee in his bonnet about being an influential producer, and he's planning a production of *A Midsummer Night's Dream*. He claims that he's always wanted to see it put on at the theatre, but I'm not convinced. He's just interested in women, that one. He'd do anything to add someone like Tatiana Okeby to his bedpost. He's a total ass. Poor woman. Someone should tell her.'

'I'm not sure I'd like to be on the receiving end of that conversation,' said Josie. 'Now, come on, let's look at those wedding dresses again. I think I'm getting an idea of what I want . . .'

Ant and Harry had moved into the bar, and Ant was beginning to feel slightly drunk. It was a while since he'd had a session this early in the day, and he wasn't as used to it as he once was.

The bar had cleared out somewhat, and most of the tourists seemed to have moved on. Tatiana Okeby hadn't stayed long either. Auberon Fanshawe had also disappeared. Maybe he'd gone to try and appease her. But Freddie Puck was still propping up the bar when they came inside.

'Have you persuaded your friend to take part in my experiment?' Freddie gave an ingratiating smile.

'What experiment?' Harry looked puzzled.

'You know, the hypnotic thing,' said Ant. 'Freddie here thinks he can hypnotise us all. It's for a TV show.'

'Ha,' said Harry. 'Hypnotise us. I don't think so.'

'Oh, well, it was worth a punt,' said Freddie. 'There's a bit of money in it.'

Harry thought about that.

'Enough to go travelling?' he said.

'Not quite,' said Freddie, 'but maybe enough to have a great weekend away somewhere'.

'That would be nice,' said Harry. 'I'd at least like to pay for our honeymoon suite. Or maybe take Josie away for a long weekend – soften her up to go travelling with me.'

'I thought Josie's folks were paying for everything to do with the wedding,' said Ant, surprised.

'Yeah, well, it would be nice to pay for something,' said Harry, 'and I would like us to splash out on our wedding night.'

'So you'll think about it?' said Freddie.

Harry looked sheepish.

'Better run it by Josie first,' he said. 'Talking of which . . .' He looked at his watch. 'I think it's time we were heading back.'

'God, she really has got you under the thumb, hasn't she?' said Ant. 'One more can't hurt.'

Harry looked mortified. 'I'm not under the thumb,' he muttered. 'Josie's mum; it would be rude to her.'

'I suppose you're right,' said Ant, unconvinced. He had

a feeling Harry and Josie might be having words when they got back. Prime reason if ever he needed one to remind him never to get married. 'See you around, Freddie.'

'So what about my show?'

'We'll think about it,' said Harry.

'I shall just have to bring all my powers of persuasion to bear on Josie, won't I?' laughed Ant.

'Don't,' said Harry, 'please don't.'

Diana found herself wandering the coastal path and getting a bit lost, before she eventually reached the Standing Stones.

It was so peaceful up here. The wind tangled her hair, and she sat down and looked over the bay. The sun was dropping low on the horizon, casting out golden rays on a sparkling sea. Seagulls whirled high in the sky above her. It was just perfect. Diana felt free and happy for once. It wasn't a feeling she was very familiar with. Much of the time, she felt grouchy and miserable. Life hadn't quite panned out the way she'd thought From such promising beginnings, when she'd got promotion after promotion in the travel company she worked for, her career had stalled of late. The global recession had meant big cutbacks in her industry. And now she was beginning to think the unthinkable; maybe her job wasn't safe. The text she'd received before losing the signal had been ominous. Perhaps her dad had been right all those years ago. She should have done that law degree. The world always needed lawyers.

She heard her phone give a familiar beep. Brilliant, there must be a signal up here. Two seconds later she wished she hadn't checked. *Sorry to have to tell you but your services are no longer required*, followed by dozens of texts from work colleagues similarly affected. Overnight the company had gone into liquidation and everyone had been given the sack. Shit, shit, shit. Now what was she to do? She could just imagine Dad's reaction when she told him.

Stop, stop, stop. Old familiar feelings of self-hatred surged through her. Dad couldn't be right. Otherwise the life she'd carved for herself over the last few years was meaningless.

That was why Ant had seemed so special, of course. He'd been the first person to see through her spiky defences and find the real Diana, the vulnerable Di she kept hidden from the world. And for a time they'd been happy. She'd been properly happy, for perhaps the only time in her life. And then . . . he'd let her down. As everyone did. Ant had reminded her why she didn't let anyone get close to her, why she didn't trust anyone. She'd vowed never to make that mistake again, and up till now, she'd been true to her word.

But Ant, here; this weekend, when it was all about Josie and Harry and their marriage (despite having eschewed it for herself, she loved her friends and was genuinely happy for them). It was unsettling looking at him, and remembering a time when life had been very different.

This was no good at all. She and Ant were history. Diana took one last look at the view, and got up. Time to get back before they sent out a search party. No point letting Ant get to her. After the weekend she wouldn't have to see him till the wedding, and then he could disappear out of her life again. This time she hoped, for ever.

Chapter Six

'Do you really think that Freddie can hypnotise people?' Josie was laughing at Ant, who was pontificating once more about the conversation he'd had with the wonderful Freddie. He'd talked about nothing else since they came back from the pub, when Harry had whispered a hurried apology for staying out so long. Josie had never seen Ant so in awe of anyone. It was quite funny, as was the idea that he thought it was so real. Josie was a complete sceptic about that kind of thing. 'I thought all of that was just nonsense for the TV.'

Laughing at Ant was at least making her not so cross with Harry, who'd been behaving like a naughty little schoolboy since he came back. Why could he not just stand up to Ant and have come back at a sensible time?

'No, straight up. I went to see him when I was still at school. He could do it, definitely. He had people dancing with complete strangers on the stage, doing handstands. All sorts. You couldn't have faked it!'

'They might have been plants,' suggested Di, who had found her way back from the Standing Stones a few minutes earlier. She seemed flushed and thoughtful, but was making an effort to talk to Ant.

Ant bridled, 'I don't see how everyone could have been

a plant,' he said. 'At one point he had the whole audience doing the *Birdy Song*. Well, I don't quite remember doing it myself – I just remember him talking and standing up in the aisles with everyone else – it's weird, I've watched that episode and *everyone* took part.'

'Mass hallucination,' said Josie swiftly. 'Don't believe a word of it.'

They were sitting round the pool sipping cocktails, while Peter made his usual song and dance about the barbie, which was the sole interest he had in family cooking. In fact doing the barbie was about the only time Peter got involved with anything domestic. Josie loved her dad, but she was glad Harry, who was a keen cook, wasn't like that; if truth be told, Harry was better at cooking than Josie.

'What are we doing tomorrow?' said Harry, yawning.

'Di, Mum and I are dress shopping,' said Josie, 'and you, Dad and Ant have an appointment at Garratt's.' Garratt's was the local gentleman's outfitters.

'No, no, no,' said Ant looking horrified. 'You didn't tell me you'd dress me up like a penguin!'

'Sorry,' said Harry. 'You don't get a say in it, and neither do I.'

'Yeah, I can see that, mate,' drawled Ant. 'You've really got him jumping to your beat, haven't you, Jose? I can see I didn't come home a minute too soon.'

Josie felt like throttling him, but she smiled sweetly and said nothing. She hated conflict, and didn't want to start a row. She waited for Harry to say something, put Ant straight about their relationship, but Harry was silent. What was it about being round Ant that turned him into a Neanderthal? Why couldn't he stick up for her? Saying nothing was much worse than anything Ant had said.

'Right, I'd better see if Mum needs some help,' she said,

more brightly then she felt. She got up to go inside, and looked back at Harry hunched over his chair looking miserable, while Ant goaded him about the loss of his freedom. At least Harry didn't look happy about his lack of support, but she wanted to tell him to get some backbone. It had been a huge mistake having Ant here. He was going to ruin everything.

'You could at least try to tone it down, for Josie's sake,' hissed Diana at Ant, as Harry got up abruptly and went to help Peter on the barbecue.

'What? What did I say?' Ant thought he'd been rather jovial and friendly. He couldn't think why Diana was being so aggressive.

'All those jokes about Harry giving everything up for love. Do you think that's fair?'

'I'm only having a laugh,' said Ant. 'Though I don't expect you'd know anything about that.'

'Mainly because it's not funny,' said Diana.

Had she always been such a sullen cow? he thought. They'd had fun once.

'Oh, lighten up will you?' he said crossly. 'I'm just teasing them. Anyway, Harry *has* gone all dappy since he's got loved up with Josie. It's my duty as a friend to point it out.'

'Just because you wouldn't know what love is if it hit you between the eyes,' said Diana with feeling.

'And I know who I have to thank for that,' Ant shot back.

'That aside,' said Diana, 'other people do fall in love. And you should leave them be.'

'Why shouldn't I point out to my best mate that he's making a big mistake?' said Ant.

'Because he's not,' said Diana. 'You're just jealous.'

'I'm not jealous,' said Ant.

'Of course you are,' said Diana. 'You know that you're incapable of loving a woman the way Harry loves Josie, and you can't stand it.'

'That's because the only woman I ever loved turned her back on me.'

There was a pregnant pause, and then Diana turned accusing eyes on him. He felt deeply uncomfortable under her gaze.

'And why not, after what you did?'

'Who said I was talking about you?'

'Weren't you?' said Di.

They sat glaring at each other.

'This is ridiculous,' said Ant, finally, breaking the silence. 'I don't have to put up with this crap.'

He got up and wandered over to the men, where he felt safer. There was a reason he was single, and Diana had just reminded him of it. He felt hot under the collar just thinking about their time together. Being tied down to a woman screwed up your life. He didn't envy Harry one little bit. Diana had got that completely wrong. He was young, free and single and quite content to stay that way. Harry could settle into boring domesticity if he wanted to. There was a whole world out there and Ant wasn't done exploring it yet . . .

Diana felt like a spare part. The boys were happily ensconced with Peter at the barbie, trying to outdo each other in their efforts to impress him. Annoyingly, she had the feeling that Ant was winning. She knew if she joined Josie and Nicola indoors she'd be driven mad within minutes by the incessant wedding chat. She was happy for her friend, really she was, but the wedding seemed to be Josie's only topic of conversation. She knew that was the point of the weekend, but still. . . . True, Josie had been suitably sympathetic when Di had told her about her redundancy, immediately offering to help out financially if she could, but Di had waved her away, with a 'don't worry, I'll be fine' response, which Josie seemed to be taking literally.

'Come on, let's take your mind off things,' she'd said. 'Here look at some of these dresses, see what you think.'

So Di had been forced to endure half an hour of flicking through bridal magazines, looking at dresses she wouldn't be seen dead in.

'You'll find another job in no time,' she'd said, when she realised Di wasn't quite as focused on the dress issue as she was.

'Will I?' Di wanted to say, but she didn't have the heart. What was the point in ruining Josie's weekend, going on about how anxious she was? She'd have to face up to what had happened when she got home. Nothing she could do about it now.

Instead she smiled, and said 'That one's lovely' (it wasn't, but Josie seemed satisfied), and tried to throw herself into wedding chatter. It was why she'd come down, after all.

Diana took a sip of her cocktail and sat back, looking up at the evening sky. It was really warm and the bats were out in flight. As the night drew in, stars appeared, brighter then she'd ever seen before in England. There was so little background light here, she realised. In London you never saw the stars.

'Oh –' she looked in wonder as a shooting star flashed across the sky.

'Beautiful, isn't it?' Harry had reappeared. 'I could sit and watch the night sky for ever.'

'Could you?' said Diana.

'I wish I knew what they were all called though,' said Harry. 'I can just about tell what the evening star is. The rest of it is a complete mystery to me.'

'Aren't you needed at the barbie?' said Diana.

'Hardly,' said Harry. 'Particularly now Ant's started talking economics with Peter. I have no idea what they are talking about. I've never felt so unnecessary.'

'Me, you both,' laughed Diana. 'I couldn't face going inside to have another dull conversation about table decorations.'

'At least you can get away from it when you get home,' said Harry. 'Feel for me. I'm living with wedding mania 24/7.'

He looked sombre and a little sad.

'Are you okay?' said Diana. 'Only if you don't mind me saying, for the groom, you seem to be a bit down.'

'I'm fine,' said Harry. 'Just, Ant being here has reminded me of how much fun I had when I was single. And that before I met Josie, I was planning to go travelling . . .'

'Harry, you're not having doubts, are you?' Diana looked horrified.

'No, of course not,' said Harry hastily, 'I adore Josie, you know that. It's just . . .'

'Just what?' said Diana, looking baffled. 'I thought you wanted to get married.'

'I do,' said Harry. 'I did. But, Christ, I had no idea how much planning would be involved.'

Diana burst out laughing.

'Oh, Harry, you poor fool. Girls love planning weddings. Surely you realised that.'

Harry felt completely stupid.

'I hadn't actually,' he said. 'I thought it would be simple. We decide to get married, we have a few friends to church, we have a party, and that would be that. But . . .'

86

'Josie is overcomplicating things?'

'A bit,' said Harry. 'At the moment, I think I'd rather just go off to a desert island and get married without anyone else. I feel we're drowning in all this wedding preparation; forgetting the reason why we're doing it.'

'Well, why don't you, then?' said Diana. 'You could do that, go on your travels, do your travel journalism. Why not? I'm sure Josie would love it.'

'But you see how happy she is,' said Harry. 'This is what she wants, this is how she wants to do it. I'm being selfish. Although I would really love to talk about something other than the wedding for a change.'

'I know how you feel,' said Diana. 'I can't talk to Josie like I used to. I told her I'd been made redundant earlier, and she barely acknowledged it.'

'Oh, no, Di, I'm so sorry,' said Harry.

'I don't suppose Josie meant to be unkind,' said Diana with a sigh.

'What are you going to do?'

'Don't know yet,' said Diana. 'I expect I'll think of something. Don't fret too much about Josie. She's just so wrapped up in the wedding she's not thinking about anyone else at the moment.'

Harry gave her a rueful hug.

'I expect she'll calm down about it eventually.'

'Sorry,' said Diana. 'I shouldn't be bitching about it. It's not fair.'

'Neither should I,' said Harry. 'I'm just feeling stressed, that's all. I hate coming down here at the best of times. Josie's dad always makes me nervous. I'm sure he'd rather she was marrying someone like Ant.'

Di glanced over at Ant, who was holding court with Peter in a suave and sophisticated way. She could see that cute, quiet, slightly bumbling Harry might feel he couldn't compete.

'But she chose you, didn't she?' said Diana encouragingly. 'And it's Josie you're marrying, not her dad . . .'

Harry was feeling more and more out of sorts. When they'd got back from the pub and seen that Josie and her mum were knee-deep in paper, sorting out menus and seating plans, he'd felt he should have been helping, but Josie had dismissed his apology with an airy, 'Oh, we don't need you for this bit,' and yet he still felt in the wrong. To his horror, their quiet little wedding had morphed into a larger and larger affair. As well as the 150 guests who were now coming to the reception ('How do we even know 150 people?' he'd asked, perplexed), a further 100 ('From the village,' Nicola had said glibly) were coming for a disco buffet in the evening. A marquee the size of Buckingham Palace had been ordered to accommodate them all, and if Nicola had her way, it would be erected on top of a cliff, which struck Harry as a mental idea. When he thought of how much this was all going to cost, Harry felt slightly weak at the knees. But Josie was blasé about it. He supposed that was what coming from a moneyed background did for you. But he couldn't help feeling it was all a bit wasteful. And he felt a gnawing worry about the honeymoon. After all this, Josie would be expecting something really special.

'I never knew that I could feel so emasculated by my own wedding,' he said to Diana.

'In what way?' Di laughed at him. She often did. Other people found Diana prickly and difficult, but Harry had always liked her. She was refreshingly honest, and never dressed things up to make them better. And – a guilty thought crept into his head – she was feistier and more vivacious then Josie.

'It's just that there doesn't appear to be much for the groom to do, other then turn up,' he said.

'Well, that is your main job,' said Diana. 'Weddings are really for mothers and daughters. If you're worried about it, why not talk to Josie about it.'

It was the obvious thing to do, Harry knew.

'She's so into it all,' he said, 'I don't want to upset her. I expect I'm making a fuss about nothing.'

'I expect you are,' said Di touching his arm sympathetically. 'It won't last for ever.'

'As long as Josie calms down after it's all over,' said Harry. 'It's enough to send me back on the fags.'

'If you're that desperate,' said Di, 'I've been sneaking down to the end of the garden for the odd puff. I've got through most of the packet this evening thinking about my lack of prospects. I can't face the thought of Peter quizzing me about my future, when he finds out I've been made redundant. That is, if Josie even remembers to tell him.'

Harry laughed. His in-laws' house was definitely not the place you could ask to smoke in. He was sorely tempted. He'd given up smoking shortly after he and Josie had got together – her dislike of them being enough to keep him on the straight and narrow. But one . . . one couldn't hurt.

'Okay, you're on,' he said.

Feeling like a naughty schoolboy, he followed Di nonchalantly down the garden, where she lit a cigarette and passed it to him.

The first puff made him light-headed. He breathed it in

deeply and enjoyed the moment. He'd forgotten how much he enjoyed the sensation. Before he knew it, he was halfway through his second fag.

'We'd better be getting back,' said Di, stubbing hers out and throwing the stub over the hedge into the field that backed onto Josie's parents' garden.

'Wouldn't do to get caught,' Harry agreed. 'Josie would be livid.'

He grinned conspiratorially at Diana. It was a relief to be doing something he actually wanted to do for once. It seemed like ages since he'd led a life of his own.

They made their way up the garden, giggling like two naughty school kids.

As they emerged from behind the bushes, Josie walked out onto the patio, carrying a salad bowl. She looked over at them and a sudden stab of pain shot across her face. She covered it up quickly, saying brightly, 'So, what have you two been up to?'

'Just had a stroll around the garden,' said Harry, trying not to feel guilty, but she looked so stricken he suddenly realised she'd drawn the wrong conclusion. 'Josie –' he began, but she slammed the salad down on the table and fled into the kitchen. Oh God, what had he done?

1986: Tatiana

'Tatiana, darling, give us your best smile.'

The cameras flashed as she spun and smiled and pouted and grimaced on the red carpet, on the way into the newly inaugurated UK TV Awards, held this year at the Royal Opera House, Covent Garden. And it was all for her. *Sail for the Sun* was a huge success, and this year, Sandy Kane's heartbreaking storyline, involving a miscarriage, a nervous breakdown, and an unfaithful husband, had ensured that *Sail for the Sun* had been topping the TV charts for week after glorious week. And she was its star. Finally, all the years of hard work had paid off and she was at the top of the tree.

'Come on, love, show us a bit more cleavage,' said Snifter Suggs, a particularly loathsome member of the paparazzi who'd gained his moniker from being able to sniff out where the good stories were to be found. Tatiana smiled sweetly but failed to oblige, and shoved back the unwelcome thought that despite her success, she was still the painted doll, preening to give men pleasure.

'Yes, Tati, do show us your tits,' a sneering voice behind her said.

Bron. That was all she needed. Annoyingly, he and Freddie were also up for several awards tonight. *Illusions* was the most-watched TV show on a Saturday night, 'great family viewing', the *Mail* had called it, and it regularly got viewing figures of over twenty million, not quite as good as *Sail for the Sun*, which had maxed out at twenty-nine million for the episode in which Sandy Kane's discovery of her husband's infidelity had led to her miscarriage, but it grated on her that Bron and Freddie were having such success. Freddie had finally got what he'd always wanted, and he and Bron were reaping the rewards.

'Bron, Tati, give us a picture together, go on,' said Snifter.

Ever the professional, Tati duly obliged, but as she draped herself seductively on Bron's shoulder, she whispered in his ear, 'Got another child bride?' and nodded at the young girl hovering awkwardly on the red carpet. Tati felt sorry for her; she was only the latest of a string of young starlets whose name Bron was being linked to. No doubt to replace the current Debbie McGee (who'd earned her spot on the show by the same means) as soon as her contract was up.

'Over here, Tati!' shouted a voice from the other side of the barrier, and Tati duly smiled as she leaned over in the other direction.

'Really, Bron, you're getting to be a bit of a joke, chasing after young women, when everyone can see that bald patch every week on TV.'

That was a low blow. She knew how sensitive he was about his hair.

'At least I have a love life.' Tatiana's last boyfriend's parting gift had been to describe their sexploits to the *Sunday Sport*.

'At least my hair's all my own,' snapped Tatiana, before smiling sweetly once more for the cameras and sweeping off inside the theatre.

Please God let me win tonight, and not Bron, she thought. If there is any justice in this world, that's how things should be. She felt nervous as hell. By rights, she should win for her portrayal of Sandy Kane, but she was up against stiff competition from her rival Candida Cordwell, whose portrayal of brave Merry Edwards coping with cancer in *Meet Me in Manhattan* had also garnered huge praise.

It was the first time Tati had been to an event like this and she was still star-struck by the comedy compere, whose TV show she'd watched since childhood, and terrified at the thought of having to speak to the Hollywood film actor who was giving out the prize for best actress, should she win. Susan Peasebottom was doing her best to hold Tati's hand, throughout the course of a long evening, in which the prize for Best Light Entertainment Show, Best TV Duo, Best Production and Best Direction went to *Illusions*, but it wasn't helping. Tati had taken two Valium before she came out but her nerves were still jangling all over the place, and despite her best intentions, she drank rather a lot of champagne. More, certainly, than she'd intended. She was just vainly looking around for another refill when Antony Hayward, the gorgeous Hollywood star of yester-year, got up to announce the winner of the Best Actress category. Tati was so tense, she didn't hear a word he'd said, and it was only when Susan prised the glass out of her hand and started steering her towards the stage that Tati realised what had happened.

Everyone in the room seemed to be on their feet; she'd never heard so much applause. And it was all for her. Tati staggered towards the bright lights of the stage, feeling more than a little tipsy, and sick to the core. What the hell was she supposed to do now? Damn, they'd rehearsed this in case she won, but nerves combined with champagne made her forget what she was supposed to be doing.

'Well, well, your little TV show made the grade,' a voice

said in her ear, and she realised Freddie Puck was raising his glass to her. Without thinking, she grabbed the glass from his hand, marched up to the stage, practically wrestled the award from Antony Hayward's unsuspecting grasp, and said, 'I'd like to thank everyone on the cast of *Sail for the Sun*, without whom I wouldn't be here today, and my wonderful agent Susan Peasebottom, thank you from the bottom of my heart, I couldn't have done it without you.' She paused and looked around the room, lighting eventually on Bron and Freddie's table. 'There are some people here who never thought I could do this, and I did. Which just goes to show you should follow your dreams. Cheers, everybody,' she raised her glass, before staggering unceremoniously offstage. As she walked past Bron and Freddie's table, she quietly poured the champagne on Freddie's head, and then went back to sit with the cast and crew of *Sail for the Sun* and bask in their adulation.

She had her crown. She had her victory. So why did it feel so hollow?

Chapter Seven

Diana was at the Standing Stones. She was standing, staring out to sea, the wind blowing through her hair. The sun was going down and the cliff was alive with burnished gold.

She heard someone call her name, and turning, she thought she saw Ant coming towards her, before the figure dissolved into Tatiana Okeby, saying, 'What angel wakes me from my flowery bed . . .'

'Rise and shine!' Josie came bounding into Diana's room ridiculously early for a Saturday, particularly one when they were away for the weekend.

'What time is it?' Diana came slowly to.

'Nine a.m., sleepyhead, I've been up for hours,' said Josie. Although she seemed bright and breezy, Diana thought she could detect a note of something else, as though Josie was determined to put on a show. An uncomfortable feeling of guilt shot through her. Josie hadn't said anything, but Diana saw how it could have looked, her and Harry coming up the garden like that. But he'd sworn her to secrecy about his smoking, and she felt it wasn't her secret to share with Josie.

'Come on, time to get out and at 'em. We're going to Penzance to do some serious dress shopping.'

'Ugh,' said Diana, pulling the duvet back. Maybe she was wrong. Maybe Josie hadn't been affected by last night.

'I'm a woman on a mission,' said Josie.

'I can see that,' grumbled Diana, but she got out of bed. Her throat was sore from smoking too much, her mouth tasted sour and her head was thumping. Drinking always seemed like a good idea at the time.

Half an hour later, she, Nicola and Josie were having breakfast. There was no sign of the boys.

'Sleeping off their hangovers, bless them,' smiled Nicola, as if she were talking about children. Diana noticed Josie give a little wince of annoyance. Diana didn't blame her. Nicola was so meek and mild it made Diana really impatient. She hoped that Josie wasn't cast in the same mould, and wouldn't turn into a carbon copy of her mum once she was settled down with Harry. Di thought her friend had more about her than that, but looking at Nicola, she did wonder sometimes.

'Where's Peter?' asked Diana.

'Working,' said Nicola. 'I never disturb him when he's working.'

No, I bet you don't, thought Diana, snaffling another piece of toast. Wouldn't want to disturb the great man, would we?

'Come on,' said Josie, before she'd finished, 'time we were off.'

'Oh, right,' said Diana, feeling a little miffed. She liked her breakfast to be relaxed at the weekends. She had realised they were going to be busy today, but not quite how regimented things were going to be. She got up with a sigh, and went to get ready.

'What are the boys going to do while we're out?' said Diana, as she climbed into the car behind Josie and Nicola.

'As little as possible,' said Josie firmly, exchanging looks with her mother. 'I've booked them in with Garratt's in the village to sort out their suits, but that's it. I don't trust Ant anywhere near the arrangements for my wedding, and as for Harry . . . Well, let's just say his efforts so far have been somewhat less than helpful.'

'Oh,' said Diana, preparing to settle down for a journey of endless bridal chatter.

After twenty minutes in the car with Josie discussing the minutiae of flowers for the buttonholes, Diana felt like slitting her wrists. Did it matter that the bride's side had pink, and the groom's white? Or how big the mums' corsages were going to be? Had she known it was going to be like this, Di might never have put the idea of weddings into Josie's head. She was beginning to feel quite sorry for Harry. No wonder he'd wanted a fag last night. By the end of the weekend he'd probably be on forty a day. Josie's search for the perfect wedding was beginning to grate.

But it was hard to remain irritated when they arrived in Penzance and Josie took both Diana and Nicola by the arm, saying, 'This is so fabulous. I'm going to choose my wedding dress with my two favourite people. What could possibly be better?'

Her enthusiasm was so infectious, Diana felt a heel. Josie was so lovely and so thrilled about getting married, it was mean-spirited and churlish not to feel happy for her. Di squeezed her arm tight and said, 'Penzance here we come!' and happily followed Josie's lead through the streets on the search for the perfect wedding dress.

'Oh, Josie, that's beautiful.'

Josie emerged from the changing room, wearing a simple but elegant gown in ivory silk, with a lacy bodice, long lacy sleeves, and a skirt that swirled as she walked.

'I don't know,' said Nicola critically. 'I think you can do better.'

'Really?' Diana was flabbergasted. 'I think she looks amazing.'

'Nah, don't think I like this one,' said Josie.

Half an hour later they left the shop empty-handed, and then proceeded to make their way through every bridal shop in Penzance. Josie tried on dozens of dresses, but none of them was right.

'It pinches too much,' she said of one dress, which admittedly looked as if it was made for a size zero American model, or 'I look all boobs and bum,' she wailed of another which accentuated her body into a Marilyn Monroe-type shape. But not in a good way.

Whichever dress Josie tried on was wrong. It was either too short, or too long, didn't show enough cleavage, or showed too much. It didn't matter that Diana and Nicola pointed out that each offending dress could be altered to suit, Josie found something to criticise about every single one, though Diana and Nicola had agreed there were at least three which made Josie look stunning. Even Nicola, whom Diana had never heard raise her voice before, said rather tetchily at one point, 'Come on, Josie, surely something must be right?'

'You're going to kill me,' said Josie. 'But you know that very first dress we saw . . .'

Diana had known the elegant lace gown, which had shown Josie off to complete advantage, was the one, but Josie wouldn't be told.

'I'm sorry,' she said, 'I just want everything to be perfect.'

Perfect. Of course she did. And of course it would be. Perfect – because Josie's life was always perfect, from her looks, personality, to her boyfriend, job and home. She didn't have messy relationships or redundancy issues. Josie's life *was* perfect.

Hang on? Where had that come from? Diana was pleased for her friend, really she was. And yet suddenly she felt herself being ever so slightly jealous . . .

Harry woke up with a thumping head. He rolled over. Josie wasn't beside him. She'd gone to bed before him last night, without saying a word, and had been fast asleep when he came to bed. And now she appeared to have got up and left without saying anything either. She must be very angry with him. He glanced at his watch. Ten-thirty already. Damn. Where was she? The thought of braving the breakfast table so late, without Josie, filled him with horror. His future in-laws always breakfasted early, and it was usually cooked. It was the only home he'd ever been in where breakfast felt formal. Josie must be furious with him to let him face the outlaws alone.

He got out of bed gingerly. Those vodka shots with Ant at two a.m. had been a mistake.

'Go on if you want, lightweight,' Ant had taunted when Harry had muttered something about going to bed, 'but since Peter has given us the full run of his drinks cabinet, it seems rude not to indulge.'

So indulge they had. Blearily, he even wondered if Peter had actually given them permission to raid his drinks cabinet. Ant certainly seemed to think so – he and Peter having bonded more in six hours than Harry had in six months. But even if Peter was fancying Ant as an alternative son-in-law (as no doubt he was), would he be happy to see quite how much they'd consumed?

Ugh. He tried to stand up and the room spun. The sun was shining in. It was very, very bright, and the sound of the seagulls outside was driving him crazy. And he thought living in London was noisy. Harry was tempted to go back to bed, but that was only putting off the inevitable. Reluctantly he showered, shaved, got dressed and tried to make himself look vaguely presentable, though the hollow gauntness round his eyes rather gave the game away.

When he finally made it to the main house, Ant and Peter were drinking coffee and eating toast, bonding some more over the *FT*. Ant, he was irritated to see, was looking distinctly bright-eyed and bushy-tailed.

'Ah there you are, old boy,' said Peter, with such forced joviality that Harry wondered if he was finding this weekend as excruciating as Harry was. 'We were about to send out search parties. The girls have gone swanning off to Penzance to buy dresses, and it's my job to take you two reprobates to try on our monkey suits.'

'Great,' said Harry faintly. 'Look forward to it.'

'You're looking quite green, mate,' said Ant. 'Hope your head isn't throbbing too much.'

'Yours is clearly fine,' snapped Harry, feeling uncharacteristically irritated with his friend.

'Some of us can take it,' grinned Ant in an infuriatingly superior manner, and Peter grinned with him, making Harry's sense of humiliation complete.

'I do find that weekends like this sort the men from the boys,' said Peter. Great. His future father-in-law clearly saw him as a total lightweight. Not for the first time, Harry wished he were somewhere else.

Josie was also feeling irritable. She'd been planning this day for weeks, and it had gone horribly wrong. She'd so wanted Mum and Diana with her to help choose her wedding dress and they'd been no help at all. Mum, who never raised her voice, had yelled at her at one point, and Di was clearly getting exasperated that Josie couldn't make up her mind. 'Surely there must be one you like,' she kept saying.

'But it's the most important dress I'll ever wear,' Josie had wailed, 'I just want it to be right.' Josie felt they were both fed up with her, particularly Di. This wasn't the way things were supposed to be. Plus, while she'd been immersing herself in dress shopping, it had kept her from thinking too deeply about what she'd witnessed in the garden last night.

Josie had played the scene over in her head from the previous evening, again and again. She had been too upset to say anything to Harry last night and gone to bed early to avoid a confrontation, but he and Di had looked so guilty as they'd walked up the path, almost as if they were hiding something. Though surely, surely, they couldn't have? Josie hadn't trusted herself to ask Harry directly, in case she'd seen something in his eyes to confirm her suspicions, so she'd gone to bed early, feeling utterly miserable. She'd tried to hint to Harry to join her, but he'd avoided her eye and seemed intent on drinking the night away with Ant. It was as if he didn't want to spend time with her. He was dead to the world when she'd got up this morning, and so she'd left with a feeling of unresolved misery.

And now Diana was acting funny too. She seemed so grumpy and stressed. What if her suspicions *weren't* unfounded? What if Di and Harry were –?

'So, are you going to make me wear this meringue or not?' Diana was standing in front of her, looking fed up in a pale pink ridiculously frilly dress. With her flaming red hair and fair complexion, it made her look washed out and anaemic. Even Josie had to admit that it would be a mistake to make Di wear it.

Perhaps I should make her wear it anyway. The thought crept into her head, although she tried to shake it off. She was being unkind; a feeling Josie was unfamiliar with and which wasn't making her feel good about herself.

'She certainly won't.' For the first time that day, Mum took charge. 'Really, Josie, what were you thinking,' she scolded. 'That colour makes poor Diana look pasty faced, and shows off her natural charms a little too amply.'

'Let's have a change of tack,' Josie said brightly. 'Why don't we go for lunch and leaf through some more of those bridal magazines, to get some fresh ideas.'

'Anything to get me out of wearing this monstrosity,' said Diana.

'Great,' said Josie more cheerfully than she felt. 'Lunch it is then.'

Ant stood in the men's changing room, feeling as if Paul Whitehouse was about to peer round the corner at any minute. Despite cockily trying to pretend he was used to these places, he'd never had a made-to-measure before. True, his suits were expensive, but they were always off the peg.

He felt uneasy and uncomfortable. He'd spent the best part of last night trying to persuade Harry he was making a mistake. 'Come on mate, admit it. You know you're going to regret this,' he said, but Harry wasn't having any of it, replying, 'Pisshoff and pass the vodka.' So Ant had to give up, and now his head was pounding from the vast quantities of vodka he'd drunk (not that he was going to admit that to Harry).

'You don't understand,' Harry had slurred earnestly. 'I love her, she's perfect.'

Ant could understand that. If Ant had Josie as a girlfriend, maybe he'd have changed his mind about marriage too. She was gorgeous, and sweet and funny. He'd known it when they'd first met all those years ago, and inexplicably, she'd chosen Harry over him. The knowledge that she was now utterly unattainable made her both more alluring to him, and viciously nastier about the wedding, despite the fact he could see it was annoying both Josie and Harry. Ant wasn't quite sure why he was behaving like such a bastard, but Diana's presence wasn't helping. Why people felt the need to get married, he had no idea. He felt the world would get on much better if the sexes kept themselves separate apart from for purely recreational reasons, or perhaps, occasionally to procreate.

'Right, sir, let me just take a tape measure to your inner thigh,' the shop assistant was unfailingly polite, but it didn't stop Ant from feeling incredibly awkward.

'Suits you, sir,' joked Ant. The guy was probably sick of that joke.

'Indeed, sir,' said the assistant, which instantly put him in his place. This was utter torture. Ant couldn't believe he was being made to go through it, or how long it seemed to take to get measured up.

'That was such an ordeal,' he said as he emerged from the dressing room, to find Peter and Harry waiting for him. 'I've never felt so uncomfortable in my life. Suits you indeed.'

Peter guffawed with laughter. 'I've always thought Mr Garratt bore a passing resemblance to Mark Williams,' he said. 'Very good. I say, that was good, wasn't it, Harry?'

'Yes,' said Harry, 'hilarious.'

But he looked down and miserable as he said it. This would never do.

'Pint to celebrate getting through that?' said Ant.

'Why not?' said Peter. 'The girls will be gone for hours. I think we deserve a drink.'

'My thoughts exactly,' said Ant, rubbing his hands.

The day was looking up already.

Chapter Eight

Harry cradled his pint, feeling miserable.

'Hair of the dog's what you need, old boy!' Peter had clapped him on the back in bonhomie, and ordered a pint of Idle Brew, the strongest beer Tresgothen had to offer. Harry's constitution was still feeling pretty delicate, and he wasn't quite ready for beer yet. By teatime, maybe he'd be up for it, but it wasn't even one o'clock. Besides, he didn't think Josie was going to be too happy with him if he came back drunk.

Knowing how exacting Josie could be about sharing out domestic tasks, Harry also felt uneasy about the state they'd left the kitchen in after breakfast. But Peter had insisted that Nicola 'wouldn't mind' clearing up, so Harry had tried to pretend that Josie wouldn't mind either. After all, it wasn't her house. But the nagging feeling that she might be cross wouldn't quite go away. And he was certain she'd be angry with him for drinking again. That coupled with the guilt he was still feeling about last night, made him sip his beer slowly, and when Ant and Peter tried to persuade him to a second, he said no.

How's it going? He texted Josie carefully.

Rubbish. was the response. *You?*

Suits ordered. In pub. Back soon.

DON'T BE LATE.

The capitals didn't bode well, but at least she'd responded, he thought.

'I really think we ought to get going soon,' Harry said. He didn't want to be back after Josie.

'Nonsense,' boomed Peter. 'Nicola's just texted me to say they're having a spot of lunch. We'll be back long before them. I just want to have a chat with Lionel Roberts about some golf club business and then we'll have another pint.'

Golf club business. Of course he did. Harry really wondered sometimes about the world he was entering.

'Harry, come on, mate, there's no hurry,' said Ant. 'I bet they'll be ages.'

'Josie asked me not to be late back,' mumbled Harry.

'And we won't be,' said Ant, wafting away his concern. 'Come on, one more pint can't hurt.'

Harry, who had only just managed to finish his first pint, allowed himself to be persuaded. Just as they sat down with it outside, a familiar figure came over to them.

'Ant, great to see you again,' Freddie Puck was pumping Ant's hand enthusiastically. 'And, Henry, isn't it?'

'Harry,' he reminded him.

'How are you both today?' said Freddie. 'Enjoying this glorious Cornish sunshine?'

'I would if my head wasn't pounding so much,' said Ant, clearly delighted that Freddie had joined them.

'So, have you thought any more about my offer?'

'Your offer?' Harry was puzzled for a minute.

'Do you want to be hypnotised?' said Freddie.

'Oh, that,' said Harry.

'Only, Bron and I are staying at Tresgothen Manor and we wondered if you guys wanted to come over there tomorrow and give it a go? What do you think?'

106

'I think it's a great idea,' said Ant. 'Don't you, Harry?'

'Er,' Harry hadn't actually talked to Josie about it yet, but judging by how sceptical she'd been, he couldn't see her agreeing to it with any great pleasure.

'Don't forget about the money,' said Ant, teasingly.

'The money isn't that brilliant,' said Harry, 'but I'll think about it.'

'Excellent,' said Freddie. 'Here's my card, give me a ring and we'll see what we can do.'

He walked away with the confidence of one who knew just what he was doing, and Harry's heart sank further. Now what had he got himself into?

'I think that calls for another pint,' said Ant triumphantly, and Harry's heart sank further. It was going to be a very long afternoon.

Lunch proved a welcome distraction, and Josie even managed to talk about something other than wedding matters, mainly because Nicola had been talking non-stop about how Mrs Bertram in the post office was sure that Tatiana Okeby was going to be staying in her yurt for a long time.

'The rumours about her playing at the theatre must be true,' said Nicola, in delight. 'It's so exciting. I hope I can get her autograph.'

'You might not have to wait too long,' said Diana drily, and she and Josie had to practically gag Nicola's squeals when she pointed out Tatiana Okeby (in what she clearly thought was a heavy disguise of sunglasses and headscarf) sneaking into the café and discreetly finding a spot in the corner. This time she was completely alone, minus her entourage.

'Ooh, I wonder what she's doing in here,' said Nicola,

who almost passed out with joy as Tatiana brushed past their table. Diana had never seen Josie's prim and proper mum so excited.

'I think I can guess,' said Josie. 'Look, it's Mike Slowbotham. Do you think he's trying to use his powers of persuasion on her?'

Mike Slowbotham swept in, in an attempt at grandeur. He clearly thought the whole café would stop to look at him.

'Tatiana, my darling,' he said loudly, greeting her like a long-lost friend.

'So much for anonymity,' said Josie. 'He clearly wants everyone to know who he's meeting.'

'Shh, shh,' said Tatiana, 'I'm trying to be incognito.'

'I've never seen anyone less incognito in my life,' snorted Diana.

They watched in fascination as Tatiana and Mike outdid one another in over-politeness.

Just then, the door of the café opened again. 'Surprise, surprise,' said Diana, as a photographer entered, along with a woman holding a dictaphone.

'Jenny Barrow, *Tresgothen Gazette*,' she thrust her dictaphone in Tatiana's face. 'Is it true you are in talks with Mr Slowbotham about bringing *A Midsummer Night's Dream* to our famous theatre?'

Tatiana drew herself up regally, as if about to hold court. She looked around in some disappointment and said, 'Only two of you?' but then, consummate performer that she was, overcame her dismay and gave a charming account of the interesting conversation she'd had with Mike Slowbotham. 'whom I'm sure can tell you more about it than I can.' Then she got up and went to leave the café.

As Tatiana walked past their table, Nicola pounced.

'Miss Okeby, I'm a huge fan of yours. Please, may I have your autograph?'

Tatiana was evidently in a hurry, but couldn't resist the lure of an actual fan who actually wanted her autograph.

'Delighted, I'm sure.' Diana noticed that it was said with some reluctance, but she consented to have her picture taken with Nicola, who had descended into simpering schoolgirl levels of idiocy. Diana had never seen Nicola anything but unruffled and in control, and it was amusing to see her so overwhelmed.

'So are we going to see you tread the boards in Tresgothen?' gushed Nicola. 'It would be so wonderful for the village if you could.'

'We'll see,' said Tatiana. 'If I have to talk to that odious little man about it any more, I might lose the will to live.'

'Oh, please,' said Nicola. 'It's a while since we've had a star in the village. It would be such an honour. Only, I'm not sure Mike —'

'I'll be delighted then,' said Tatiana graciously. 'I can't let my fans down.' And with that, she swept out.

'I was going to warn her about Mike Slowbotham,' said Nicola.

'I think she's got his measure,' laughed Diana. 'Look at him.'

Mike was still deep in conversation with the journalist. Every other word seemed to be 'Tatiana, said this, or Tatiana has promised that.' Unbeknownst to him, the journalist was edging away, trying to wrap it up.

'That has been the perfect end to the morning,' sighed Nicola.

'And the day's not over yet,' said Josie. 'Time to look at some more dresses.'

'Oh, God,' groaned Diana.

'Just kidding,' said Josie, 'we're going back to the first shop, and I'm going to buy the first one I tried on, and you are going to choose whichever dress you really want to wear.'

'Thank God for that,' said Diana.

Two hours later, Josie was feeling relieved that at least she'd got her wedding dress sorted, and Diana had chosen a sensational strapless turquoise gown, which showed her colouring off to perfection. God alone knew what kind of flowers would go with it – the pink and white theme was clearly going to have to go out – but Josie was past caring. At least they hadn't come away empty-handed.

They'd been so long, Josie was sure the boys would have been back by now. She hadn't heard from Harry since a text a couple of hours earlier saying they were in the pub, and when she tried to ring him, his phone was off.

'Tea, anyone?' said Nicola, going into the kitchen, and then saying, 'Oh.'

Josie followed her in. The kitchen, which they had left neat and tidy, now looked like a bomb had hit it. The boys had clearly had breakfast and left everything for someone else to clear up.

'I'll kill Harry,' said Josie. 'I asked him specifically before we came to help out in the kitchen.'

'It's all right, dear, I'll tidy up.' Josie's mum took on a martyred air which she knew too well, and was precisely why Dad never did anything round the house. And why Josie had sworn she wasn't going to spend her married life running round after Harry the way her mum had after her dad. Mum always said she didn't mind. 'It gives me something to do,' she'd say, but Josie was often frustrated by her lack of ambition. Surely there was more to life than keeping her house clean, especially when you had two cleaners who came in every week?

Josie wanted to protest that Mum should leave it for the men to do when they came back, but cross and all as she was, it wasn't her house, and they weren't her rules. She was furious that Harry hadn't at least tried to improve the situation, but resorted to slobby behaviour just because Ant and her dad did.

'I can't believe they're not back from the pub yet,' she said, starting to help Mum as she couldn't bear the thought of her doing everything. It was another thing that was making her cross. Harry would be fit for nothing for the afternoon at this rate.

'Boys will be boys,' said Nicola indulgently. 'And really, you don't need to help. I'll do it. You two sit by the pool, and enjoy the sunshine while it lasts. Heaven knows when we'll get another weekend like this.'

Reluctantly feeling like she was dumping on her mum, while simultaneously seething that the boys had got away with it, Josie joined Diana at the pool. It was shaping up to be a boiling hot afternoon, and Di was already slathering suntan lotion on and didn't seem to share Josie's irritation.

'If your mum wants to be a martyr, let her,' she said. 'I bet she gets her own way with other things. I wouldn't want to cross her too much if I were your dad. Come on. Your mum's right. You need to take a break from all this frantic wedding planning and relax for five minutes. It won't kill you.'

Josie slid into place next to Di. She felt churned up and miserable and now Diana seemed to be saying . . .

'You don't think I've turned into the bride from hell, do you?'

'No,' said Diana, 'but you could calm it down a bit. I think you're terrifying poor Harry.'

'Harry?' Josie felt jumpy and suspicious again.

'Yes, Harry, your fiancé, Harry,' said Diana.

'What's he been saying to you?' said Josie, really wanting to know and *when* had he been saying it?

'Nothing. Just last night, he hinted. Well, he mentioned – he's feeling a bit overwhelmed.'

'What, when you had your nice little tête-à-tête in the garden?' the words were out before Josie could stop herself.

'Look, Josie, that wasn't what you think –' Diana started to say before the boys marched in, loud and leery. Just what Josie didn't want.

'I think I will go and help Mum after all,' Josie said, and ignoring Diana's hurt look, went indoors. Not trusting herself to go into the kitchen in case Mum asked if anything was wrong, she hurried into the lounge instead.

'Oops,' she thought she heard Ant say, 'Think you're in big trouble, mate.'

Not as much as me, Josie thought, not as much as me.

When they finally made it back to the house, Harry was like a cat on hot bricks.

'Calm down, mate, you'll give yourself a heart attack.'

Peter seemed to have the right attitude, as far as Ant could tell. The girls would all have been chatting about the wedding and wouldn't have missed them. Ant couldn't see what the big deal was, and was dismayed that his best mate was so domesticated now he seemed to be unable to enjoy himself for five minutes without Josie's company.

But when they got in, and he saw the way Josie glared at Harry, even Ant felt a slight twinge of guilt. Bugger, he might have unwittingly caused a domestic, which meant this weekend could only get more unpleasant. Maybe he ought to help them out.

Peter, who seemed oblivious to any awkward atmosphere that had built up, tried to fix Harry a drink, despite Harry half-heartedly saying he only wanted an orange juice.

'You'll have to do better than that on your stag night,' Ant heard Peter say as he slipped into the house and went in search of Josie.

He found her in the lounge, flicking through wedding magazines in a desultory manner. She looked pale, and he thought she might have been crying. Ant was good at telling the signs. Women seemed to cry a lot around him, for some reason. Even when he laid it on the line and did the whole consenting adults thing, they always seemed to cry.

'Oh, it's you,' she said with barely concealed distaste.

'Er, is everything all right, Jose?' he said.

'Not really,' said Josie, 'No thanks to you.'

Ant sat down, 'I'm sorry, Josie. It's not Harry's fault we're late, he's been trying to come home for hours and it was your dad who was stopping him, mainly.'

'And I expect you had nothing to do with it,' said Josie, unbending a little.

'Maybe a bit,' he said. 'But your dad is pretty determined when he gets going.'

'That is true,' said Josie, managing a small smile. That was better.

'It's not just that, though,' said Josie. 'I'm probably being silly . . .'

'But . . .?'

Josie shook her head. 'I must be going mad. Why on earth am I talking to you, of all people?'

'Because despite it all, you know you're making a huge mistake and should marry me?'

'Definitely not that,' said Josie, giving him a shove.

'Then, what?'

'Then . . . It's . . . last night,' she burst out miserably. 'I saw Harry and Di coming up the garden together. And I'm sure I caught him giving her a hug earlier. They looked so . . . secretive. I'm sure it's nothing, but . . .'

'You thought?' Ant burst out laughing.

'It's not funny!' said Josie.

'You dozy cow,' laughed Ant. 'Harry didn't tell you, then?'

'Tell me what?' said Josie, looking puzzled.

'He was feeling so stressed about this weekend, he cadged a fag off Diana and the stupid twat didn't tell you.'

'Oh.' Josie looked simultaneously relieved and annoyed. 'Now I feel really stupid. God, I was thinking all sorts.'

'You are daft, Josie,' said Ant. 'Harry adores you. You're all he ever talks about.'

'That's as may be,' said Josie, 'but if he does it again, I am going to bloody kill him.'

Chapter Nine

'Surprise!' Harry, who'd made his excuses and gone back to the annexe for a lie down and a think about how best to tackle Josie, woke up bleary-eyed as Ant came bounding in, followed by Josie, a sheepish look on her face.

'What?' said Harry.

'I think it's time you two had a little chat,' said Ant.

'Sorry?' Harry still felt totally befuddled.

Josie was looking a little awkward, so Ant pushed her towards Harry and said, 'Go on, lovebirds. Do what love-birds are meant to do – kiss and make up.'

Feeling sick with misery, Harry tried to work out how to say sorry for making Josie suspicious, when all he was doing was having a fag, which sounded lamer than lame, and sorry for coming home drunk.

Josie helped him out.

'Why didn't you just say you'd been smoking?' she said.

It sounded pretty stupid when she put it like that.

'Because I'm an idiot?' said Harry. 'I knew you wouldn't like me smoking, so I didn't tell you. But that's all I was doing. Honestly. I'm sorry.'

'I know,' said Josie, sitting down on the bed. 'But since we've been here, you've been . . . so distant, like you're not interested in the wedding . . . and you came to bed so late

115

last night, I thought you were avoiding me . . . and then I thought . . . I thought . . .'

Her composure faltered, and to Harry's dismay, he saw she was about to cry. He couldn't bear that he'd made her cry. She was his gorgeous Josie, and he wanted to spend every day of her life making her happy, not making her cry.

'Oh, Jose,' he said. 'You mean everything to me. I could never ever let you down. Come here, you dope.'

He pulled her close and held her tight.

'My work here is done,' said Ant and left the room, but Harry barely noticed. He drank in the smell of her, felt her respond to his touch. His gorgeous, gorgeous Josie. He only ever wanted to be with her.

'Sorry about staying out so late,' he said. 'Your dad's a hard man to resist.'

'Tell me about it,' said Josie laughing as she snuggled back up to him. 'Years of Mum putting up with him, means he does more or less exactly as he pleases.'

'I shall have to take a leaf out of his book, then,' teased Harry.

'You most certainly will not,' said Josie. 'I'm not going to spend the next twenty years playing the little wifey at home, or there'll be trouble.'

'Hmm, I like the sound of that,' said Harry, and started tickling her. They romped around on the bed for a bit and then Josie stopped and sat up. She looked at him really seriously and said, 'Harry, you are okay about all this, aren't you?'

'About this?' said Harry snaking his arm up her back.

'Not that,' said Josie, smacking his hand, 'though that of course is very nice. No, I mean about the wedding. Only you don't seem to be as enthusiastic as you once were. I know I've been a bit OTT about it . . .'

Harry smiled, 'A bit?' he said.

'That bad?' said Josie looking stricken.

'Worse,' said Harry.

'I'm sorry. I just want everything to be right.'

'And it will be,' said Harry.

'So you're okay?'

'Apart from being super intimidated by your dad,' said Harry, 'I'm fine. Don't worry, it's all going to be wonderful. Now, where were we?'

Josie sank back onto the bed with a blissful expression on her face. Harry gently bent over her and stroked her face. 'It's all going to be brilliant,' he said, 'you wait and see.' But as he took her in his arms, he wasn't sure if he was convincing Josie or himself . . .

Everyone seemed to have disappeared. Peter, ostensibly to his study to work, but Diana suspected he was having a little snooze. She'd spotted a recliner in there when Josie had shown them round. Nicola had disappeared into the kitchen again to prepare another huge meal, and Ant, Harry and Josie had all gone off to the annexe. Diana didn't know whether to join them or not.

She was just thinking about going in, when Ant came strolling back, dressed in the briefest of swimming briefs. His tanned torso was broad and rippled in all the right places. Clearly he still worked out. Diana watched him carefully from underneath her sunglasses, while pretending to read her magazine.

He certainly still had it, she thought, what a bod. If she didn't know him, it might have been fun to have a pre-wedding flirty fling with Ant. But she did know him, and despite her hormones betraying her horribly, she wouldn't go there again.

117

Being Ant, he was acting as if he had an audience anyway. His every move was slowly calculated. He walked up to the pool, dived in and swam several lengths of perfect crawl, scything his way through the water with impressive speed. Then he hauled himself lightly out of the pool. Diana had to smother a giggle. Any minute now he'd shake himself off like a springer spaniel.

'Move over Michael Phelps,' said Diana. 'Is there no end to your talents?'

Ant glared at her. He'd clearly been hoping she was impressed. She *was* impressed, but she certainly wasn't going to let him see that.

'You didn't honestly think I was going to fall for that little piece of peacock behaviour, did you?' said Diana.

'No more than I'd fall for you baring yourself to the world, like some floozy,' sneered Ant.

'Floozy, am I?' said Diana. 'That's rich, coming from the biggest male stud I know.'

They glared at each other angrily, and then Ant burst out laughing.

'What's so funny?' said Diana crossly.

'Us,' said Ant. 'I told Freddie Puck it would never work.'

'What would never work?'

'He reckons he could hypnotise a couple and make them fall in love on Midsummer's Eve at the Standing Stones, like in the legend. He's invited us all over to Tresgothen Manor tomorrow to give it a go. He even thought he could make it happen for us.'

'Ha, ha, ha,' Diana nearly spilt her drink. 'I don't think so.'

'That's what I told him,' said Ant. 'In fact, I've got a bet on it.'

'A bet I think you'll win,' said Diana. 'Maybe we should

118

get him to work on Josie and Harry, though. I'm a bit worried that Harry's getting cold feet.'

'It's all right,' said Ant. 'I sorted it. Put Josie right about your little rendezvous in the garden with Harry last night.'

'It wasn't a rendezvous,' snapped Diana, cross again. 'Poor guy was feeling stressed and I gave him a fag.'

'Which is what I told Josie,' said Ant. 'Anyway, they should be okay now.'

'Why do you care?' said Diana curiously. 'You've hardly been the biggest fan of this wedding.'

'Harry's my best mate,' said Ant, looking a little embarrassed. 'I don't like seeing him down.'

Diana felt something unfamiliar squirm inside her. A small nasty part of her had been slightly enjoying Josie's misery today, and here was Ant thinking about their friends, trying to put things right for them. It shamed her to think it, but since being here, she'd felt jealous of her friend and unexpectedly drawn to Harry. Shut up, she said to herself, shut up. You're not to think that.

'So what do you think?' said Ant. 'Shall we do this stupid experiment? We even get paid a bit for it.'

'We get paid?' Diana's ears pricked up. She'd got some savings, but any little extra was a help till she found a new job.

'Didn't I say?'

'Nope,' said Diana. 'As it happens, I could do with the money. We know it will never work, but it might be a laugh.'

Ant was feeling quite pleased with himself. Josie and Harry had arrived together for dinner, looking pleasantly flushed and slightly coy. No prizes for guessing what they'd been up to. Maybe Josie would get off his case now. Despite Diana's admiration of his actions, he hadn't been entirely straight with her. If Josie thought he was on her side, maybe she wouldn't be quite so hostile. It had alarmed him this weekend how much Harry seemed to take store by what Josie said, and how little time he was prepared to give his friend. Once they were married Josie could stop Harry seeing Ant altogether, and that would be a disaster.

Personally, Ant thought Harry should take a leaf out of Peter's book. He seemed to have got things completely sussed. Nicola seemed happy pottering around at home and Peter seemed to do exactly what he liked. Ant suspected he would have happily stayed out all afternoon, had Harry not insisted they get back. Peter had been far more relaxed about things. 'Nicola won't mind,' he'd said. Ant was overcome with admiration. What a man. And Nicola really *hadn't* seemed to mind, rustling up sandwiches when they got back without a murmur, despite the fact the girls had eaten in town. And now producing another delicious meal. She must spend her whole life in the kitchen, but she seemed quite content. If you had to get married, the answer was clearly to marry someone like Nicola, Ant thought. Yup, Peter had it sorted; he got to do what he liked, when he liked, and had a pretty appreciative wife when he came home. If Ant did ever settle down, he was going to have that kind of marriage.

'Everything okay now?' he whispered, as Josie came to sit down.

'Yes, thanks, Ant,' she glanced fondly over at Harry, and squeezed Ant's shoulder in thanks as she sat down. Ant grinned. Project win over Josie was underway. Now if he could get this hypnotist thing to work and have Diana fall for him again as a laugh, his cup of happiness would be complete. It might even have been worthwhile, his coming for the weekend . . .

Josie was feeling much better as they sat down to dinner. Mum had produced yet another fantastic meal – braised lamb and onion stew, with new potatoes and asparagus from the garden, followed by raspberry cheesecake and steaming apple pie. She could tell Harry was in heaven. He loved her mum's apple pie. She wondered if that was what had won Nicola around.

'I thought you could have done better than a journalist,' had been her mum's plaintive complaint when she'd first been introduced to Harry, but she softened when Harry had used all his natural charm on her, including helping her with the washing up; something Dad never did.

'So what's the plan for the evening then?' said Diana as they passed the pudding around.

'I thought a stroll to the Lover's Rest might be in order,' said Ant. 'Unless Harry's still recovering from his hangover. Freddie Puck said he might be in again.'

'You're not still thinking about that stupid programme, are you?'

'Why not? At least let's find out more about it,' said Ant. 'It might be a laugh. We can earn some dosh and we'd be on the telly.'

'Sounds ridiculous,' sniffed Peter.

'Is it dangerous?' said Nicola. 'You do hear such funny things.'

'I don't think so,' said Ant. 'Otherwise they'd never get anyone to do it.'

'I still think it sounds silly,' said Josie.

'I don't know,' piped up Harry. 'It could be fun.'

'I bet it won't work.' Diana looked levelly at Ant when she said this.

'What? Frightened you'll fall for me?' said Ant.

'Frightened I won't?' shot back Di.

'Children, children,' said Nicola. 'Go on, off to the pub with you. I'll clear up here.'

'No, Mum, you *won't*,' said Josie firmly. 'You've been running round after us all day.'

'Yes, let me help, Nicola,' said Diana, jumping up.

Harry sat where he was, until Josie nudged him.

'Of course,' he said. 'Here, let me. Sit down, Josie.'

He took the plates out of Josie's hands and followed Nicola and Diana into the kitchen.

Peter and Ant had no such qualms and much as she loved her dad, Josie felt like thumping him. That was never ever going to happen to her.

Harry smiled at her as he went out, a secret, shared smile that warmed her to her core. He was hers, not Ant's, and for the first time all weekend, Josie felt herself relax.

1988: Tatiana

Tatiana held the phone as she rifled through her Filofax, wondering if she should really go ahead with it. God, how many numbers did she have for him? Bron seemed to have moved around such a lot since she'd left him, never staying in one place or with one woman for very long.

Aha! Here was the latest number. She felt shaky, this might be a big mistake, but she didn't want to do this without hearing his voice; without, she could admit now, having his blessing.

She'd waited till she was completely alone in her hotel room, having dismissed everyone, even her mum, saying she wanted a lie down before dinner. When really she wanted this. One last chance to hear his voice.

'Darling, how are you?' Tatiana hadn't been sure of the reception she'd get. Hell, she wasn't even sure till the last minute she was going to dial his number. She'd had to down nearly a bottle of wine to have the confidence to ring him. And when he answered the phone, her knees sagged, and she thought she might faint. His voice resonated on the other end of the phone. So near, and yet so far. How could he still have this power over her? After all this time, it didn't seem possible.

Help, I think I'm drowning, is what she wanted to say. *Save me.* She was shouting inside.

This was stupid. Why was she ringing Bron of all people? As if he'd be interested in her now.

Instead, she said, 'I'm getting married tomorrow.'

There was a pause, and then, 'I know, I read it in the papers.'

Below the belt, but fair point. They hadn't spoken to each other in months.

'Sorry, I didn't know how to tell you.'

'Tati, my darling, it is of no consequence to me,' his voice was light, ironic, wounding. 'We're both grown-ups and we've moved on. I'm thinking of settling down myself. Time we both did, don't you think?'

Tatiana felt a punch in the stomach. He didn't care any more. She'd been idiotic to phone. She was getting married in the morning. What on earth had she expected? Auberon to come riding along on his white charger and rescue her at the last minute? And rescue her from what? She and Simon were in love, and were going to live happily ever after. The tabloids told her so daily. It must be true.

'Oh,' she squeaked. 'Good for you.'

Inside, she felt herself die a little. That chapter of her life was finally over. Bron was closing the door. And it was all her own fault. She let out a half sob, but suppressed it, hoping he hadn't heard.

There was a pregnant pause.

'Tati, is everything all right?' It was the old Bron, the one she fell in love with, all touching concern.

He's only being nice, she reminded herself, it's what he does.

'Of course it is,' said Tatiana brightly. 'I'm a marrying a

124

wonderful man tomorrow. I suppose . . . I just wanted your blessing.'

No, no, she screamed inside, I want you to stop me. I want you to come over here and tell me you can't live without me.

'You have it, always,' Bron said. 'Good luck, darling. Be happy.'

'You too,' she whispered. 'You too.'

She put down the phone, blinked the tears back from her eyes. He was never coming back to her. Finally, it was over. Time for her to move on.

Be happy. If only it were that simple.

Part Two

Ill Met by Moonlight

'Love looks not with the eyes, but with the mind;
And therefore is wing'd Cupid painted blind.'
        A Midsummer Night's Dream: Act I, Scene 1

'It's not a trick. You don't have to do anything you don't
want to. I make suggestions. Some people are more
susceptible than others, that's all.'
        Freddie Puck: The Art of Illusion

Chapter Ten

It was another warm, balmy evening as they walked down to the pub. Everyone was feeling pleasantly mellow and relaxed. Diana, in a post-meal, alcoholic-infused warm glow, was feeling a little more positive about her future – she had a lot of experience, she was still young, something would turn up – and even more kindly towards Ant, keeping up a steady banter about how easy it was going to be for Freddie Puck to dupe him.

'You're already half in love with the guy,' she teased, 'if he hypnotises you, you'll do anything he says.'

'I am not, as you put it, in love with him,' said Ant, prickling a little, 'I just respect his abilities, that's all.'

'It was a joke,' said Di, touching him lightly on the shoulder. 'I'm a real sucker for this kind of thing, so he'll probably persuade me more.'

'Do we really want to do this?' said Josie, as they sat down with their drinks in the pub. She scanned the pub, looking to see if Freddie had turned up yet. 'I'm not sure it's a good idea.'

'Oh go on, Josie, it might be a laugh,' said Diana. 'Haven't you always wanted to be on TV?'

'Not especially,' said Josie. 'Besides, Harry and I are already in love, so what can a hypnotic experiment do?'

'Ah, but he hasn't plighted his troth to you at the Standing Stones, has he?' said Ant. 'Perhaps hypnosis will bring out his romantic side.'

'I thought Harry had been showing Josie his romantic side all afternoon,' said Diana.

Josie and Harry blushed, and even Ant laughed at the joke.

'You people all seem to be having fun.' Freddie Puck appeared as if by magic. 'May I buy you all a drink?'

'Ha, that's how hypnotism works is it?' snorted Diana. 'Get us all plastered and then we'll do what you suggest? Not really rocket science is it?'

'Oh ye of little faith,' said Freddie, with a hurt look on his face. 'Let me show you what I can do. If you come to Tresgothen Manor tomorrow, I can take you through it properly. But I could do a simple demonstration here, tonight, if you'd like.'

'Like what?' Josie still seemed suspicious.

'I could hypnotise someone else, so you can see how straightforward it is.'

'I'll think about it,' said Diana. She was sipping an elderflower wine, a local brew known as Love in the Mist. It was stronger than it looked and on top of the wine she'd had at dinner, was making her feel a bit giddy. 'Do I have to sign anything?'

'Disclaimers at the ready,' said Freddie with a wolfish smile.

'No, seriously,' said Diana, 'I do like to know what I'm getting into. Do you have a contract or anything?'

'Bron's sorting out the finer detail, and we can go through it properly tomorrow,' said Freddie, 'but here's a basic version. Honestly, I have been doing this for a long time, I am properly licensed. You really have nothing to worry about. And you can put an end to the experiment at any time. I won't make you do anything you don't want to do. You don't have to go through with it, if you change your mind.'

Reading through the disclaimers Freddie had given her, Diana felt a bit better. There didn't seem anything too horrendous there, and the few hundred quid on offer was enough to put aside her qualms. Beggars couldn't be choosers.

'Right, gather round folks.' Ever the showman, Freddie had worked the crowd in the pub, and they were all gathering round a chair in the middle of the room, where his victim was waiting.

Harry pushed forward and nearly burst out laughing when he realised that Freddie's first punter was Mike Slowbotham.

'Am I okay here?' Mike was saying. He looked simultaneously nervous and proud. See, he appeared to be saying, the great Freddie Puck has chosen me to be his first subject. It was all Harry could do not to giggle out loud. Little did Mike know how little the locals were impressed with him.

'You're fine,' said Freddie. 'Now I want you to take a deep breath, while I count you down.'

'Look into my eyes, look into my eyes, you're under,' said Mike, in a very poor attempt at a *Little Britain* impression.

'It's not quite like that,' said Freddie. 'Just try and relax and think soothing thoughts. Imagine you're climbing down a spiral staircase, and at the bottom, something really pleasant and lovely is waiting for you.'

Harry watched in fascination as Freddie put Mike under. He didn't seem to be asleep, although he had shut his eyes. In actual fact, it seemed like no big deal. All Freddie suggested was that when he awoke Mike would think he was a donkey, until Freddie clicked his fingers. It didn't seem like a lot. Just a bit of light entertainment. Much like he'd used to do in his TV shows.

'Do you think it will work?' said Diana, equally fascinated.

'I guess the proof will be in the pudding,' said Harry. 'Shh, watch.'

Freddie was bringing Mike round. '. . . and three, two, one – you're awake.'

'Eee ore,' said Mike, promptly going down on all fours, much to the amusement of the pub at large.

He put his hands above his head to make ear shapes and said 'Eee ore,' again, more loudly this time, making the place erupt.

'Do you think he fancies a carrot?' shouted a wag.

Mike eee-ored enthusiastically, and one of the bar staff fetched one from the kitchen, which Freddie fed to him while patting him on the head, saying 'Good donkey.'

'I'm not sure I like this,' said Josie uneasily. 'Freddie could do anything to us when we're asleep.'

'It's only a bit of fun,' said Harry. 'Freddie, you wouldn't do anything like that to us, would you, right?'

'Of course not,' said Freddie, 'I'm just showing how easy it is to hypnotise someone. I promise I won't make you look silly.'

Josie still looked unconvinced, but Harry gave her a hug and said, 'You worry too much. I'm sure it will be fine.'

He sipped another sip of Idle Brew. God this stuff was good. His hangover had completely cleared and he felt up for an adventure. This hypnotism lark didn't look too onerous and – who knew? – it might even be fun.

* * *

132

Josie was still feeling uncomfortable about the whole hypnosis thing. She'd watched Freddie put Mike under, which she had to admit had been quite a mesmerising experience in itself. But while the atmosphere was joshing and light-hearted, Josie didn't like the fact that Mike didn't realise he was being made a figure of fun. Granted the guy was self-delusional – he'd promised more than one woman over a certain age in the village fame and fortune – but this seemed cruel. And maybe a little dangerous.

Josie wasn't the only one who was having doubts.

'What the hell's going on here?' Tatiana Okeby arrived and her retinue; camp M'stard, willowy little Ariadne, and fussy Gypsy, tumbled in after her.

'I'm conducting a little experiment, and I've hypnotised Mike here to think he's a donkey.'

'You're making a laughing stock of the poor man.'

'Eee ore,' said Mike and the pub erupted.

'What's wrong with that?'

'What's right with it?' Tatiana was furious. 'This is typical of you, Freddie. You always have to make people look foolish, don't you? And as for you, Bron, isn't it about time you stopped putting up with all this crap? I despair, I really do.'

'What would you have me do?' said Freddie, shrugging his shoulders to his audience as if to say, look what I have to contend with. 'Be reasonable. Mike here consented to be hypnotised –'

'The man is a well-respected member of this community, and you are making a mockery of him,' said Tatiana, oblivious to the sniggers in the audience. 'Go on, snap him out of it.'

'You are such a spoilsport, Tati,' sighed Freddie, 'but if you insist. Three, two, one and you're awake.'

Mike came round, looking a little confused.

'I was dreaming I was a donkey,' he said, 'and how come I'm holding a carrot?'

'This idiot played a rotten trick on you,' said Tatiana. 'I think he should apologise.'

'Oh, no need, no need, all in the spirit of the thing.' Mike took her hand earnestly and planted a kiss on it, 'but thank you dear lady, for thinking of me in my hour of need.'

'See, no problem,' said Freddie. 'All a bit of harmless fun. I was just demonstrating what I could do to these lovely people who are going to join in an experiment with me tomorrow. You could come along too if you want.'

Josie looked anxiously at the others; she was even less sure now than she'd been at the beginning.

'Over my dead body,' said Tatiana. 'I wouldn't trust you with a bargepole. Come on, everyone, party's over. Let's get back to the yurt.'

With that, she swept out, leaving Freddie smirking in the corner.

'So is that how it works?' said Josie. 'You make us look idiots? I can't speak for the others, but I'm really not up for that.'

'No, no, no,' said Freddie. 'That was my little joke. Mike understands, don't you? And if he's prepared to have another go, I'll show you that there really is nothing to worry about.'

'I'd be delighted old boy,' said Mike, preening himself. It didn't look as though he'd been harmed by his encounter. Maybe she was worrying over nothing.

'All right, Mike, now let's try and relax you once more . . .'

Ant came back from the bar with another round of drinks, as Mike slipped under again. This time he was snoring really loudly. Ant couldn't see what Tatiana was making a fuss about. The guy was a prize idiot. He could make himself look like an ass without Freddie's help.

'I think we could have a bit more fun with this,' he said to Auberon Fanshawe, who was sitting nearby looking sardonically amused by it all. 'Just to stir things up a bit for Tati.'

'Go for it,' said Auberon. 'She deserves everything she gets in my opinion.'

Ouch. Still no love lost there then. Their fiery relationship had clearly not been exaggerated in the press. Bron made Ant feel he was being positively charitable to Di.

Freddie turned to the still-snoring Mike and said very solemnly, 'When you awake you will be convinced that you are a famous London producer with lots of connections to the stage, and you can bring a certain famous actress back into the fold. Tatiana Okeby is going to be the key to your golden future. Three, two, one . . . now you are awake.'

'That's so mean,' said Josie, who still looked uncomfortable. 'I really don't like this at all.'

'It's only a bit of fun,' said Di. 'I bet it won't work. And doesn't that guy have ideas above his station anyway?'

'Yes, but I feel sorry for Tatiana Okeby,' said Josie. 'She's clearly the butt of the joke.'

'So,' Freddie grinned. 'What do you think? Are you going to come by my place tomorrow and sign yourselves up?'

'I'm your man,' said Ant. 'What do the rest of you think?'

'I think it looks like a laugh,' said Diana, who had clearly slightly overindulged in Love in the Mist. 'I'm game if everyone else is.'

'Ditto,' said Harry.

That only left Josie.

'I'm really not sure,' she said.

'There's nothing to it,' said Freddie. 'I promise I won't

do anything you don't want me to, and you can stop the experiment at any time.'

'Go on, Josie,' said Harry, putting an arm round her. 'It doesn't look too bad, and I'll be there. What could possibly happen?'

'I suppose,' said Josie.

'Brilliant, it's agreed,' said Freddie. 'So you'll come by Tresgothen Manor in the afternoon, then? Say two-ish?'

'You have a deal,' said Ant, shaking Freddie by the hand.

The hypnosis session over, the rest of the pub returned to what they were doing. The four of them sat back down at a table and carried on chatting – Josie clearly making strenuous efforts to talk about something other than the wedding.

'I'm really tuckered out,' Harry yawned eventually. 'I think I'm ready for my bed.'

'Me too,' said Josie.

'Are you sure you'll be getting any sleep?' said Diana with a grin.

'Behave,' said Josie.

Bed. Yes, bed seemed like a good idea. Ant suddenly felt very sleepy. Too much beer on top of a heavy session the previous night.

'Yeah, let's go,' he said.

They got up to leave. It wasn't actually that late. And the cool evening air was refreshing, and suddenly Ant felt more wakeful. The evening sky was a darkening blue, and a blood-red moon sat huge and still over the sea.

'Wow, that's amazing,' said Josie.

'Wouldn't it look better from the cliffs?' said Diana. 'And we could check out what it's like up there in the dark, so we know whether we'll be safe if we do go along with the hypnotism.'

'That's a great idea,' agreed Harry. 'The fresh air's woken me up a bit.'

'Sounds like a good plan,' said Josie. 'Besides, I feel there's magic in the air tonight.'

Ant followed them up the path with a growing sense of excitement. Like Josie, he felt as if something momentous was about to happen. He just didn't know what . . .

Chapter Eleven

Josie walked up the hill in a dream. The evening had taken a surreal turn. Several glasses of Love in the Mist had taken the edge off her slight anxiety over the whole hypnosis thing. She was probably making a fuss about nothing, and Mike seemed unharmed by the experience. She should probably relax a bit more.

It was another lovely warm evening as they made their way up the cliff path. Harry strode forward, lighting their way with the torches that Dad had fortunately made them bring as it got so dark walking home from the pub. The moon was so bright, it was scarcely necessary. Although it was shrinking slightly, it still looked amazing against the blue-black sky, and the calm shimmering sea. Josie felt like she was floating on air.

It was harder going in the dark. Although moonlight still lit the path, the trees and shadows meant you occasionally tripped on a hidden rabbit hole. Josie was regretting wearing her strappy sandals. She always forgot when she came home how unsuitable London footwear was for day to day living, and twice now she'd ricked her ankle. In the end she took her shoes off. The path was sandy rather than stony, and it hadn't rained in a while. The top of the cliff was full of soft heather and grass, and it was good to feel the sand between her toes, just as she had done when she was a child.

'Are we nearly there yet?' Diana plaintively called behind her. She was wearing flip-flops, which were equally unsuitable and she kept having to stop when they pinged off her feet. 'It seems so much further than in the day time.'

'Not much further now,' said Josie. 'I think Harry's made it to the top.'

'Come on you lazy sods,' shouted Harry, from high above them. 'We're nearly there.'

Josie scrambled up, needing to use her hands to pull her up the last bit, till she got near the summit, and Harry stretched out his hand before her.

Diana soon followed, and Ant came up last.

Josie walked towards the Standing Stones and looked at them in awe. She'd been coming here all her life, and yet it was as though she were seeing them for the first time. The moon was higher in the sky now, still with a hint of red, but bathing the stones in a shimmering silvery light. The stones themselves cast dark mysterious shadows across the grass, which waved softly in the gentle sea breeze. Josie felt that if she reached out and touched the air she would be transported somewhere, different; other. For the first time, the myths felt they could almost be real. You really could imagine fairies here.

'Wow,' she said. 'Just wow. This is amazing.'

'Isn't it?' said Harry. He came over and squeezed her hand tight.

'Love you,' said Josie as he pulled her towards him, and kissed him. The air seemed full of promise and mystery. She was glad she'd come.

* * *

139

Ant climbed down into the Faerie Ring, his sense of anti-cipation growing. There was a strange atmosphere in the air. Harry and Josie had gone all moony on each other, and even Diana seemed chilled and less aggressive.

The sea rose and fell below them, and the moon shone as bright as day. A soft breeze ruffled his hair, and the silvery beams of the moon cast weird shadows on the grass. For all that Ant didn't believe in this nonsense, he had the shivery sensation that something – unusual? – was about to happen. It even made him feel more warmly to Diana for a moment. But only for a moment, because she opened her mouth and spoilt the atmosphere.

'So when do the hordes of fairies arrive?' she said. 'I can't believe we've walked all the way up here in the middle of the night. We must be off our trolleys.'

'But you have to admit it is rather beautiful,' said Josie. 'I'm so pleased we came up here.'

'Me too,' said Ant, surprising himself. He felt almost poetic as he looked out to sea; this feeling was unlike one he had ever experienced before. 'And I feel . . . different. As if I could do anything. As if I were invincible.'

'In your dreams,' snorted Diana. 'You've had too much beer, and allowed yourself to get sucked into the whole stupid hypnotism thing. We should all just go home to bed!'

'Don't be so bad-tempered,' said Josie. 'Come on. Lie down on the grass, and look up at the stars. This is a perfect evening. Enjoy it.'

'Yes, Di,' said Ant, 'don't be so bad-tempered.'

Diana looked as if she was going to bite off a retort, but then changed her mind, and sat down instead.

'So, you two, isn't it time you plighted your troth in the light of the moon?' said Ant, also sitting down.

'Not while anyone's looking,' said Harry. 'What about you and Diana? Maybe being hypnotised tomorrow will change your feelings towards one another.'

'No!' shrieked Ant and Diana in unison.

'I'm as likely to plight my troth with Harry,' Diana added. 'Which is not at all likely.'

But Ant wasn't sure it was entirely true. There was something odd in the air tonight, and he felt suddenly quite nervous around Diana. Once upon a time, she'd meant everything to him. Could you ever put those feelings away for good?

Diana was feeling very strange. She'd been quite happy when they left the pub. But the nearer they got to the top of the cliff, the more anxious she felt. What were they doing up here, in the middle of the night? And what if Freddie Puck had secretly hypnotised them, without them realising it? She'd been quite clear in her own mind that she wasn't going anywhere but home to bed after the pub, and yet, here she was.

And Josie and Harry had gone into sappy mode again. She felt shut out of their world and it made her feel lonely. When she and Josie had first flat-shared, they'd both been single and then Harry had moved in, and she'd moved out – and nothing had ever been the same again. Diana hadn't realised how difficult she was going to find it without Josie. She felt she was in mourning for the best friend she'd ever had, and it was all her own fault. She'd pushed them together. Thanks to Diana, Harry and Josie would be married next year, and she'd be on the sidelines for ever.

She looked over to where Josie and Harry were sitting up, talking quietly together. Ant was lying on his back, looking dreamily up at the stars. He'd been giving her some funny looks all evening. She did hope he wasn't going to try anything on. She wouldn't put it past him to pretend the past hadn't happened, and see what he could get away with this weekend. From what Josie had said about him, eventually Ant tried it on with every woman he met. She hoped given their past history she would be the exception.

She tried to relax, and remember the happy feelings drinking Love in the Mist had induced in her. She'd been having fun then, but now she felt edgy and irritable. Everyone seemed to be enjoying the moment but her.

This was no good, Diana admonished herself; she should try to cheer up. No one liked people who behaved like a wet weekend in November, as her mother was fond of saying. She was the only person responsible for her own happiness. Maybe she just needed to liven things up.

'I know,' she found herself saying, 'let's play a game of Truth or Dare.'

Harry was leaning his head on Josie's lap and looking up at the stars. He was feeling deeply content. This was turning out to be a quite magical evening. He smiled happily up at Josie, who smiled happily back.

'Penny for your thoughts?' she said.

'Thinking how lucky I am,' said Harry, 'that I nabbed you.'

'And me you too,' said Josie, leaning over and kissing him on the lips.

'Ugh, you two. Do you have to?'

'Sorry,' said Harry. 'Did you just say something?'

'I thought it might be fun to play Truth or Dare,' said Diana.

'Why?' said Josie.

'I don't know,' said Diana. 'I feel like it. Sorry, I don't know why I suggested it, it's a silly idea.'

'No it's not,' said Harry, suddenly feeling this could be the funniest thing ever.

'I'm game,' said Ant.

'Me too,' said Josie.

'Who's going first?' said Ant.

'I will,' said Harry.

'So what's it to be, Truth or Dare?' said Ant.

'Truth,' said Harry.

'Okay,' said Diana, 'what do you want most of all in the world?'

'To spend my life with Josie,' said Harry. 'Simple.'

'Okay, my go,' said Diana, 'I'll do a dare.'

'I dare you to kiss Ant,' said Josie sneakily.

Diana blushed, but went and kissed him on the cheek.

'Don't put yourself out too much,' said Ant. 'Okay. Josie, your turn.'

'Dare,' said Josie.

'Finish this bottle of Idle Brew I brought with me,' said Ant.

'Down in one, down in one,' they shouted, as Josie finished it triumphantly.

'Now you, Ant,' said Harry. 'Truth or Dare?'

'Truth,' said Ant.

'What's the question you want to know the answer to most in the world?' said Josie.

'That's easy,' said Ant. He turned to Diana. 'What did I do to make you hate me so much? I've never really known.'

Chapter Twelve

'So what's the score today?' Nicola said brightly over the breakfast table, as if sensing a bit of an atmosphere. After Ant's question, which Diana had refused to answer, they'd given up on Truth or Dare and come home. Diana had gone straight to bed, and this morning was barely speaking to Ant. Ant and Harry were both looking pale and wan, thanks to their overindulgence the previous day, so Josie had decided a more active day was in order.

'I think we've spent enough time in the pub this weekend,' she said. 'We need to get some fresh air. Let's go kayaking. I was thinking we could do it on my hen night, so I'd like to try out the new centre near St Ives.'

'Kayaking? You are joking,' said Diana, who had been very quiet since last night. 'Who goes kayaking on their hen night?'

'Me,' said Josie. 'I don't want a strippogram. I'd just like us to have some active fun in the day, before we get down to drinking later.'

'Are you sure you wouldn't prefer a spa?' said Diana. 'That was more what I had in mind.'

'Nope,' said Josie. 'It's my hen night. And if I want to go kayaking, that's what we're going to do.'

'I wouldn't bother arguing, dear,' said Nicola, 'Josie's just like her father, stubborn through and through.'

'I'm not getting in a boat,' said Diana. 'Even if you pay me.'

'Oh, go on,' said Harry. 'I've been before. It's fun. If I can do it, anyone can.'

'That's true,' laughed Josie, 'he was pretty hopeless at it.'

'What about going over to Tresgothen Manor?' said Ant. 'We agreed we'd go and see Freddie at some point today.'

'We can go after the kayaking,' said Josie.

'Okay then,' Ant said, 'I'm in.'

'I hope you haven't got any other mental ideas planned for your hen night,' said Diana.

'I was thinking about a parachute jump,' said Josie. 'I've always wanted to do one.'

'You are joking –' Diana looked pale.

'Of course I am, you idiot. I don't want to hobble up the aisle.'

'Right, are we all set?' Twenty minutes later, Josie had marshalled everyone together. She was determined to have a good day today, and was doing her best to keep the W word out of the conversation. But it was so hard. She kept having to sneak off and look through the dozens of bridal mags Mum had saved for her. And despite having suggested the kayaking, a part of her just wanted to sit chatting to Mum about place settings and table decorations. Although the wedding was still a year away, Josie felt a crippling worry that she had to organise as much as possible, as soon as possible, in order to avoid mishaps. No one else felt like that clearly, but she did. She couldn't help it.

Harry drove faster down the country lanes than he'd intended. Every bump felt as if the car was lifting in the air, and he had to slam his brakes on a couple of times, eliciting a 'Harry!' from Josie, but he didn't care. He wasn't that keen on going kayaking, but Josie was so determined, he wasn't at all likely to get his own way. He'd noticed she'd started doing that to him; making little decisions (mainly about the wedding) without him, and then confirming them in public with that lovely smile of hers. Which meant he couldn't do anything but seethe quietly. He wished she'd be a bit more inclusive sometimes.

'Woah,' said Ant as Harry slammed on the brakes so as not to hit a passing tractor.

'Sorry,' said Harry, 'thinking of other things.'

But he drove more soberly till they got to the outdoor centre where the kayaking was taking place. Harry's heart sank. It looked very outdoorsy and energetic. The sort of place he hated and Josie, he was beginning to realise, loved. He still hadn't quite got round to letting her know just how much he wanted to go travelling. He'd hinted at it several times, but she'd not picked up on the hint. Harry had the horrible feeling that his future plans would just slip away from him without him being able to stop them.

'So what's it going to be?' asked Harry, as he looked at the activities on offer. 'Are we going on the lake, or are we going to brave the sea?'

'I am not going in the sea,' said Diana firmly. 'I want to make it back in one piece, thank you very much.'

'God, you're dull,' said Ant. 'Bags I don't go with you.'

'I know,' said Harry peaceably, 'why don't you and Josie go together and I'll go with Diana, as she's not done it before.'

'Fine by me,' said Ant. 'You've done this before, right, Josie?'

'Once or twice,' said Josie. 'I've been kayaking since I was a little girl.'

'Ha,' thought Harry uncharitably. That would teach her.

Ant was not in the slightest bit capable of listening to instructions. Particularly not from a girl.

'Right, Di,' he said with a smile. 'Are we all set?'

Diana was terrified. She'd hated boats ever since she was a kid and had gone adrift in one with her dad. They hadn't been far from the shore, but she'd never forgotten the feeling of panic when the motorboat's engine had shut down, or the look of fear on his face, and the way it felt to be drifting, helpless, further away from the shore. The whole incident had probably only taken ten minutes or so. But she'd never really got over it.

'You okay?' said Harry. 'Only you seem a bit nervous.'

That was Harry all over. Kind and thoughtful. She was glad he'd opted to have her in his boat. She could imagine all too well how unkind Ant would have been, and to a degree, Josie. Josie always failed to understand how other people found difficult the things she made look effortless. It was a really irritating characteristic, and today would be shown to its full, no doubt.

'Okay,' said Harry once they were sorted with lifejackets, helmets and sculls, 'it really is quite straightforward. You take your lead from me.'

Blanching at the reason why they were wearing headgear ('So if you fall out of the boat, you minimise any head damage,' said the cheerful instructor), Diana gingerly climbed into the boat, while Harry nobly stepped into the water. God, Josie was lucky to have him. What a gent. She noted with some amusement that Ant had leapt in first, leaving Josie to push their boat into the water. Not that Josie seemed to mind. She was in her element, teasing Ant when he complained about the cold.

The boat rocked alarmingly when Harry clambered in

and Diana let out an involuntary scream, and then felt really stupid.

'Sorry,' she said, 'that was really pathetic of me.'

'Don't worry,' said Harry. 'If I can do this, anyone can. Honestly, it's easier than it looks.'

Harry turned out to be right. Soon, with his gentle instructions, she found they were skimming across the water, and gradually her nerves deserted her.

'This is actually quite a lot of fun,' she said, surprising herself. It was the first time she'd felt comfortable on the water for years.

'Isn't it?' said Harry. 'I think we should race the others to the island and back.'

'You're on,' said Diana. 'I don't think we're going to have too many problems.'

She pointed Harry in the direction of Josie and Ant's boat, which was going round in circles.

'When I say right, I mean you paddle to your left, you idiot,' Josie was saying, 'so we can turn right. I thought you'd done this before.'

'I have,' said Ant.

'Could have fooled me,' said Josie grumpily. 'Right.'

Ant pushed to his left.

'No, I meant left that time!' Josie's exasperation was obvious. 'Come on. Let's start again. I want us to go left, so we paddle to the right. Okay?'

Gradually they got the boat under control and Harry shouted across, 'Race you to the island and back. Loser buys the first round.'

'That's like a red rag to a bull,' said Diana.

'You're on,' said Ant, and with that, he and Josie flew away.

'Bugger, we'll never catch them.'

'Oh yes we will,' said Harry. 'Steady as she goes. Ant will cock it up by wanting to go too fast. You mark my words. It's in the bag.'

Ant was beginning to regret going out with Josie. She was much bossier than he'd thought she would be, constantly nagging him about which oar he was supposed to be using. The very unwelcome sight of Harry and Diana gliding effortlessly through the water while laughing their heads off at him was deeply irksome.

So it was with some satisfaction that when Harry (foolishly, in Ant's opinion) proposed a race, that Ant and Josie finally got it together and were soon flying across the waves.

'Go for it, Ant!' Josie shrieked in delight.

He glanced round to see her flushed face, sparkling eyes and fair hair flying back, and he was reminded of the vivacious girl whom he'd met all those years ago. He remembered spotting Josie in the uni bar, surrounded by male admirers, and at the time he'd been as smitten as the rest. Funny that he'd forgotten how attractive she was. But it was a long time since he'd spent so much time in her company.

'We'll show them, Josie,' he said, 'make up for them laughing at us.'

'I think they were laughing at you, actually,' said Josie. 'But let's not quibble.'

Then the race was on in earnest. The little kayak scythed through the water, which sparkled and shone in the June sun. Ant felt like he was flying. He'd never felt so elated. This was so much fun. Before too long, they'd reached the island. They were miles ahead of Di and Harry, who were ploughing steadily through the water. Josie's expertise and his brute strength were going to win the day. Except . . .

'Right, Ant. You need go to right.'

Ant ploughed on to the right and the boat spun in the opposite direction.

'I mean left,' said Josie. 'You should be paddling left to go right.'

'What?' said Ant paddling frantically to his left.

'That's right,' said Josie.

'Did you say right?' said Ant paddling to his left again, and making the boat veer suddenly to his right.

'No, left,' said Josie, 'paddle on your right.'

Ant tried to do as he was told, but there were some big waves coming up, and one slurped alarmingly in the boat.

'Bugger,' said Josie, 'we're taking on too much water. We need to bail out.'

'Do I go left or right?' said Ant, before a wave crashed over his head, and the next thing he knew, he was in the water, without a paddle, and a very, very long way from his canoe.

1992: Bron

Bron was exhausted. They'd just finished filming series 4 of *Illusions*, and they still had all the brouhaha of interviews and other nonsense to get through. It seemed to get worse every time. Especially as the inevitable questions about his love life always seemed to come up. Couldn't journalists think of anything else to ask him about?

One more drink with the crew, and he was done. He still had the age-old problem that had beset him ever since Tati had left, of how to say goodbye to his latest assistant. He would only let Freddie employ them from now on.

'It would help if you didn't keep shagging them, Bron,' Freddie would drawl, and he knew in that at least, Freddie was right.

Ever since Tati had gone and got herself married – hell, ever since she'd left (could it really be ten years ago?) – Bron had been looking for a substitute. But no one had ever matched up. There could never be another Tati, not on stage, nor in his bed. And yet he still kept searching, kept kidding himself he could find her. Sometimes he toyed with ringing Tati up for old times' sake. But what would he say? She'd made her choice a long time ago, and she hadn't chosen him. Nothing was ever going to change that.

He sipped mournfully at his pint, unable to join in the

high jinks of the rest of the crew, who were persuading Freddie it was a really good idea to try out one of his mind games on them now. That was a waste of time, as Freddie rarely drank, and he'd clean them all out in minutes.

'Well, well, well. Look what the cat brought in.' A very familiar voice cut into his thoughts. 'Auberon Fanshawe, as I live and breathe.'

'Tati,' Bron couldn't help but be cut to the quick that she'd used his full name. His heart sank. It was one thing thinking about her, imagining what he'd say to her, but to have her there in front of him was too much to bear. He felt stifled, like he couldn't breathe, and his clothes suddenly felt uncomfortably tight. His palms were hot and sweaty and he was aware that he was breathing faster than normal. A small knot formed in the pit of his stomach. She was just the same. Beautiful; distant; unattainable. Why did she still have this effect on him, why?

'Mind if I join you?'

'Be my guest.' As he said it, Bron knew it was a really bad idea. They'd been apart now longer than they'd been together. All they ever did was hurt one another. He was tired of it, and didn't want to open himself up to any more pain.

Tati sat down next to him, and he was overwhelmed by her perfume. Word on the street was that her marriage was on the rocks, and so, the whispers went, was her career. Drunk on set, was what people were saying. But there were always rumours about Tati; it went with the persona she'd created for herself. She'd never made it her business to make friends, and had plenty of enemies, not least among his cast-offs, who'd sought to emulate her career trajectory. If they were hoping for a friendly helping hand from one of the sisterhood, they were certainly mistaken.

'You look lovely,' he said. 'How's Simon?'

'Fine,' she said coolly. 'And how's – is it Emily?'

'Amelie,' said Bron. 'And she's not – we're not together anymore.'

'A drink for old times' sake?'

'I'm not sure that's a good idea, Tati,' he said uneasily. 'Your marriage –'

'Is over, in all but name,' she said. 'Come on. One drink. What harm can it do?'

Chapter Thirteen

'You have to admit, it was funny,' Harry said for the hundredth time as they got in the car, ready to drive to Tresgothen Manor. They'd all agreed that it was worth giving Freddie the benefit of the doubt, even though Josie was still expressing her doubts.

'Ha bloody ha,' said Ant, whose mood didn't seem to have improved since he'd had to be fished out of the water by the people running the kayak hire. Josie had managed to get back into the kayak, but had ended up drifting round the wrong side of the island, and it had taken her nearly half an hour to get back.

'Lucky one of us knew what we were doing,' she said, looking over her shoulder as she buckled her seatbelt.

'Shame you don't know your left from your right,' said Ant grumpily.

'Me?' said Josie. 'I was giving you perfectly clear instructions. It's you who have the problem with left and right.'

'Oh do shut up, you two!' said Harry, looking in the rearview mirror as he did a nippy three-point turn out of a very crowded spot in the car park. 'Let's not squabble.'

He was feeling much happier than when they'd come out. He'd actually enjoyed rowing with Di. When he'd kayaked in the past with Josie, he was always aware of his inadequacy in the face of her eminent superiority in the rowing department. Not that she rubbed it in or anything, but he could feel her impatience. By contrast, it had been nice and restful being with Di, who knew less than he did and was willing to learn. And she'd impressed him with her courage. Scared as she'd been when she got in the boat, once she'd stopped shrieking, she'd settled down.

'I'd have hated going in the water,' said Di. 'You've actually gone up in my estimation, Ant. You dealt with it pretty well.'

'Wonders will never cease,' laughed Josie, 'that's the first nice thing you've said to Ant all weekend.'

'I suppose it *was* funny,' said Ant grudgingly.

'Funny,' said Harry, 'it was bloody hilarious.'

He felt quite triumphant. It wasn't often he got one over Ant, and he was enjoying the unusual feeling of having come out on top.

'Harry's right,' Josie started to giggle, breaking the mood, 'the look on your face . . .'

Her laughter was infectious, and before long Diana had joined in, and in the end, even Ant started to smile. 'Okay, okay,' he said, 'I made an idiot of myself. But Josie, I never want to go kayaking with you ever again.'

'Deal,' said Josie.

She wound down the window, and the scent of freshly mown grass and roses drifted past them, as Harry sped down the country lanes.

'You sure you know the way?' he said.

'Of course I do,' said Josie, 'Tresgothen Manor is on the road past Mum and Dad's, about a mile from the open-air theatre. You can't miss it.'

Josie put one arm out of the window and sat back, enjoying the ride.

'Are we still sure about this?' she said. 'Freddie made Mike Slowbotham look pretty stupid in the pub last night. I don't want to look like an idiot.'

'He did deserve it though,' laughed Diana. 'The guy's a total ass.'

'. . . Hole,' joked Ant. 'I'm sure Freddie won't be making us look that stupid.'

'I hope not,' said Josie. 'I'm still not sure this is such a good idea.'

Harry looked at the others. 'What do you think?' he said.

'So long as I'm not made a fool of, I'm up for it,' said Diana, 'it sounds like fun.'

'And the cash will be handy,' added Ant.

'I don't know . . .' said Josie.

'Oh don't be such a stuffy bore,' said Diana, 'it'll be fun. What can possibly go wrong?'

Harry had a funny feeling that possibly a lot could go wrong, but then he thought about the money. It wasn't a great deal, but enough for the two of them to go to a really nice hotel on their wedding night, and maybe have enough left over for a weekend in Europe. Maybe if he took Josie somewhere fun and interesting, she'd get the travel bug too. He could but hope.

Diana was enjoying herself. She'd beaten her demons and proved she could kayak with the best of them. A slightly ignoble part of her also felt quite triumphant. Josie was so damned good at *everything*, it felt quite nice to have done better for once. And as to having seen Ant ending up in the water, she hadn't enjoyed anything so much in ages. It had even made up for the shakiness she'd felt after Ant had asked her that question last night. Why he had to bring it up during the game and not when they were alone, she couldn't fathom. She hadn't bothered to answer him. A memory of sitting alone in a hospital bed, waiting for him, came searing back into her consciousness. How could he possibly not know why she hated him? If it wasn't obvious to him by now, it never would be.

Deciding to put thoughts of Ant out of her mind, which wasn't as easy as all that, with him sitting right next to her, Diana leaned against the window and stared out dreamily as they sped through the beautiful Cornish countryside. It really was a glorious day, and above the car engine, she could just make out the murmur of bees, and the summer breeze blowing through the fresh green grass. It was so lovely here. Part of her wished she could stay for ever.

She lay back and shut her eyes, letting her mind drift.

She wasn't exactly daydreaming, but her thoughts wandered to a scenario where a tall dark stranger came striding up the beach and whisked her off her feet. He was lovely, soulful, caring and looked like – *Harry*? She jerked awake suddenly, feeling herself blush. She'd never looked at him that way before, and after what had happened on Friday night, didn't want any more misunderstanding. She flushed again, as Josie said, 'Are you okay? You look a bit flustered.'

'Yes, fine,' said Di, brushing away the guilty feeling that her daydream had left her with. It was only a dream. Nothing had happened.

'Daydreaming about anyone nice?' teased Josie.

'No one nice,' said Di, and glanced at Ant to throw Josie off the scent.

Josie giggled and whispered something to Harry.

Phew. That had worked. But how strange. To be dreaming about Harry. Strange and embarrassing. Best she forgot all about it.

* * *

157

Ant's temper had finally improved as they pulled up at Tresgothen Manor. If Ant had been impressed by Josie's parents' house, this was mind-blowing. A long driveway, lined with poplars, gave way to a massive drive with a cultivated lawn, which looked as though someone had cut it with nail clippers, and led up to a massive Elizabethan-style house, with red brick chimneys and a huge oak door, which was thrown dramatically open as Freddie came out to greet them.

'Welcome, welcome,' said Freddie, 'do come in. We're having drinks on the lawn, and we can sit down and go over the finer points of the contracts.'

He ushered them through the house, and Ant looked around him at the cool interior, with marble floors and a magnificent wooden staircase, paintings of long-dead aristocrats lining the walls, before they were led out into a glorious garden.

If the front garden had looked impressive, the back garden was magnificent. A large lawn, with neat flowerbeds at either side, led to a terraced garden at the bottom which was a riot of colour. A rose arch made way for a sunken garden, from where the tinkling sound of water suggested the pond at the bottom of the terrace had been carefully laid to create the illusion of a waterfall. Even Ant, who knew nothing about gardens, could see it was amazing.

'I'd heard they'd done up the gardens here,' said Josie, 'I hadn't realised they were quite so beautiful. When I was a child they were a wilderness.'

'Aren't they magnificent?' said Auberon Fanshawe coming towards them, his hand extended in greeting. 'I've stayed in lots of wonderful places over the years, but I can honestly say I would really love to make this my permanent home.'

'Drink, anyone?' Freddie clicked his finger, and as if by

magic a waiter appeared bearing a tray of champagne and Bucks Fizz. Everyone took a glass except Harry, who opted for orange juice.

'To all of you,' said Freddie, raising his glass, 'and thank you for sharing in my experiment.'

'Are you sure it's safe?' said Josie, who still seemed down on the whole idea.

'Quite sure,' said Freddie. 'Look, Jack here, our lawyer, will go through it with you, but honestly, as I told you before, you don't have to do anything you don't want to, and we can stop the experiment at any time. Why don't I demonstrate how easy it is on one of you? And we'll take it from there.'

Ant put his hand up.

'I'm up for it,' he said.

'All right,' said Freddie, and led Ant to a chair in the middle of the lawn. A blank screen had been set up behind the chair, and a camera was also in place.

'This is Will, our cameraman,' said Freddie, 'and he'll be with us tonight, to record what happens.'

Ant sat down, slightly nervous now that it was about to happen, but Freddie put a light hand on his shoulder.

'Nothing at all to be worried about,' he said. 'I just want you to think about something that makes you relax.'

Ant immediately imagined himself on a beach in Australia.

'Take a few deep breaths, and imagine you are descending a spiral staircase,' began Freddie. 'I'm going to count down from two hundred, and when you get to one, you will be at the bottom . . .'

Ant was vaguely aware of Freddie counting, and before he knew it, Freddie had reached one.

'Now you are completely relaxed,' he heard Freddie

saying; his mind was drifting and Freddie's voice sounded as if it came from a long way away. 'I'd like you to go and let the person you're closest to here know how you feel about them.'

Overcome with a strong emotion and fuzzy warmth, Ant got up and walked over to Harry and gave him a huge bear hug.

'Aw, mate,' he said, 'Aw, mate.'

Harry squirmed a little under his embrace, but Ant didn't mind, he just felt a beatific sense of warmth that he was here on this lovely day with Harry, Josie and Diana.

'Now go back and sit down and go to sleep.'

Ant wandered back to his chair, and sat down, and within seconds was fast asleep. He was dreaming about Diana, about how she'd been when they were young; remembering the joy he'd felt in her presence, when he heard Freddie say, '. . . and one and you're awake.'

He shook his head, and said, 'Was that it?'

'That was it,' said Freddie. 'Now, that wasn't so bad, was it?'

'I still don't like it,' said Josie, even though the others were convinced by Freddie's display, and had eagerly agreed to meet Freddie at sunset at the Standing Stones so they could begin the experiment.

She couldn't put her finger on why, but Josie had a sudden bad feeling about this. There were strange undercurrents in the air. Diana and Ant were still on edge with each other, and she had the distinct impression that Harry was not telling her something. Having seen Ant suddenly come over all affectionate to Harry made her wonder if under hypnotism, they might all reveal things they'd rather keep hidden. Josie wasn't sure she wanted to know his innermost thoughts at the moment. She had a horrible feeling they wouldn't chime with hers.

'I'm not sure,' she said. 'I think we should let things lie.'

'Oh, don't be a spoilsport, Josie,' said Harry, tickling her.

'Yes, go on, Josie,' urged Diana. 'Nothing happened to Ant, and I know it was a bit mean, but seeing what Freddie did to Mike was quite funny.'

Everyone but her seemed to think being hypnotised was a huge laugh. But Josie had the weirdest feeling that she'd regret it if she did.

'What if we cause things to happen that we don't intend?' said Josie.

'What things?' laughed Harry.

'I don't know. We might all turn into axe murderers, or kill ourselves.'

'I doubt that is going to happen,' said Harry, laughing. 'You have far too vivid an imagination.'

'Maybe that is a bit extreme,' said Josie. 'But I think we're playing with fire. All I'm saying is that I don't want to get burnt.'

Chapter Fourteen

The sun was dipping low in the sky as they clambered up to the Standing Stones, casting long shadows across the grass. It was a warm balmy evening, but Diana kept shivering. She was slightly apprehensive about what was going to happen, especially as Nicola had been quite frantic when she found out about it.

'But what if you all get attacked, or fall off the edge of the cliff,' she'd wailed.

'I really don't think that's going to happen, Mum,' said Josie, which was a bit rich considering she'd also been worrying about it.

Nicola had only consented when they'd promised to go well prepared, with proper trainers, warm clothes, torches for when it got dark, and even a food parcel, but she was still fretting about it when they set off.

Luckily Peter was more worried about being late for a golf dinner dance they were attending at a hotel fifty miles away where they were staying the night, and told them they were idiots, but it was on their heads. Diana didn't like to say, 'I'm only doing it for the money'; she didn't imagine for one moment they'd understand. But it was her only motivation.

'Okay,' said Freddie, as they gathered by the Standing

Stones at eight thirty. 'You met Will earlier. With your permission, he's going to follow us round this evening and film anything interesting that happens.

'What I'd like to do, if you have no objections, is to take each of you individually, and make some suggestions that the others can't hear,' continued Freddie. 'Don't worry, Bron and Will are going to be sitting with me all the time. Nothing's going to happen.'

'So who's first?'

'Okay,' said Diana, 'I'll go for it.'

She followed Freddie to the middle of the Standing Stones, where Freddie had set up two chairs, and Will had his camera set up.

The sun's last rays cast golden shadows on the grass, the sound of seagulls keening floated from high in the sky, and there was the constant thrum of waves crashing against the rocks below.

It was quite breathtakingly beautiful, and Diana felt her misgivings fade away. Somehow, she knew this was going to be a night to remember.

'Where do you want me?' she asked.

'If you just sit there, we'll check out the sound and lighting,' said Freddie.

Another ten minutes of fiddling went on before Freddie appeared happy.

'No need to be worried,' he said eventually, 'just let your mind empty.'

'Do I have to look into your eyes?' said Diana.

'No, nothing like that,' said Freddie calmly. 'I just want you to relax, take some deep breaths and imagine somewhere that makes you feel safe and happy. If at any time you feel worried, go to your safe place, and everything will be fine. Shut your eyes if it helps.'

'Okay,' said Diana. She felt a little shiver of excitement. Now it came to it, it was quite thrilling being hypnotised. She shut her eyes, and tried to think of the last time she'd felt safe. A picture popped into her head of her being eight years old, and lying by the fire, staring into the flames. She saw sprites, and fairies and magic in those flames, and she knew somewhere in the house her mum would be cooking dinner for her. She felt secure in a way she hadn't done for years.

'Now I want you to imagine climbing down a spiral staircase, till we get to your safe place. I'm going to count down from ten. Ten; you are descending the first couple of stairs . . .' his voice rolled over her like warm melted hot chocolate. 'Think calming thoughts.'

Despite herself, Diana began to relax. Freddie's voice was like a summer's breeze blowing gently through every corner of her mind, making her feel safe, warm, content. She was vaguely aware that when they reached the bottom of the stairs, a picture came into her head of playing by the fire with a small furry black and white kitten. He'd been a present for her eighth birthday. A deep feeling of content-ment stole over her and she felt utterly relaxed.

'I'm going to unlock your deepest desires,' Freddie purred. 'When the film crew have gone, you're going to have a little sleep, and when you hear an owl hoot, you will wake up, completely refreshed. The first person you see when you wake will be the person you plight your troth with at midnight, tonight.'

Diana felt detached from herself, but very happy. She let out a deep sigh. Slowly she became aware that she was resurfacing, 'Three, you are climbing back up the stairs . . .' Freddie's voice soothed her, and she could see the next step, feel the metal handrail, 'Two, nearly at the top now . . . One, wake up . . .'

Diana shook her head, blinking a little.

'Was that it?' she said, feeling a little disorientated.

'That's it,' said Freddie. 'Now go and join your friends, and we'll have the next person. Let's say, Ant.'

Ant came strolling into the centre of the circle. He was feeling more confident tonight. Whatever suggestions Freddie might think he'd planted earlier, nothing had happened, apart from him feeling mildly affectionate towards Harry which was undoubtedly the booze talking, proving the whole hypnotism thing was pure bunkum. Easy money.

'So, Ant, how do you feel tonight?' said Freddie, as he sat down.

'Fine,' said Ant. 'I still don't think you can do it.'

'Really?' said Freddie, with an amused smile. 'We'll see, shall we?'

Ant settled into his seat, vaguely aware that Freddie had started speaking again. Once more he was descending a spiral staircase, one step at a time, 'three, two, one, you're asleep . . .' said Freddie, and then Ant had the strangest sensation of floating. He was soaring high above the earth, feeling that the stars were almost within his grasp. It was a dizzying, intoxicating sensation. Looking down, he could see his own body slumped over a chair, while Freddie was leaning in and whispering in his ear. Freddie was saying something like, '. . . as this was your idea, you are responsible for your companions. If anything goes wrong tonight, it is up to you to put it right . . .'

That didn't seem too bad, Ant thought lazily, wondering if he could float as high as the gulls. It was a pleasant sensation up here, with the soft sea breeze on his face, and the sensation of wheeling, arching up, up and away.

He felt freer then he'd ever felt, and almost wished he could stay here for ever. '. . . Three, two, one, and you're awake.'

Ant sat up with a jolt. For a minute, he felt cheated, as if deprived of some great treat, and then a little foolish. Had he really imagined he'd been floating up in the sky? How daft was that?

'We done?' he said, to hide his embarrassment.

'We're done,' said Freddie.

'I think your wallet is going to be somewhat lighter by the end of the evening,' said Ant. 'I don't feel any different at all.'

'We'll see,' said Freddie. 'We'll see.'

Josie went next. Despite her forebodings, Diana and Ant had come back seeming very chilled and relaxed about the whole thing. Maybe she was making a fuss about nothing.

'Still nervous?' said Freddie, as she sat down.

'A bit,' said Josie. 'Are you sure you're not going to do anything bad to us?'

'On my life,' said Freddie. 'Hypnotism is really harmless. I've done it on Bron dozens of times, haven't I?'

'Absolutely,' said Bron, 'there's nothing to it. And I promise you, I won't let any harm come to you.'

'Okay,' said Josie, slightly mollified. Bron was like your favourite uncle. She couldn't imagine him letting anything bad happen. 'Now what?'

'I'm just going to chat to you for a bit. Think of lovely things, and things that make you happy.'

Josie could hear Freddie's voice floating over her, tinkling like a running stream. 'I am going to take you to your safe place,' she heard him say and then she was walking through a beautiful forest that had a river running through it, filled with flowers, birds, sunshine and laughter. It was wonderful, she had the sensation of being truly alive and at one with nature. She had never felt so incredible in her life.

'You will find your heart's desire tonight,' Freddie's voice flowed overhead from a long way off. 'The first person you see when you wake up is your life's partner. You know you are meant to be together for ever . . .'

Josie smiled happily as Harry came running through the woods towards her, and she flung herself into his arms.

'. . . And, two, you are at the top of the stairs, and one, you're awake.'

Josie felt absurdly happy, as if someone had just given her the best present in her life, if only she could remember what it was.

'I feel fantastic,' she said in surprise.

'And you will continue to do so,' assured Freddie. 'You're in for a magical and surprising evening.'

By the time it was Harry's turn, he was feeling both a little bored and a little concerned about what they were doing. He couldn't help but feel that maybe Nicola was right and they were making themselves very vulnerable out on the cliffs after dark.

'Don't be daft,' joshed Ant, when he mentioned his fears. 'We're all going to be together anyway. And it probably won't work. What's the worst that can happen?'

'What indeed?' agreed Harry; put like that, his fears seemed foolish.

'Okay,' he said, as he sat down in the circle. 'How do you want me?'

'You're fine, just there,' said Freddie. 'Now sit still, and breathe deeply and cast your mind back to a happy positive point in your life.'

Josie. Harry's heart leapt as his thoughts automatically turned to Josie.

'You're getting married soon, I gather,' Freddie's smooth mellifluous tones continued. 'Think of that happy day.'

Harry felt a jerk of concentration. Josie made him happy, but the cheerful positive feelings fled away the minute he tried to picture her in a wedding dress . . .

'Sorry, lost concentration for a second.'

That's okay . . .' Freddie's voice soothed. 'Think only good thoughts. You are very, very relaxed. Now, I want you to find your safe place . . .'

Harry resisted the urge to giggle. What was he doing here? A grown man. This was ridiculous. But he couldn't seem to keep hold of Freddie's words, they seemed to flow over and past him, sounding meaningless, yet dragging him further down into himself. Until eventually he found himself at the bottom of a spiral staircase, rooted in the earth, his arms round Josie, the safest place he could possibly be.

'. . . And you will reveal the secrets of your heart,' he heard Freddie say as he pulled his arms tighter still round Josie.

Harry stifled a yawn and heard Freddie say, 'You are ascending, slowly climbing back up the stairs . . .' again the words flowed around him, and he could barely remember what Freddie was saying till he heard, 'Three, two, one. Now you are awake.'

Harry roused himself, feeling a bit confused about what had just happened.

'Now what?' he said.

'Now you go back to the others,' said Freddie, and when you hear me count to three, all four of you will fall asleep.'

Harry went back and sat down next to Ant, as Josie and Diana were preoccupied in a giggling girlie session.

'What are you doing?' said Harry to Josie.

'Look, I'm making daisy chains,' she grinned. 'Here's a crown for the king of my heart.'

Harry blushed, but accepted the gift and the kiss Josie gave him.

Then Freddie was standing before them.

'When I click my fingers, you will all go to sleep. But when you hear an owl hooting, you will wake up.'

Harry let out a yawn; he felt enormously tired, as if he just had to lie down. He saw the others were also struggling to keep awake too. And then Freddie clicked his fingers.

'Just might put my head down for a bit,' said Josie sleepily.

'Me too,' yawned Diana.

'This is ridiculous, I'm not going to sle –' Ant's words were muffled by the sound of his snoring.

Sleep washed over Harry. No point fighting it. He lay down, curled up and in seconds was fast asleep.

Chapter Fifteen

Ant was wandering through a forest, feeling kind of dreamy. He had never been out at night like this in the country. The silver beams of the moon danced through the trees, casting a light shimmer, which meant he wasn't afraid. He heard the snuffling sounds of woodland creatures in the undergrowth.

It was such a lovely evening, such a pretty copse. He felt that no one would mind if he lay down here and stayed for a while. Ant lay flat on his back and looked up at the stars, feeling pleasantly detached, and then suddenly the dream changed . . .

It wasn't summer any more, it was winter, and he and Diana were holding hands, laughing, at the top of a mountain. He could feel the crisp cold air against his cheeks, see the majestic mountains around him. He was with her and nothing mattered at all. He could hear the others falling out of the bar, screaming and laughing, but nothing else mattered but this moment, with Diana by his side. He had never felt such exquisite happiness.

'I will never ever let you go,' he whispered, kissing her softly on the lips.

Laughing, she tugged him by the hand, and then they were tobogganing down the mountain at a dizzying and thrilling rate. Time and time again they ended up in heaps of snow, only to remount and carry on. It was mad, furious and funny and he never wanted the moment to end. But end it did, with a bump, as they fell off the toboggan for one last time and ended up in a soggy giggling heap in the snow.

'I'm so lucky to have found you,' he said, 'don't ever change.'

'Tony –' she began, just as he heard the sound of an owl hooting. 'I need to tell you something . . .'

'What?' Ant asked, but the dream was already fading, and the snow and Diana disappeared as quickly as they'd come.

What? What was she going to tell him? He felt sure it was important, and simultaneously sad, as if he'd lost something very dear to him.

He felt his cheek and realised to his surprise that tears were coursing down them. He remembered more then. Diana had never answered his question, and two weeks later she'd dumped him in front of everyone, by pouring a pint of beer over his head. At the time he had no idea, why. And by the time he'd found out why, it was too late.

Ant sat up and looked around him, and gasped. He was alone in a beautiful copse, the silvery moon casting its light in the gaps between the trees. How had he got here? He glanced at his watch, nearly ten o'clock already. He must have been sleepwalking. Suddenly it felt imperative he get back to them, especially to Diana. He'd done her a great wrong and it was time he put it right.

Diana was dreaming she was lying on pillows in the base of a boat, being rowed down a river. Kingfishers darted across the bows, and fish jumped up out of the river. She lay back drowsily, letting her hands drift in the river, feeling the warmth of the sun on her cheek, deeply content. She wondered idly who was rowing the boat; all she could see were strong arms rhythmically rowing back and forth. She had never felt so safe and secure.

She heard the sound of a bird – an owl at this time of the day? – and sat up to see what it was. Smiling, Diana took in the face of the rower, but the dream faded before she could tell who it was. The warmth of the sun was gone, and she was completely alone in the midst of the Standing Stones. She felt sure she'd woken up earlier and looked over and seen Harry next to her. Where had he and the others gone? What was happening? She should be feeling alarmed, she supposed, but somehow she wasn't. They would probably turn up in a minute. Perhaps she should go and look for them? Although there was no sense of urgency.

'Hello?' a voice called out to her. 'It's Freddie, just wondering how you are?'

Freddie? Oh. Then Diana remembered. She'd been hypnotised, they all had. Not that she felt any different.

'Fine,' she said, looking up as Freddie came towards her, shadowed by the cameraman, Will. 'Where's everyone else?'

'They're scattered about,' said Freddie. 'Part of the experiment is waiting to see what happens now.'

'Okay,' said Diana. 'Should I go and find them?'

'If you wish,' said Freddie. 'Is there anyone in particular that you'll be looking for?'

Diana thought for a moment.

'I don't think so,' she began, and then realised it wasn't true.

Her mind flashed back to the dream, and the face she'd just glimpsed when she woke up. No, it couldn't have been.

172

'Well?' prompted Freddie gently.

'There's only one person I want to see,' said Diana, puzzled, 'and I have to find him now.'

'And who's that?' Freddie smiled at her, and she was vaguely aware the camera was still rolling.

The face from the dream swarmed in front of her again.

'Harry,' she said slowly. 'I need to find Harry.'

Harry was on a boat – no, not on one, *driving* one. He was powering a speedboat across the waves, blinking into the sun. The wind was blowing through his hair, and he was exhilarated by the speed and the spray. He was wearing sunglasses, tee shirt and jeans, but felt like something in a James Bond movie. Even more so when he realised there was a beautiful girl by his side, shrieking her pleasure as he sped up, causing waves behind them.

'This is awesome!' she shrieked.

'Isn't it?' He turned and smiled. 'I'm so glad we're doing this together.'

'Me too,' said Josie. 'Me too.'

Harry woke with a start, a smile on his face. What a great dream. He wondered if he could perhaps persuade Josie to go travelling after the wedding. His dream had left him feeling restless, as if something were missing from his life.

He looked down, and realised he'd been sleeping curled up with Josie on a bench at the top of the cliff. He had vague memories of them waking up after Freddie had hypnotised them, and deciding they wanted to sit here together looking out to sea.

Josie was still asleep, and he didn't like to wake her. She was so beautiful, so precious. Their relationship was still new enough for him to be grateful that he'd found her. Not for him any more the thrill of the chase, the misery of the rejection. He'd found the woman of his dreams, and he wasn't ever going to let her go.

Josie stirred in her sleep and then blinked and looked up at him. She stretched and yawned.

'Where are we?' she said as she sat up. 'I was dreaming I was wandering through a vast forest, and I couldn't find you. I'm so glad you're here.'

'Me too,' said Harry. 'I was dreaming we were taking a round-the-world trip on a massive speedboat. It was amazing.'

'Ha,' Josie sat up properly now, 'I can't see you ever being able to drive a speedboat.'

'You never know,' said Harry, 'I've never had the chance.'

'And aren't likely to,' said Josie.

'Is it such a mad idea?' said Harry.

'Is what?' said Josie.

'Us going travelling together?'

'Woah,' said Josie, 'where's this come from? Have you been talking to Ant again?'

'Ant has nothing to do with it,' said Harry. 'You know before I met you I was planning to go travelling?'

'I didn't think you were serious,' said Josie. 'How can we go travelling? We can't afford it, not with the wedding and everything.'

The wedding. Harry suddenly felt as if he'd been hit between the ribs. He was beginning to hate the sodding wedding.

'We could go afterwards,' said Harry. 'Save up and . . .'

'No,' said Josie, 'I'm sorry Harry, I don't want to go travelling. I can't believe you've suddenly suggested it. We need to get ourselves straight first.'

'Oh,' said Harry, feeling deflated. He hadn't realised till now just how much it meant to him. 'I suppose you're right.'

'You know I am,' said Josie. 'You've got commitments now. You can't just up sticks when you feel like it anymore. That's Ant's department.'

'Then maybe,' said Harry slowly, 'we should have a rethink.'

'About?' said Josie.

The words were out of his mouth before he could stop them.

'The wedding,' he said.

Josie stared at him in dismay. It was the last thing she'd expected. She'd woken up feeling unaccountably anxious, after uncertain dreams in which she was searching for Harry and unable to find him. And now Harry had started wittering on about doing some kind of grown-up gap year, which was the last thing she wanted to do at the moment, and now he seemed to be saying . . .

'What about the wedding?' said Josie.

'We could put it off,' said Harry. 'Wait a couple of years, have some fun. Then get settled. What's the rush?'

'I thought you wanted to marry me,' said Josie in a small voice. A feeling of cold dread washed over her. Had he changed his mind?

'I do,' said Harry.

'But?'

'But, I think we're rushing things,' he said. 'We've been together less than a year. We have still so much to learn about one another. You didn't know I wanted to travel that badly, for example . . .'

'More than you want to get married to me, it would seem,' Josie felt as if her world were crumbling. Harry couldn't be saying all this stuff.

'That's not what I meant,' said Harry.

'So, what did you mean?' said Josie. 'Do you still want us to get married or not?'

There was a pause, before Harry said, 'Yes, of course I do.'

The pause hadn't been long, but it was long enough.

'But you'd rather go travelling first?' said Josie. 'Thanks for nothing, Harry.'

'It's not like that,' protested Harry.

'Then what *is* it like?' said Josie. 'It feels like my fiancé has cold feet, is what it's like from my perspective.'

'I love you,' said Harry.

'Really?' said Josie. 'You could have fooled me.'

Shaking with anger, she got up and walked away. Harry had taken her completely by surprise. She thought that everything was perfect, that he was happy, and wanted to get married. But now it appeared he wasn't. He said he loved her, but seemed to be unable to prove it in the one way she felt mattered. What did it mean? Could they still be together and not get married?

1995: Bron

'So it's over then?' Bron said sombrely.

'Sorry, mate, but I'm afraid it is,' said Freddie sighing. 'They've said the viewing figures are really down from last series. And to be honest, I want to look at doing something new. Time for a change for both of us, old boy.'

'I suppose,' he replied. He'd hated the last two seasons of *Illusions*, but even so Bron felt cast off. It was work, and it was regular. It stopped him having to think too hard about what happened next.

'There's always producing and directing,' said Freddie. 'You have been banging on about doing both forever.'

That was true. Maybe he'd have time for that now . . .

He felt melancholy though. And he knew the reason why. Bloody stupid after all these years to be still hankering after her, but he'd always imagined that Tatiana Okeby would be the first leading lady he'd ever direct. But then, he'd always imagined that they would have been together with a horde of kids by now. What had stopped him? He could have had that future, and it was his own fault for not making it happen.

Tati had more or less intimated that to him on their last, and he hoped final, meeting. One drink had led to another, and another, and then, of course the inevitable. And he thought it was their chance to put things right. They'd talked about everything that night; about their hopes, their fears, their failures, the pain they'd caused one another, and he'd really thought it was a new beginning. But whereas he had been over the moon, thinking that finally, here was the second chance he'd been wanting all those years, Tati had made it very clear to him what it was all about for her.

'It's called a revenge shag, darling,' she'd said in the morning. 'Poor little Bron, did you really think I was coming back to you? After all this time? Give me strength.' But she'd been so drunk by the time they went to bed, he didn't even think it had been that calculated.

And then to make matters worse, the next thing he knew it was all over the Sunday papers. 'Bron and me: The True Story', 'Bron the Bastard'; 'How Auberon Fanshawe broke my heart'.

Poor lovely Tatiana. Such a waste. They said she was in rehab now, but he didn't enquire too often. He really thought they'd cut through the bullshit of the last few years on that evening. But he'd been so wrong. Bad enough that she had rejected him in the morning, but to sell their story to the papers: his heart had broken all over again.

However much of a mess Tati was in, Bron was staying well clear. He knew he was still vulnerable to her charms. Probably always would be. The problem was, she was bad for his mental health.

178

Chapter Sixteen

Diana's happiness from earlier on had completely dissipated. She'd been wandering around for over half an hour and was now grumpily lost. After her chat with Freddie, she had left the Standing Stones to find the others, feeling unsettled by the emotions she'd had when she woke up. She'd just been having a weird dream, with Harry rowing her in a boat. It didn't mean anything, surely? Diana felt sure that once she saw him again, she'd put it all in perspective, but couldn't rid herself of the stomach-churning excitement she felt at the thought – which was ridiculous, especially as he was getting married to Josie. Your best friend, Diana reminded herself. How could she harbour feelings for her best friend's fiancé? Especially since she'd never let herself fall for anyone properly since Ant.

Diana's mind fled back eight years, to when she and Ant had been an item. They had been so happy, or so she'd thought. But he'd let her down in her hour of need. And when she'd come looking for him – afterwards – she'd found him cosied up in the bar with Sian. Sian, who'd been her best friend. Ant claimed to have had no idea why she'd poured the glass of beer over his head. He'd denied anything was going on – yeah, right. Diana had seen first hand how flirtatious Ant could be, and Diana had never known anyone resist Sian's seduction technique. All Diana knew was that during the most traumatic experience of her life, her boyfriend had been betraying her with her so-called best friend. Josie was the first proper friend Diana had trusted since then, but now she seemed to be harbouring feelings for Harry. She couldn't do to Josie what had been done to her. She had to put these thoughts out of her mind.

The moon was really bright and shone on the path, which gave way to some woods. Where the hell was Harry? Or Josie? Or even Ant? Or *anyone*. Diana wasn't really a country girl, and the sound of hooting owls freaked her out. But the path shimmered in the moonlight, and something drew her on. Despite her anxiety and irritation, Diana felt a sense that something magical was about to happen, and if only she could find her way through to the right path, she could almost reach out and touch it.

Harry was not feeling the magic. His head was thumping, and he felt heartsick at what he'd said to Josie. She had looked so hurt when he'd talked about delaying the wedding and the last thing he'd ever wanted to do was cause her pain. Harry wished she'd given him time to explain properly, but she'd run off into the darkness and now he didn't know where she'd gone.

He wasn't even sure which direction he should be looking in. Perhaps he should think about heading home. Maybe Josie had gone straight back there. He'd find her, sit her down, have a proper chat, and sort it all out. They'd had a silly misunderstanding, that was all; it could be easily resolved. Descending the cliff path, he found himself walking through woods which swayed gently in the breeze.

The soft calls of owls and the odd rustling in the bushes were the only sounds to disturb him. After he'd been walking about ten minutes, he found himself in a clearing. In the far distance he could hear the rhythmic roar of the waves. There was a real sense of something – magic? – in the air. Harry paused for a moment and then sat down. He didn't know why.

Then he heard voices. He got up gladly. Maybe it was Josie. But as the voices came nearer, he realised they were male voices.

'Oh,' he said, 'it's you.'

'Hello, Harry,' Freddie was all urbane charm, while Auberon Fanshawe huffing and puffing behind him nodded hello, and Will wandered nonchalantly behind them with a camera.

'I thought you were going to show me where Tati is,' Auberon grumbled. 'Where in God's name are we?'

'I believe we're not too far away from the farm where she's camping,' said Freddie with a smile.

'Tati, camping? I'd like to see that,' snorted Auberon.

'I believe it's more of a glamping experience,' said Freddie, 'she's holed up in a yurt with all mod cons. But I'm hoping she might be up for a little midnight adventure.'

'What did you say to her?' said Auberon.

'I may have possibly suggested subliminally that if she wanted that part, a late-night assignation at the theatre might be the thing,' said Freddie. 'You're not getting cold feet, are you? It was your idea.'

'No,' said Auberon, but he didn't sound too convinced.

'Ah, Midsummer Eve,' said Freddie, breathing a deep sigh. 'Such a magical night, don't you think? You could almost believe fairies and elves and Cornish piskies exist, couldn't you?'

'Tommy rot,' said Auberon.

'Um, I think I gave up believing in fairies some time ago,' said Harry.

'Oh well,' said Freddie. 'How's the experiment going?'

'Not well at all,' said Harry. 'I can honestly say that if I get through this evening, I will never be hypnotised ever again. Thanks to you, Josie's run off and I don't know where she is.'

'So no one's plighted their troth yet.'

Harry rolled his eyes.

'The likelihood of Diana and Ant ever making it is somewhat less than zero, and thanks to me getting a dose of verbal diarrhoea as a direct consequence of your hypnotism, my fiancée isn't speaking to me.'

'Ah,' said Freddie. 'I'm sure it will all be all right in the end. Why don't you go and find her and have a chat?'

'That was the plan,' said Harry, 'but I'm not sure where she's gone.'

'Well, we're heading for the theatre,' said Freddie. 'If I see her, I'll tell her to meet you there.'

'Okay,' said Harry. 'It's a deal.'

Josie had planned to go back to the Standing Stones, to see if the others were there. She really wanted to talk to Diana and ask what she thought. A bit of her thought maybe she'd been unfair on Harry. Perhaps he was right, maybe they *had* rushed things – but it had been a bit of a shock, hearing that he still wanted to go travelling. He'd mentioned it when they first got together, but she hadn't realised he was serious about it. Josie felt a little stab of guilt. She knew Harry really wasn't happy in his job. Working on a local rag for London suburbia covering school fetes, lost pets and the occasional petty crime wasn't exactly what Harry had had in mind when he left the journalism course he'd taken after uni. Josie could remember all those years ago, when they first met, he'd had the burning ambition to be a prizewinning journalist. That wasn't going to happen at the *Hornsey Echo*, but she hadn't twigged that he was so determined to do travel writing. Harry had mentioned it once or twice, but in such a diffident manner, Josie had assumed he wasn't that serious.

She couldn't help feeling it was partly Ant's fault. No doubt he'd been stirring Harry up with thoughts of getting away and finding his freedom again. Despite Ant's intervention the previous day, Josie didn't quite trust him. He was so against marriage – or commitment even, Josie had read the excoriating email he'd sent Harry when Harry told him they were moving in together – he couldn't seem to bear it happening for other people.

Josie had reached a fork in the path; one way carried on round the coast, and another path went down to the open-air theatre. A third made its way down to a pretty little beach where she'd spent much of her teenage years having illicit barbies on the beach.

Josie struck off for the cliff path and, hearing voices, thought for a moment it must be Diana or Ant, but as she came further up the path, she realised the sounds were coming from a field where she could make out a brightly lit campsite – oh of course, this was the new place Mum had mentioned recently. A smart young couple from London had moved in and converted an old farm into a luxury caravan site, complete with yurts, and log burners, and 'massage parlours', according to Mum. Josie had checked, and it turned out there was a healing tent offering everything from Ayurvedic massage to hot stone therapy.

And according to Mum, it was where Tatiana Okeby and her entourage were staying.

'Please don't go, Tati,' she heard the high-pitched voice of Gray M'stard pleading, 'Darling, you might get lost out there.'

'Who knows what creatures are lurking in the woods,' said the flighty little assistant, whom Josie had heard Tati refer to as Gypsy.

Their voices were getting nearer, they were clearly heading across the fields for the path she was on.

'Will you all stop making such a fuss,' said Tatiana grandly. 'I am going for a little walk down to the woods, where I am going to meet Mr Slowbotham and discuss this part further.'

'But why so late?' said the final member of the entourage, Ariadne, Josie thought she was called. 'What if he's an axe murderer?'

'Hallo there,' called Josie, 'it's me, Josie, I met Tatiana yesterday. You really don't need to worry. 'I've known Mike all my life, I can promise you he isn't an axe murderer.'

'You see,' said Tatiana triumphantly. 'There really is no need to worry. Mike wants me to perform for him at midnight, so as to get the ambience right. I think it's a wonderful idea. Now please, children, leave me be. I'll be fine. This young lady seems to know her way round, so I'm sure she won't mind escorting me to the theatre.'

'Er,' Josie was going to mention that she was looking for her friends, but didn't get a chance as Tatiana bowled past her, grabbed her arm and said forcefully, 'Now, I believe it's this way, isn't it?'

* * *

Ant was lost in the woods. He'd walked round and round in circles, and was no nearer to finding anyone, least of all Diana. Which in a way was a relief. Although he still had the strongest feeling that he needed to find her, a part of him was hoping he didn't. From her reaction last night, when he tried to talk about what had happened between them, she didn't seem too keen to go over old ground. Maybe he should let sleeping dogs lie.

He was just about to throw the towel in and take any path down the hill, just so he could get out of this wretched wood, when he heard voices. Female voices. It must be Josie and Diana, he decided. Well, it was now or never.

He walked towards them and then realised Josie was with someone else entirely.

'Oh,' he said. 'Where's everyone else?'

'I haven't seen Di,' said Josie, 'and Harry's still on the cliff somewhere. Tatiana was a bit lost, so I said I'd show her the way to the theatre.'

'Thank you so much,' said Tatiana graciously, 'I couldn't have found my way on my own.'

She was wearing highly inappropriate clothing; a light gossamer dress, which was far too revealing for a woman her age, and high strappy sandals, which looked like they'd break your ankles if you fell over.

'I must say, the countryside is rather tiring,' she continued. 'I don't sleep a wink in that yurt. All I can hear is strange snuffling noises all night long. It is most concerning.'

Ant suppressed a laugh. What did the woman expect from camping?

'At least you've got the glamorous version,' said Josie tactfully. 'Now, if you just follow the path that way for five minutes, you should be able to find the theatre. You can't miss it.'

'Thank you, my dear,' said Tatiana, 'it was very kind of you.'

'Are you sure you don't want me to take you all the way?'

'No, thank you,' said Tatiana, 'I think I can manage.'

And with that she walked off dramatically in the wrong direction, till Josie pointed her the right way again.

'God, what a drama queen,' said Josie. 'I'm glad to see the back of her. What's been happening with you?'

'Not a lot,' said Ant. 'I'm glad I've met you, as I've been getting hopelessly lost.'

'Where were you trying to get to?'

'Back to the Standing Stones to find Di,' said Ant.

'Really?' Josie looked confused. 'So the hypnotism thing actually worked, then?'

'No!' said Ant, 'I just want to talk to her.'

'About what?' said Josie. 'Only after last night, I wouldn't have thought bringing up the past is a good idea, do you? Diana hasn't even told me what really happened, what makes you think she'll discuss it with you?'

Ant shrugged his shoulders.

'She probably won't, but it's worth a try,' he said. Ant looked around him. 'Where did you say Harry was again?'

Josie shrugged.

'I left him on the cliff,' she stubbed her toe in the ground. 'We had – we had a row.'

'About?'

Josie looked miserable. 'He wants to delay the wedding and go travelling. I said I didn't. And then we fought.'

'Come on,' said Ant, suddenly feeling he wanted to make her smile again. 'I'm sure you two can sort this out. Let's go back and find him.'

'Okay,' said Josie.

They turned back up the path together, Josie leading the way. She seemed so sad, which upset Ant for some reason. He felt an overwhelming urge to make sure she was happy again, and as he followed her up the path, he couldn't for the life of him think why.

Chapter Seventeen

Harry was struggling to find the right path to the theatre. The one and only time he'd been there, on his first date with Josie, they'd come from a different direction altogether. And now with the light of the moon fading, and the beginnings of a sea mist slowly curling its way across the cliffs, he was getting quite disorientated. All he knew was that he must find Josie. Surely she'd understand how he felt if he explained it to her better? He'd been clumsy and spoken without thinking. Maybe he could persuade her that instead of a honeymoon and buying a house, they should take a year off and travel instead. That would be a good compromise, he felt.

As he came out of the woods, he ran into Diana, who was looking pale and ghostly; ethereal almost.

'Harry,' she said, flushing slightly, and he thought with a jolt that she was very pretty. He hadn't really noticed it before.

'Di,' he said, 'have you seen Josie?'

'No,' she said, 'I assumed you were together.'

'We were,' said Harry with a sigh, 'but we had a row, and I've lost her.'

'Never mind,' said Diana. 'I expect she'll turn up.'

'I hope so,' said Harry, feeling morose and out of sorts. 'I can't bear the thought that I've made her upset.'

'I hope she realises how lucky she is,' said Diana. She sounded rather sad, and Harry looked at her in surprise.

'Is everything okay, Diana? Only you seem a little different.'

'Do I?' said Diana. She gave him a shy and tender smile, which was rather disconcerting, to say the least. If she hadn't been Josie's best friend, he might have thought . . .

Suddenly she grabbed hold of him, and said, 'Have you ever danced under the light of the moon?'

And then he did think, very rapidly and in an increasingly panicky manner. What on earth was happening? Di was Josie's mate; could she? – was it possible? – was she coming on to him?

'Er, no,' said Harry.

'Everyone should try it at least once,' said Diana, starting to croon Frank Sinatra lyrics at him, which was a tad alarming. She'd just got to the bit about there being trouble ahead, when he managed to extricate himself from her embrace.

'I think we really ought to be looking for the others,' he said, but she pulled him back to her. 'Oh, Harry, you're so staid,' she said. 'Live a little.'

'Are you drunk?' said Harry. It was the only way he could account for her behaviour.

'Yes, I'm drunk on love, and high on you,' said Diana, grabbing him and spinning him around.

Harry was stunned.

'Diana –' he began, just at the moment Josie burst down the path.

'Harry,' she said. 'What's going on?'

Josie stopped dead in her tracks. Diana and Harry? Diana and *Harry*? She'd been prepared to be conciliatory when she was talking to Ant, but here was Harry, *her* Harry, dancing with Diana, looking for all the world as if he had forgotten all about their argument.

'So now we know the real reason you want to put off the wedding,' she said; 'you're more into the bridesmaid than the bride. Great. Absolutely great.'

Josie's legs felt like jelly and her heart was pounding so loudly she thought it might explode.

'I *thought* there was something going on on Friday, but I told myself I was being stupid. But now, this . . .'

She turned to run back down the path, and Harry ran after her.

'Josie, it's not like that.' Harry looked aghast, urgently grabbing hold of her hands to try and remonstrate with her. 'Diana, well Diana's in a bit of a funny mood.'

'And was Diana in a funny mood when you were dawdling together down the garden the other night?' said Josie. 'I can't believe you two. I trusted you both.'

Her voice cracked, and she wiped furious tears from her eyes. Why was Harry doing this to her? This weekend was supposed to be perfect. And now it was all ruined.

'Josie,' Harry looked gobsmacked, as if the truth of what had happened had only just dawned on him. 'Josie, you're wrong. Nothing is going on. I love you.'

'I don't believe you,' said Josie, flinging his hands away.

Just then, Ant came panting up the path. 'What's wrong?' he said.

'Nothing,' said Josie, 'and everything.' And with that she was gone again, unable to stand it one moment longer. The world had gone mad and she wasn't sure what to do next.

'What? You did what?' Ant felt like smacking his head against a brick wall. What on earth did Harry think he was doing? Why was he mucking around with Diana, when he had Josie? He couldn't have made a bigger fool of himself if he'd tried.

'Nothing,' said Harry, 'I did nothing. Diana launched herself at me, and we were dancing when Josie came up. She got the wrong idea, that's all.'

He was standing as far away from Diana as he possibly could, so perhaps he was telling the truth, though it would be difficult to persuade Josie of that.

Diana was leaning against a tree, looking slightly defiant.

'What about me?' said Diana in a small voice.

'What about you?' said Harry. 'I'm sorry, Di, I'm not sure why you did that. But thanks to you, Josie thinks I'm cheating on her. I need to find her, now.'

'What do I do?' wailed Diana. 'I love you.'

She started to walk towards him, but Harry pushed her away, and took off in the direction that Josie had taken. She looked so undignified, Ant snorted to himself, and then felt bad. Poor Di was going to end the night disappointed, he felt sure of it. Poor Di? When had Diana become poor Di? Good God, he was losing the plot too. It was bad enough that he felt the need to become friends again with Diana, it was a bit much to have to feel sorry for her too, especially as he felt miffed that she'd chosen his friend above him. It was about time he found Freddie bloody Puck and got him to sort this mess out once and for all.

'Excellent, excellent,' he heard a voice in the bushes. 'Did you get all that?'

'Who's there?' Ant said suspiciously.

'It's only us,' said Freddie, emerging from the bushes with a debonair smile, followed swiftly by Bron and Will, whose camera seemed surgically attached to his body. 'We've been catching up with what's happening. Oh, dear. It's all gone a bit pear-shaped, hasn't it?'

'You're enjoying this, aren't you?' accused Ant. 'Did you do this on purpose?'

'No, of course I didn't,' said Freddie, 'but the course of true love never did run smooth. I'm sure it will all work out.'

'It better had,' said Ant. 'Otherwise you'll have me to answer to.'

Again, that feeling of responsibility. Where had that come from? It was becoming rather annoying.

Di was well and truly lost this time. The moon had vanished, hidden by swirling clouds which made the place resemble something from a Daphne du Maurier novel. Bushes rustled in the wind as she walked past, and she had never seen anywhere so dark. She lit her way with the torch, but its light didn't spread very far. Diane shivered; it was a bit creepy out here on the cliffs. Suddenly she felt foolish for having come.

Oh, dear God, what was she doing here? There was no point in chasing after Harry. Whatever moment of insanity had led her to dance with him had passed. She could see how pathetic she looked now. Harry was in love with Josie. Josie was in love with Harry – she had no right to interfere. But Diana felt very strange. She was in the grip of a really strong emotion which possessed her whole being. She loved Harry with all her heart, and the pain of knowing that he could never be hers was sharp and intense. As usual, Diana's timing was off, and she'd made the mistake of falling for the one person she couldn't have. How she could have been so dense as to not see it before, she didn't know.

'There's nowt so stupid as folk in love,' she muttered to herself.

'You can say that again,' a voice startled her in the darkness.

192

'Jesus!' Diana nearly leapt out of her skin. 'Who's there?'

'We met in the pub, I think,' a woman got up from where she was crouching on the ground, and Diana saw it was Tatiana Okeby. 'Your friend, Josie, was showing me the way to the theatre, but then the mist came down and I got a little lost. I sat down here and I think I might have dozed off. 'I feel sure I'm meant to be meeting someone, only I can't remember who.'

'Is it the guy we saw you with at the café? Mike, isn't it?' said Diana. 'Something about a play?'

'Ah, yes, that's it. He wanted to meet me at midnight in the open air theatre, so I can audition to play Titania. How immensely thrilling.' 'I'd best be off,' Tati said and, surprising Diana with her sprightliness, walked very fast towards the theatre.

Diana couldn't think where else to go, so she got up and followed her.

Chapter Eighteen

'What on earth have you done?' said Ant. 'Harry and Josie have fallen out, Di thinks she's in love with Harry and I have this overwhelming urge to look after everyone.'

'Aah . . . I think that might have been a small thing I did,' said Freddie.

'Which was?'

'When you were under, I might have made a few suggestions to liven things up. Josie is supposed to find her deepest desire, Harry was supposed to reveal his true thoughts, and Diana was to find her true love.'

'And me?'

'Ah, yes,' said Freddie, 'I did suggest that you might have to take responsibility for everyone, as this was all your idea.'

'When? When did you say that?' Ant couldn't remember Freddie saying anything like that. Mind you, the hypnosis itself felt blurry now anyway.

'Earlier on, when you were at the Standing Stones,' said Freddie.

'Oh,' said Ant, vague memories of the words, 'You will take responsibility,' seeping through his memory banks.

'I'm sorry, I was just trying make things more interesting,' said Freddie.

'You certainly did that,' said Ant.

'It was part of the experiment,' said Freddie. 'I had no idea that all this would happen.'

'But you can fix it, right?'

'I *should* be able to,' said Freddie, but he didn't sound too convinced. 'Where are they all now?'

'Harry followed Josie to the theatre, I think,' said Ant. 'God knows where Di's got to.'

'Well, best foot forward,' said Freddie.

'No,' said Ant firmly, 'I want you to rid me of this responsible behaviour thing. It's cramping my style.'

'First things first,' said Freddie, 'I think we need to find Josie and Harry, don't we?'

'All right,' said Ant, 'but I'm next. I don't want to be the one in charge.'

He turned to Will who was following behind with his camera clamped to his shoulder. 'And will you please stop filming my every move?' he said. 'It's making me paranoid.'

After it turned out that the open-air theatre was further away than they thought, Tatiana decided to take a breather. 'Need to rest my legs,' she gasped. 'You go on.'

Diana had never been to the open-air theatre before and, intrigued, she walked on till she found the entrance, which was covered in weeds. Apparently it wasn't in use as much as it had been. She wasn't even sure if the gate was locked. But then she pushed it and it swung open with a creak.

Diana stepped through the entrance and was immediately entranced. A stone gateway lead through to a grass stage, surrounded by seats in a half circle looking out to sea. The mist rolling from the sea, was swirling around the theatre, reflecting the silvery shimmer of a moon just trying to peep through the clouds. Shafts of moonlight caught the stone seats, and cast long shadows on the grass. It felt magical and mysterious.. Diana felt herself shiver in anticipation. Of what, she wasn't quite sure.

'Josie? Harry?' she called. 'Are you there?'

But there was no answer, just the crashing of the sea on the rocks below and the cries of the seagulls. She shivered. What was she doing here really? She had a sudden feeling that coming at all had been a mistake. Josie and Harry were meant to be together. She was Josie's friend. She should never have entangled herself in their love life, should have seen her feelings for what they were. Now, she risked losing the best friend she'd had since . . . Sian. She'd never allowed anyone to get that close again. And now Diane had pretty much done to Josie what Sian had done to her. She'd never felt so bad about anything in her life before.

'Is that you, my love?'

Diana nearly jumped out of her skin.

'Um – no, I don't think so,' she said cautiously. Oh God. She was on a cliffside at midnight with a weirdo. To her relief, the weirdo turned out to be Mike Slowbotham.

'I thought you might be Miss Okeby. We have an assignation.'

'She's heading this way, but just stopped for a rest,' said Diana. 'Are you quite sure she's expecting the same thing you are?'

'I know it,' said Mike, dramatically. 'I saw it the first time we met. We're kindred spirits, you see. Fellow thespians. Mere mortals couldn't begin to understand. But through her, I'm going to revive the fortunes of this place. This theatre will live and breathe again. She will be a glorious Titania, and magic our way back on to the map. It is going to be wonderful.'

'If you say so,' said Diana, edging away nervously. The guy was barking. 'I think I really must just go and find my friends.'

'And if you see Tatiana, tell her I'm waiting, won't you?'

'Of course,' said Diana escaping thankfully, and striking out on a path back to the forest. The mist had come down really heavily now, and it wasn't long before she was hopelessly lost . . .

Harry ran and ran, frantically calling Josie's name. But if she was there and listening, she certainly wasn't answering. And who could blame her, after what he'd done? She had every right to be angry with him. Every right.

Eventually he caught sight of her sitting by the edge of the forest. She looked beautiful, wistful and lost.

He longed to go and hug her, but held back in case she turned away from him.

'It's all right, Harry,' she said. 'I know you're there.'

'Oh.' Harry came forward feeling foolish.

'Look Josie, I'm so sorry. Nothing happened with Diana, honestly. It's been a strange evening and a pretty odd weekend. Can we just start again?'

'It's okay,' said Josie, 'I'm sorry too.'

She took his hand and held it.

'But I feel a bit strange. It's been such a weird night, and I think I need a bit of space. I've clearly been pressurising you about the wedding, and I feel stupid I didn't know how serious you were about your travel plans. Sorry, Harry, but I need some time to think this all over.'

Whatever Harry had been expecting, it wasn't this. He opened his mouth and shut it again.

'What is there to think over?' he asked weakly.

'Everything,' said Josie, holding his hand, but it felt cold to the touch. 'I'm worried we may have rushed things. Perhaps we should slow it all down, delay the wedding –'

Delay the wedding? Harry felt seriously alarmed now. He'd not been sure about the wedding itself, and should have felt pleased. But a cold clutch of fear held him in its grip. What if *delay* the wedding, meant *cancel* the wedding? He'd always felt so lucky to have found Josie, and amazed that someone as gorgeous as her had chosen him. Maybe *she* was the one getting cold feet? Perhaps she didn't want him at all, and his worst fears were going to come to pass.

'Look, all this hypnosis stuff has clearly played around with all our minds,' he said. 'This is nothing. We'll get over it. I'm sure we can work it out. I never meant to hurt you.'

'You haven't,' said Josie. 'It's okay, really. I hope you and Di are very happy together. Now if you don't mind, I have some serious thinking to do. I'll see you later.' With that, she got up and walked away.

Harry slumped back with his head in his hands. Now what? Josie sounded like she had been really serious. What if she left him? He loved her now more than anything. He'd been a prize idiot, and it could cost him dear.

Josie walked away from Harry, feeling oddly numb. It was as if a veil had been lifted from her eyes. Once she'd got over the shock of seeing Diana and Harry together, she'd known what she had to do. If Harry was having doubts about their relationship, now was the time to say it. Better now than later, and at least it would stop her worrying that her parents secretly felt she was making a mistake.

She had been so thrilled to see him again at Amy's wedding, remembering how well they'd got on when they dated at university, and had thrown herself headlong into the relationship. She'd wanted it to work, she'd wanted to get married. She'd got so caught up with the excitement of a wedding, she'd forgotten the important person, Harry. And maybe she'd pushed him away. If he ended up in Di's arms, she only had herself to blame.

The mist had come up even thicker now, so Josie was a little uncertain of the way. Which path had she come down? The trouble was, in the dark and in this mist, they all looked the same. She struck off to the left, feeling sure that was the direction she'd come in, but in only a few moments, she realised she'd lost her way.

Bushes loomed at her alarmingly and the path she was on grew smaller and smaller until it vanished altogether, and she found herself scrambling through undergrowth to get out into the open.

'Oh.' She'd arrived by chance at the open-air theatre. Should she go in, or should she just call it a night? There seemed no point pursuing this hypnotism thing, it had been such a disaster.

She was about to turn back, but then she noticed the gate was open, and a faint voice was declaiming, 'I know a bank where the wild thyme blows . . .'

Intrigued, Josie pushed open the gate and walked in.

1998: Bron

She was coming out of the hotel, just as he was entering it. Swathed in furs, her hair covered with a scarf, eyes hidden behind dark glasses, her lips, bright red in a cruel smile. He hadn't seen her for five years, but he'd have recognised her anywhere. Still the same, beautiful Tati. A bit sadder and wiser now, perhaps, but for all the talk in the tabloids of how Tati had lost 'it' – whatever 'it' was – she would always remain beautiful to him.

'Bron,' she said, 'what a delight.'

Her voice was dripping with sarcasm, and he felt a sharp blow in the pit of his stomach. Why did she always have to be so unkind to him?

'The pleasure's all mine,' he responded, cursing himself for still getting that weak-kneed feeling in her presence. It was that damned perfume. Got him every time.

'Still toiling away behind the cameras?' her smile said it all; you've lost it, career over, just like me.

'How's rehab?' It was a low blow, but the pain she perpetually caused him, and the memory of the way she'd treated him still rankled.

'I've been clean for three years!' she snapped. 'I've just been meeting my agent, if you must know. A possible part in Hollywood.'

'London's loss is Hollywood's gain,' said Bron, with only the slightest trace of irony.

'Hmm, well it's not a done deal,' she said, 'so not a word, understood?'

'My lips are sealed,' Bron bowed politely.

She softened slightly. 'You always were a gentleman, Bron,' she said.

There was a pause and then she said quickly, 'I hear you're married. I hope you're luckier than I was.'

And then she was gone in a blur of scarves and perfume, and Bron stood looking after her, not sure if he felt happy or sad.

Part Three

The Course of True Love

'I know a bank where the wild thyme blows,
Where oxlips and the nodding violet grows.
Quite over-canopied with luscious woodbine,
With sweet musk-roses and with eglantine.'
                    A Midsummer Night's Dream: Act II, Scene 1

'People enjoy what I do. I enjoy what I do, otherwise I
wouldn't do it. Do I owe them anything? No, I don't
think so. It's their choice after all.'
                    Freddie Puck: interview with Loaded; 2000

Chapter Nineteen

Diana was hacking her way through the bushes. Leaving the theatre, she'd decided the best thing she could do was to go home and get some sleep. This evening had turned into a total farce, and she just wanted it to be over, so she could forget all about it, before she made an even bigger fool of herself.

But with the mist now fully entrenched on the cliffs, she had become lost within minutes and ended up in some woods, where owls hooted, creatures rustled and there were all sorts of mysterious and intimidating noises. Before long the path petered out, and she found herself scrambling under branches and pushing her way through nettles and brambles, before tumbling into a hedge, from which she was now unceremoniously pulling herself. She was grateful for her fleece, which not only was keeping her warm as the temperature dropped but had stopped her arms from being completely scratched to bits, though she'd stung her hands after grabbing a nettle by mistake, and her hair, which had been in a very fetching up-do, was now straggling round her face. She was filthy dirty and very, very cross. So the last voice she wanted to hear was Ant's.

'Di, is that you?' he said.

Emerging from the mist like a phantom, Ant hove into view.

'Hang on, I'll help you out of there.'

Great, now her humiliation was complete.

'Don't you dare laugh,' Diana said, trying to summon what little dignity she had left as Ant pushed brambles and bracken out of his way to reach her.

'Watch out, there are some stingers there – oh.'

Ouch. Ant's warning had come too late; Diana simultaneously put her hand in among the nettles, and accidentally dragged her leg through them as she stumbled through the gap.

'Damn, that hurts.'

Diana wrung her hand, and checked Ant suspiciously for laughter, but he seemed surprisingly solicitous. Perhaps she'd underestimated his capacity for chivalry.

'Here, let me find you a dock leaf. Hang on.'

Ant half dragged, half yanked Diana the rest of the way out of the bushes and sat her down.

'Where's it stinging?'

'Everywhere,' said Diana crossly, then, aware that she might be appearing like a prima donna, said, 'I'm scratched everywhere, but the sting's on my leg.'

'Oh, I'm just going to rub this dock leaf on it.'

'What are you doing?' said Diana in alarm. The first time Ant had touched her leg, on around their second or third date, she'd got into all sorts of trouble. She could still remember the treacherous feelings of excitement, nerves and delicious anticipation as if it were yesterday. She had no intention of her body betraying her in that way now.

'It will make it feel better, honestly,' he said.

And to Diana's surprise, it did. Whatever was in the leaf

soothed the stinging sensation, and soon it had gone altogether.

'That's amazing,' she said. 'How did you know how to do that?'

Ant shrugged his shoulders.

'Dunno, I just do. Seriously, did you never rub dock leaves on your leg as a kid? I thought everyone did.'

'City girl through and through, me. I don't think I ever saw a nettle till I left home,' Diana said. She looked at Ant suspiciously. 'What's with you? You're not normally this helpful.'

'Blame it on Freddie. He apparently threw in a little, *you're going to be responsible for everyone* thing into my hypnosis experience. It's a right pain in the arse. I've sent him to find Harry and Josie and get them talking again. *Then* I'm going get him to make me irresponsible again.'

'I think I prefer the responsible version,' said Diana.

'I don't,' said Ant with feeling.

'That's because the real you is an arse,' said Diana. 'Take it from one who knows, you're much better like this.'

'We'll have to disagree on that,' said Ant. 'I do not want to be responsible for everyone. Especially not you.'

'There's no need for you to,' Diana bristled. The real, obnoxious Ant was in there after all.

'Di, you can't have Harry. I saw the way you looked at him,' said Ant, more gently then he expected. 'It'll ruin everything.'

'I don't know what I feel about Harry,' said Di, 'I'd never thought of him like that till tonight. This hypnotism has muddled everything up.'

'Maybe Freddie can fix it so we go back to normal,' said Ant.

'So now what?'

'I said I'd wait here for Freddie and Bron,' said Ant.

'I suppose I could stay with you,' said Diana, though not entirely relishing the prospect. 'I doubt Harry and Josie want to see me, and I've nothing else to do.'

Harry wandered through the mist, also lost in more ways than one. He wished he'd kept his mouth shut, and not mentioned anything about his travel plans. Then he might be lost, but at least Josie would be at his side. Why had he opened his big mouth?

Because it's true, a voice said in his head, and he realised with sudden clarity it was. He loved Josie, truly, with all his heart, and would do anything for her, but he also wanted to travel, see the world, have a proper attempt at being a travel journalist, instead of marking time at the *Hornsey Echo*. If he hadn't met Josie again, he'd have probably been off by now. But he had, and fallen head over heels with her. In the first flush of new romance and the excitement of getting married, his plans had fallen by the wayside. No wonder she hadn't taken them seriously. He'd forgotten to take them seriously himself. If he found her, Harry thought, and explained it properly, maybe she'd understand. This was just a blip in their relationship, the first no doubt of many. He needed to find Josie as quickly as possible and put things right.

He'd been walking aimlessly for about an hour before he realised he must have gone round in a circle. The bush and rock he'd seen half an hour ago loomed up once more.

'Can this sodding evening get any worse?' he said, sitting down in exasperation. If ever he needed a fag it was now.

'Harry? Is that you?' A voice came out of the gloom, and Auberon Fanshawe lurched towards him. 'I keep getting lost in all this fog.'

'Me too,' said Harry. 'What are you doing?'

'The idea was that I'd find you and bring you back to Freddie for a little – erm – hypnotic readjustment, so we can start again.'

'So it *is* Freddie's fault,' said Harry. 'I should have known this hypnosis thing was a bad idea.'

'Steady on,' said Auberon. 'You were supposed to wake up next to Josie. But you didn't.'

'No, because when I got back, she was chatting to Diana and oh –'

'Diana fell in love with the first person she saw – you. So if I can get you back to Josie and Freddie and he puts you all under again, Josie can forget what she saw, and then Freddie can make Diana forget she's in love with you.'

'That easy?'

'That easy.'

'Okay, what are we waiting for?'

'Right, good,' said Auberon. 'Off we go, then.'

'Er, which way?' said Harry.

'This way,' said Auberon firmly. 'I know I haven't been down here before.'

Harry followed Auberon down a path that had cleared a little as the mist escaped. He was damned if he was going to get lost again. Not now there was a chance to put things right.

Josie came into the theatre to see Mike Slowbotham standing dramatically declaiming his lines.

'Miss Okeby,' he rushed forwards expectantly.

'Erm, sorry, no,' said Josie. Oh, God, please don't let Mike come on to her. That would be too much to bear after the trials of this evening.

'Oh, it's you. Darling little Josie, how are you?' he said exuberantly. Nicola had spent many years on the committee

209

of the local theatre, and Josie had been darling little Josie nearly all her life, much to her disgust.

'I have the most exciting news to impart,' Mike said portentously. 'We will soon be graced with the presence of that angel of the small screen, that beauty, that wondrous being, the divine Tatiana Okeby, treading the very ground we walk on. And then I hope she will consent to be mine.'

'Right,' said Josie. 'And she knows this, does she?'

It sounded most unlikely, and she wondered if Freddie Puck could be somehow involved.

'Without a doubt,' said Mike. 'Tatiana and I are soulmates, two halves of a whole. You saw her last night, in the pub, how she stood up for me. I've finally met someone who can match me in every way. Tatiana is perfect.'

'Well, good luck with that,' said Josie. 'I think she's just intending for you to give her a part in your production.'

'Production? Of course she's going to have a leading role, as befits the leading lady in my life.'

'Oh, God, you really mean it, don't you?' Josie laughed out loud, forgetting her own troubles for a moment. Mike had always had delusions about his ability to attract women, but this took the biscuit. 'Sorry to disappoint you, but I think you might be punching a tad above your weight, there.'

The door creaked open behind them and Tatiana swept in.

'Where do you want me, darling,' she said. 'I can't wait to begin.'

Mike looked as if all his Christmases had come at once.

'Right, erm, okay,' he began, voice squeaking (perhaps he wasn't as confident as he appeared), 'I thought we could start with . . .'

Josie wondered what she should do. She still hadn't sorted out the mess in her head about Harry and the wedding yet, and wasn't quite ready to find him. She sat down instead. This could be fun, she thought. May as well stay and watch.

Ant felt very strange, sitting here with Di. Something about the intimacy of putting the dock leaf on her leg had sparked something. Regret? Maybe . . . Why had he let her go all those years ago? Till their split, he'd thought her the best thing that had ever happened to him. Yes, he knew the reasons she'd given him later, but why had he never told her how he'd felt about it? *Because she never gave you a chance.* The thought came unbidden, and he realised it was true. Suddenly he wanted her to hear him out, as she hadn't all those years ago.

'So go on, now we're alone, answer the question I asked you last night,' he said.

'What question was that?' said Diana, looking uncomfortable.

'Why you hate me so much,' he said. 'You do realise you never actually told me.'

Diana rolled her eyes.

'You're bringing that up now?'

'Why not?' he said. 'It's the first time we've had a chance to properly talk all weekend. You never gave me the chance before.'

'Maybe I don't want to talk,' said Diana.

'And maybe I do,' said Ant.

'Why? What good will it do? It's a long time ago. We were in love. You were a bastard. End of story.'

'Because it was good, wasn't it?' he said softly. 'I'm not making that up. At one point I thought . . .'

A memory sprang unbidden into his head, of having brunch with Di and looking across the table at her and realising how very lucky he was. It hadn't just been good; it had been amazing.

'Well, you thought wrong,' said Diana, savagely ripping out his memory. 'Look, what is this? Do you want to make amends for what you did? You had your chance. It's too late.'

'That's the thing, though,' said Ant. 'I've never known what it was that I did wrong. As far as I knew everything was fine, and then you ditched me in front of everyone. It was humiliating.'

'Humiliating? Humiliating?' Diana practically screamed. 'I'll give you humiliating. Ant, I lost our baby all alone in a foreign hospital and you weren't there. It wasn't just humiliating, it damn near broke my heart.'

Ant felt like he'd been punched in the stomach. Despite what Diana may have thought of him, he still felt the pain of that loss, though over the years he'd buried it deep.

'But at the time I didn't even know you were pregnant,' he protested. 'And it was my baby too.'

'And when I came out looking for you, there you were, cosied up with Sian. All those messages I left. And you never came.'

He heard the catch in her throat, and instinctively leaned over to touch her. But she shook him off and got up.

'You broke my heart, Ant,' she said, getting up. 'And I don't think I can ever forgive you.'

'What messages?' said Ant, puzzled, to her departing back. 'I never got any.'

Chapter Twenty

'Okay,' said Harry, after they'd gone round in circles for the tenth time. 'Admit it, you're just as lost as I am. Have you any idea where Freddie is?'

'Can't get a signal on this damned phone,' admitted Bron sheepishly. 'The only thing it's good for at the moment is as a torch.'

'You won't get one up here,' said Harry. 'I think there are only about three places in Tresgothen that you can get a signal. I swear one of them is on my in-laws' roof.'

Possible *ex*-in-laws, Harry corrected himself. Auberon was putting a lot of faith in Freddie's skills, and what if he got it wrong again?

'I think we should try going downhill,' said Harry. 'We keep heading upwards, and I really don't fancy tumbling off a cliff in the fog.'

'Good idea,' said Auberon.

They found a path that Harry didn't think they'd taken before, and wandered down it before it gave way and opened up towards a clearing, at the edge of which a gate attached to a stone wall lurched out of the fog.

'Aha!' said Harry. 'I do believe that's the theatre. Isn't that where Freddie was headed? Josie seemed determined to go there.'

'With any luck,' said Auberon.

'With any luck, what?' said Freddie, who was leaning against the wall looking nonchalant. 'Shh, I've got Will in there, secretly recording Tati and that Slowbotham fellow. It's hilarious.'

'Sorry?' Harry was confused.

'Another little unexpected bonus of the project,' said Freddie with a mischievous grin. 'Bron has a long-running feud with Tati which goes back into the mists of time. We thought we'd have a little fun with her while she's here.'

Bron looked a tad uncomfortable when Freddie said this. 'You won't be too unkind, will you, Freddie?'

In the dim recesses of his mind Harry seemed to remember his mum going on about how Bron and Tati were like the Taylor and Burton of light entertainment. He could even vaguely remember how distraught she'd been when their relationship had ended for good. 'It's so tragic,' she'd said, 'those two are star-crossed lovers if ever I saw them.'

'Do you know if Josie is in there?' said Harry. 'I have to see her.'

'Hold your horses, mate,' said Freddie. 'This requires very careful handling. I think the best way to do this is if we go back to basics. I put you under again, and we'll start from scratch.'

'And Josie won't be angry with me anymore?' said Harry. He wondered if this actually was the best way to resolve their differences; there was the small matter of him wanting to go travelling to sort out.

'Can guarantee it,' said Freddie, 'don't you worry about a thing.' Harry just had to hope he wasn't crossing his fingers behind his back.

*   *   *

Diana strode away from Ant in a blind fury. She was shaken, rocked to the core. Why had Ant had to go and bring that all up again? She'd just about coped with seeing him this weekend by blanking out all the really bad stuff, but having him bring it up again had really shocked her. She'd worked so hard at forgetting, hardening herself up, never letting herself get too close to anyone, and now . . . With a few words he'd ripped away those barriers. She felt pathetic, but the gentle way Ant had touched her leg had awoken something in her, brought her back to the time when they had been into each other.

Back then, she remembered now, she'd woken every day to a fuzzy world of blissful imaginings. A world where every day she'd known she would meet Ant, that Ant (or Tony as she'd known him then) was in her life and all was right with the world. It hadn't even been all about the sex either – though that had been fantastic, which was a new experience for Diana at the time. But there had been something more. Every time she saw him, she'd felt dizzy with delight that he was hers and that she was his. Every hour spent away from him had been an agony; every reunion sweeter than the last. And then, like the greenest girl in the world, she'd fallen pregnant and her world had collapsed.

She'd tried to tell Ant, the night they'd been tobogganing together, but the moment had passed and then she hadn't known how. A further two weeks had elapsed, when she and Ant had been so busy working separate shifts there'd barely seen each other. Thinking about it now, Sian had been in charge of the rotas. She wondered if?– no, surely Sian hadn't been that devious?

And then on the evening she'd planned to tell Ant, she'd started bleeding. No one else knew about the pregnancy, Diana had hugged her secret to herself, not wanting anyone

215

to know till he did. Frantically she'd tried to get hold of Ant, but he wasn't at his chalet, and she remembered too late that he'd agreed to do a late shift. She told Sian, sure that she would pass the message on, and then gone alone in a taxi to the hospital, where they'd confirmed she was losing her baby. Sian had offered to come with her, but at the time, Di had been so desperate for her to find Ant, she'd begged her to stay and look for him.

She'd stayed overnight, waiting and waiting for Ant, certain he would have got away, and come to find her in her hour of need. But he hadn't come, and she'd sat in her wretched hospital bed, sobbing and alone. It was the greatest betrayal of her life, and part of her had never got over it.

And when she'd been discharged and got back, there was a text saying *You OK Babe? Missed you earlier. Bar later?* She'd left her phone at home in her hurry to get away.

So she'd gone to the bar, and he'd been with Sian. The full force of that betrayal and the sense of loss she'd had that evening hit her again. She'd marched straight up to him, tipped beer over his head and vowed to never let another man hurt her like that again.

Ant had tried to get in touch, but she refused to see him. She'd assumed that he'd got her messages, and couldn't be bothered to come. And that knowledge had kept her hatred of him burning long. But tonight for the first time she had doubts. 'What messages?' he'd said. Maybe he hadn't received them after all.

Ant was also lost in the past. He had been so shocked that night when Di had poured beer over his head. He'd had no idea what had happened. That poisonous cow Sian had been whispering sweet nothings in his ear – not that he'd been in the remotest bit interested in her. But Sian seemed to have been always there, drip-feeding him stuff for weeks about how Di was changing shifts to avoid him; feeding his insecurities about why a girl like Di would be with someone like him. And when Di had ditched him, Ant had assumed it was true, she'd never loved him. Like an idiot, rather than sorting it out with Di straight away, hurt pride meant he'd fallen straight into Sian's arms, as no doubt Sian had always intended. By the time he'd found about the miscarriage from a message Diana later left on his answerphone (Sian had never once mentioned it) it was too late. Diana wasn't answering his calls and refused to see him. She'd left soon afterwards to go back to the UK, and so had he, and he'd put her out of his thoughts ever since.

And the baby. He'd tried not to think about the baby. If it had lived it would have been seven or eight by now. Instead of the self-indulgent life he'd lived up until now, he'd have been a dad — been responsible. Normally the thought terrified him, but tonight it made him feel sad. It was a long time ago, but the thought of what might have been was heartbreaking. This evening, something inside him had changed. Despite insisting that Freddie de-programme him, Ant suddenly felt he was taking the easy way out. He'd ruined Di's life all those years ago, albeit unintentionally. Till tonight, he'd had no idea she'd tried to contact him before she went to hospital, believing instead she hadn't wanted to have anything to do with him. No wonder she hated him.

And thanks to his idiocy in pushing this hypnotism thing, his best friends had fallen out. He needed to go and make sure that Freddie was really making things better. And he needed to make his peace with Di. After all this time, he owed her.

*   *   *

'I pray thee, gentle mortal, sing again:
Mine ear is much enamoured of thy note . . .'

Tatiana was really getting into character, and to her surprise, Josie was enjoying the performance. She was very good. A shame she'd never had the chance to prove it. Josie found herself hoping that this could actually be her comeback to the theatre world. She only prayed if Mike managed to put on the play he didn't elect to play Bottom himself. He was dreadful. As Tatiana lay languidly back, he pawed over her, and was blurting out 'Methinksmistressyoushouldhavelittlereasonforthat. Andyettosaythetruth –' before Tatiana stopped him and said, 'Maybe we should run that through one more time, a little slower, perhaps, with pause for feeling.'

Mike's response to pausing for feeling was to take such long pauses between words that Josie was liable to nod off waiting for the next sentence. She was giggling to herself about this when there was a tap on her shoulder.

It was Freddie Puck.

'I feel responsible,' he said.

'What for?' said Josie.

'For everything that's happened tonight,' he said. 'It's my fault that you and Harry have had a row.'

'It's okay,' said Josie. 'I think I might just need some space away from him. Maybe we rushed this marriage thing.'

'Oh, bugger, much worse than I thought,' said Freddie, 'Time for you to find your safe place again. I'm going to snap my fingers and you'll fall asleep, and when you wake up the first person you meet will be the one you love.'

Josie stretched sleepily, and lay against the seat in the theatre, feeling cosy and warm. Over her head, she could hear Auberon saying anxiously, 'Isn't that a bit risky? Suppose she doesn't see Harry straight away?'

'Shh, I know what I'm doing,' said Freddie. 'Now let's leave her and go back to Harry, just to make sure he is the first person she sees when she wakes up . . .'

Josie stretched herself languorously on her seat. It was turning out to be a strangely entertaining evening. She dozed off, and was soon dreaming. She and Harry were in the woods dancing. It was lovely, she felt all happy and floaty. Then she turned, and there was Diana, coming towards her. Oh, good, she'd had a feeling they'd fallen out, but here she was smiling. 'Oh, Diana,' said Josie, giving her a hug. 'I'm so glad we're friends again . . .'

Slowly, she became aware of someone shaking her.

'Oh, Josie,' Diana was saying, tears pouring down her cheeks. 'I've been such an idiot. I'm so sorry. I've let you down so much. You're my best friend in the world.'

Josie sat up, feeling bewildered.

'Di, it's okay, sweetie. You've got nothing to be sorry about. You know I love you.'

'And I love you too, Josie,' said Diana. 'Are we still mates?'

'Of course,' said Josie. And leant forward and planted a smacker on Diana's lips. 'I'll love you for ever. You're my one and only.'

Chapter Twenty-One

'You what?' Diana was stunned. Had she heard what she thought she'd just heard? As Josie leant forward to grab her, she realised she had.

'Gerroff me, what are you doing?'

'Don't be like that, Di,' said Josie. 'Don't you see we're meant to be together?'

'No,' said Diana firmly, 'we really really aren't. I mean you're my best mate, and I love you dearly, but . . .'

'See, you said it,' said Josie, 'you said the L word.'

'I meant love as in a *sister*,' said Diana.

'Oh, you silly,' said Josie. 'Don't be shy. We're all grown-ups here. You know you feel the same way.'

Diana started to edge her way backwards.

'I don't, Josie, honestly I don't,' said Diana. 'Hot-blooded hetero me. I mean, I've got nothing against lesbians. Some of my best friends are lesbians, including apparently you, which is a surprise – and is fine – but seriously, girls don't do it for me.'

Josie had a scary gleam in her eye, as if she wasn't prepared to be thwarted.

Oh dear.

'Look, I understand,' she said grabbing Diana's hand

and clutching it hard as if she'd never let it go. 'You're in denial. It's been sudden –'

'You can say that again,' said Diana.

'But you don't know what you're missing. Just think of it, how wonderful it would be if the two of were living together.'

'Yeah, I remember that,' said Diana, 'we were flatmates, I used to nag you about tidying up. And then you fell in love with Harry.'

'Harry, Shmarry,' said Josie airily. 'I was blind then. But now I can see. Don't you get it? We're meant to be together?'

'I don't think so,' said Diana.

'Just think of the fun we'll have,' urged Josie. 'Two girls, chilling out in our onesies, being able to watch all the chick flicks we want to, whenever we want to –'

'I'm more of a horror film girl myself,' said Diana.

'The house will be spotless –'

'Yeah, right,' said Diana. Josie, having been waited on all her life, didn't 'do' housework.

'And best of all –'

'What?' said Diana, wondering at what revelation was about to pour from Josie's lips . . .

'The loo seat will never be left up!' said Josie triumphantly. 'Come on Di, embrace your inner lesbian. You know it makes sense.'

'Right, going now,' said Diana, extricating herself from Josie's hand with difficulty. She ran down the aisle to escape her friend. But Josie was too fast for her.

'Ooh, playing hard to get,' she said. 'I like it.'

'Nooo, this cannot be happening,' said Diana. 'This isn't real, Josie, Freddie's hypnotised us, remember?'

'It's real to me,' laughed Josie.

Di tried to run in the opposite direction, but Josie blocked her.

'You won't get far,' said Josie with a grin. 'You know I'm faster than you.'

Of course, another sodding thing that Josie was better at than her.

'Oh God,' moaned Diana, 'someone, please get me out of here!'

Ant had pounded all the way down the path and quickly reached the theatre, where he found Freddie standing over Harry saying, 'When you wake up, you will see Josie and it will be as if your argument never happened . . .'

'Did you tell Josie the same thing?' said Ant.

'More or less,' said Freddie.

'What was it, more or less?' said Ant.

'I told her when she woke up she'd fall in love with the first person she saw.'

'You idiot,' said Ant, 'what happens if the first person is one of us?'

'But it won't be,' said Freddie, 'because you're going to stay back while Harry goes in.'

'Did Di pass this way, by the way?' said Ant, trying to keep things casual.

'Not that I've seen,' said Freddie. He turned his attention back to Harry.

'Now, Harry, go get her.' Freddie gently propelled Harry through the creaking gate to the theatre and underneath the archway, where Ant suddenly heard a squeal of, 'Bloody hell, Josie, don't you dare do that again!'

As Harry walked into the theatre, arms wide open, saying, 'Josie, I am so sorry, I truly love you, please let's start again,' Diana leapt over the seats and came tearing towards them.

'You've got to help me, please!' she said. 'Josie's gone mad and thinks she's in love with me.'

'I don't think,' said Josie with a lascivious wink, 'I know. Diana, you're what's been missing all my life.'

'That should make bedtime more interesting,' said Ant. 'Honestly Harry, you lucky bugger.'

'Who said anything about him?' said Josie. 'I'm so done with *him*. All men are good for is providing sperm. I'm sure Diana and I can get along just fine without you two.'

'Freddie, what on earth's going on? Josie's gone mad,' said Harry in disbelief.

'You have to admit it is quite funny,' said Freddie. 'I've never had a reaction like that before. Fascinating.'

'Fascinating? You think it's *fascinating*? You wouldn't say that if it was happening to your fiancée,' said Harry. 'Do something!'

'Okay, point taken,' said Freddie looking a tiny bit remorseful. 'Josie, sweetheart, I think you need to have a little sleep again, while we think things through.'

'No chance,' said Josie. 'You're not going to get me that way again, not now I've found the love of my life.'

And with that she bounded down the stage and headed off round a path at the side of the cliff.

Harry raced after Josie and Ant followed him.

'Sorry,' he shouted as he barged past Tatiana Okeby and Mike Slowbotham who were standing open-mouthed, looking at them. 'Bit of a crisis.'

Good God, could this evening get any madder?

Josie felt ridiculously light-hearted. Falling in love with a girl was the most fabulous thing. They could paint each other's nails, sit down and chat about make-up for hours. It would be so much fun. Like having a sister as well as a lover. Josie had always wanted a sister. Josie felt all girlish and giddy. She'd never felt so light and happy before. It was the most wonderful feeling.

After a while, she grew weary, and finding a bench that looked out to sea, sat down. Never in her life had she felt more content. Josie yawned slightly. All this excitement had made her feel sleepy. Maybe she could just lie down and take a little nap . . .

Soon Josie was dreaming. She was in a wood, a dark, spooky wood, and she had lost her way. Somehow, she knew she had got things wrong and she needed badly to find her way back to someone, but who? Her path was blocked with brambles which scratched her arms, as she fought her way through. She had to find her way back; had to make things right.

Eventually, she saw a light flickering on and off in the distance, and she made her way towards it. She could just make out the shape of a large wall, and a tower behind it. Gradually she hacked her way through the branches, more determined than ever that she must find her way to whoever was on the other side of the wall.

Breaking through the last tangles of brambles, and could it be? Roses? Josie ran towards the wall, where she found a gate creaking slightly open. Without thinking, she pushed her way through, and saw the source of the light, a lantern hanging above a gate, by the entrance to the tower. She grabbed the lantern, and raced up the stairs two at a time, determined now to find the person she knew was waiting for her.

And finally at the top of the stairs, there he was curled

up on a sofa, fast asleep, with a gentle smile playing on his lips.

'Oh, Harry,' said Josie, and kissed him.

Ant and Harry were both exhausted by the time they found Josie curled up asleep on the bench.

'She can't half run fast,' grumbled Ant. 'I'm knackered.'

'She's used to it,' said Harry, leaning over and breathing fast. He had a massive stitch in his side. 'She grew up doing cross country round here. Even at home she does mad long runs all the time. I can't keep up with her. Now what?'

'Wait for Freddie to sort this out, I guess,' said Ant, 'and hope she doesn't wake up before he gets here.'

Harry threw himself onto the grass and let out a snort. 'I suppose it is quite funny in a way,' he said.

'What is?'

'Josie, falling for Di. The look on her face ... priceless.'

'I still think you should go for a threesome,' said Ant. 'I mean, you and Di ...'

'... Was never meant to happen,' said Harry firmly. 'It's this bloody hypnotism. It's all gone horribly wrong.'

'I know,' said Ant. 'Sorry. It's my fault. I should never have suggested it.'

'You've found her then,' Freddie came puffing up the hill, Diana and Bron behind him. 'I'm sorry, I had no idea she'd do that. I think the best thing now is if we start again.'

'Don't you think you've done enough damage?' said Harry. 'Can't you just get us back to square one?'

'As you wish,' said Freddie. 'Let's have a little reboot.

When I snap my fingers you will all go to sleep. And when you wake none of this will have happened. Everyone will be in love with the person they should be.'

Harry wasn't even aware of feeling sleepy this time. One minute he was awake and the next he was in a deep dreamless sleep, feeling utterly content.

2002: Tatiana

'You can't even get me on *Celebrity Big Brother*? What kind of agent are you?' Tatiana practically screamed down the phone. 'I cannot possibly be less well known than Melinda Messenger.'

'Sorry, Tats,' Sally Peasebottom said. 'They say you're not well remembered enough.'

'Me, not remembered? God, the public are fickle.' Tatiana took a drag on her cigarette. 'What about this new Jungle thingy. I hear Tony Blackburn is up for it. If an old has-been like him can get in, surely it must be a shoo-in for me?'

'I'll try,' said Sally with a sigh, 'but don't hold your breath. Word on the street is they've signed everyone up already.'

'So it's another season doing panto for me, then?' Tatiana drooped. Oh, God. How had it come to this?

'Looks like it,' said Sally, 'but I'll do my best.'

Tatiana put the phone down and stubbed out her fag. She looked at herself critically. A few crows' feet here and there. But not too bad. Maybe she should try this new Botox thing people were talking about. Or a face-lift. Her hair still had a natural sheen and bounce, thanks to the magical hands of her favourite stylist, Colin. He could do amazing things with a bottle, that man.

She was still looking good for her age. Despite the drinking, she'd managed to invest her soap star money wisely, which meant the odd nip and tuck had been available to her. In the good times she'd always remembered the bad, and now the bad were rolling round again, it was just as well she had . . .

But what would she do when the parts dried up? She was still occasionally in the papers with stories about her latest toyboys – usually an escort she'd paid to hang on her arm – but that wasn't enough to keep the wolf from the door. She was in danger of being a washed-up has-been.

And that wasn't even the worst of it. The thing was, her life felt so empty. There had been no one significant for a number of years, and she'd screwed up the one fleeting moment she might have had to get back with Bron. How she could have done that kiss and tell demolition with the *News of the Screws*, she couldn't now tell. She still curled up in shame when she thought about it. No wonder he didn't want anything to do with her, even though she'd read recently he'd split from his wife. Tati couldn't blame him either. If Bron had done that to her, she'd never have wanted to see him again. But she'd been a different person then. Drink and drugs had a lot to answer for.

And now, here she was, middle-aged, fast losing her looks, with her career going down the pan. And so very, very alone.

Chapter Twenty-Two

Ant stretched and yawned. He was sitting on the ground, on top of a cliff, looking out at a calm and placid sea. It was very dark, the moon shining faintly through the mist, swirling clouds spreading their tendrils across the cliffs. What was he doing here? He had only vague memories of the evening so far. They'd come up to the Standing Stones and then . . . it was all a bit patchy. Though he had a feeling he'd been doing an awful lot of running; he was aching all over.

He looked around. Josie was asleep on the bench and suddenly it hit him square between the eyes, and he realised how blind he'd been. Holy crap. He felt like his heart was about to explode with happiness. *Josie.* Josie was what he'd been searching for his whole life. How could he not have seen that before? Beautiful, gorgeous Josie. It had always been her, from that very first moment in the uni bar. If she did but know it. But how could he have forgotten?

Next to him, he heard a groan, and a 'Where the hell are we?'

Oh. Diana. He had a feeling they had been at odds this evening and somehow it was important – that he was supposed to have sorted something out. But he couldn't remember.

'On top of a cliff. Last thing I remember, I was talking to Freddie, and –' he suppressed a yawn, 'then I woke up here.'

'Do you think this daft experience is over yet?' said Diana. 'I really want to go home.'

Harry stirred. Ant hadn't clocked him next to Josie, and suddenly feelings of utter jealousy flooded over him. It was so unfair. Why did Harry – quiet, dull Harry – get someone as gorgeous as Josie? It was all wrong.

'Hi, Josie,' Harry said, a little shyly. 'Are we okay now?'

Josie woke up and the smile on her face made Ant light up inside. But then she ruined it by flinging her arms around Harry and saying, 'Oh babe. I was dreaming I'd lost you, and then I found you.' Ant felt a knife twist in his heart.

Josie got up, a little flustered. First she'd flung her arms around Harry, thinking they were alone, and then she'd spotted Ant and Diana were there; and Ant seemed to be radiating negativity on a major scale – but why? Surely he was happy about Harry and Josie, wasn't he? She vaguely remembered she and Harry had been arguing, and that Ant had been supportive, but now the evening's squabbles seemed to have diminished from a major storm to a minor squall. Josie couldn't work out what all the fuss had been about, why she'd got so angry. She and Harry could sort whatever it was out. They could do anything together. She was sure of that.

'I think I've had enough of this nonsense,' she said. 'Let's go home.'

'Good idea,' said Diana. She looked quite sad and lonely, and Josie felt for her friend. She hoped that Di didn't resent her own good fortune. 'I think I've had enough. Is this the way back?' She got up and walked off in the wrong direction, till Josie called her back.

'This has been an odd evening and no mistake,' said Harry, holding her hand and squeezing it tightly as they made their way up the track towards the theatre. 'But everything's fine now, isn't it?'

'Yes, of course it is,' said Josie, kissing him on the lips.

'Do you have to?' Ant sounded quite put out, which was unlike him. He was normally the one to make a bawdy comment.

'Sorry,' said Josie. 'I'm just so glad everything's back to normal.'

They had nearly reached the theatre when Freddie emerged. 'Everything all right now?' he said. 'Good, good. Then we can start filming again.'

'Actually, Freddie, we were all thinking of calling it a night,' said Josie. 'We're knackered.'

'But it's not yet midnight,' said Freddie persuasively. 'And in order to see if my experiment has worked, you should be up at the Standing Stones at midnight plighting your troth. At least hang around till then.'

'Do we have to?' groaned Diana. 'I want my bed.'

'It was in the contract you all signed,' said Freddie. 'And I'm afraid there won't be any money if you don't fulfil that part of the contract.'

Josie hesitated. She knew Harry had wanted the money to do something special for their wedding night. And although it wasn't much, now Diana had lost her job, she probably couldn't afford to turn it down.

'The money would be nice,' said Harry.

'I could do with some extra dosh,' said Diana grumpily. 'Okay, I'm in.'

'What about you, Ant?' Josie asked.

Ant shrugged his shoulders. 'I'm happy to go wherever you are,' he said enigmatically. 'Come on, let's get it over with.'

Harry felt he'd spent a whole night climbing up and down this wretched cliff. He'd know his way round perfectly by the end of the night. Freddie was keen for them to go back to the Standing Stones where they'd started from. It seemed like a daft idea to him. Ant and Diana were hardly likely to declare undying love and he and Josie – well, if he were going to do anything like that, he'd rather do it in private, without a camera crew watching. But money was money, and he couldn't afford to be choosy.

They made good time back to the Stones. The mist was beginning to clear, and there was a clear view of the moon again, and the stars sparkled and shone. Harry looked up at the sky, getting a sense of how small he was in an infinitely huge universe. Whatever troubles he and Josie had had seemed petty now.

It was still quite warm, despite being so late, and a soft breeze played on his face. He looked at Josie as the wind ruffled her fair curls, marvelling at how someone as beautiful as her could have chosen him. He loved everything about her: the way when she smiled it lit up her whole face, the little dimple on her chin; her clear blue eyes; her heart-shaped face; her flawless complexion. If nothing else came of tonight, at least he'd learned how utterly, irrevocably in love he was with Josie. There was still a huge discussion to be had about what they did about his career, and whether or not to go travelling after the wedding, but he felt they could weather anything now. They were together, united, a complete pair. And nothing else really mattered.

When they arrived, everyone sat down looking more than a little self-conscious.

'Now what?' said Diana, who seemed very grumpy, and, he felt, somewhat sad.

'Now we wait,' said Freddie with a smile. 'We wait and see . . .'

Diana had never felt so discontented in her life. Unlike the others, who appeared to either have blanked out what had happened, or had genuinely forgotten, she remembered snatches of the evening so far. She was filled with mortification at the memories; her dancing with Harry and *Josie* kissing her were two moments that were making her go hot under the collar. How could Josie be acting as if neither had happened? And then there was that painful conversation with Ant. Diana was uncomfortably aware that she might have got it a bit wrong with Ant, who had been kinder to her then she'd expected. She didn't want to let him back in her life, ever – least of all by being sympathetic. She could bear his scorn, but not his pity.

Her watch showed that it was nearly midnight. Midnight on a Midsummer's Eve . . . She took a sharp intake of breath. Maybe anything was possible. Diana had a feeling of anticipation, of waiting, as if something momentous was about to occur . . .

'We should have dressed up as druids,' said Josie dreamily, leaning back on Harry, clearly feeling the same. 'I feel all tingly, as if something amazing is about to happen.'

'Yeah, right,' said Ant. 'I didn't know you were some New Age hippy.'

'I'm not,' said Josie looking a bit hurt. 'But the setting calls for it, don't you think? I really feel that there's magic in the air tonight. . . .'

The moon was brighter than it had been all night, the sea breeze gently blowing the remnants of the mist away.

Perhaps Josie was right; perhaps it was a night when magic could happen. Diana looked at Ant, and was overcome with a sudden impulse which, try as she might, she couldn't resist. All those long-repressed feelings came rushing back – images of them kissing, of them being in bed, of them laughing, of them being together, the pair of them against the world, just the way that Harry and Josie were – came flooding back.

'Ant,' she said, slowly, as if a great truth had just been revealed to her, 'Ant.'

'Why do you keep saying my name?' Ant looked confused.

As if in a dream, and despite knowing that once the words were said they couldn't be unsaid, Di walked over to Ant's side, knelt down and said, 'This midnight, on a Midsummer's Eve, I plight my troth to you.'

Chapter Twenty-Three

'What? You like Ant now?' Josie was as stunned as Ant, who was standing open-mouthed.

'What's it to you?' said Diana. 'You've got Harry. Why should you care who I'm in love with?'

Which was true – Josie wasn't remotely interested in Ant, but for some reason it niggled her that Di suddenly was. After everything she'd said. It was none of her business, but it felt like Di wasn't being true to herself.

'I'm your friend,' she said lamely. 'And I just do. Ant's hurt you before – remember he's Teflon Tone, the guy you've hated for years – I don't want you to be hurt again.'

'It's none of your business,' said Diana. 'Besides, you can hardly take the moral high ground, considering you were chasing me round the theatre not so long ago.'

'I – I . . .' Oh, God, the theatre; it all came flooding back. Josie flushed deep red. She'd thought she'd dreamt the theatre, and now the memories of pursuing Diana were returning with dreadful clarity.

'That wasn't me,' she said. 'That was the stupid hypnosis. And so is this. You don't really love Ant. Freddie's just been messing with your mind, like he has with the rest of us.'

Of course. It all made sense. Di was jealous of her. Josie had money, looks, Harry. Diana had nothing. Not even a

235

job anymore. Josie took a deep breath and said, 'Look, I know you've had it tough and you've screwed things up in the past. But what makes you think Ant would suddenly be interested in you?'

'Well, Ant?' said Diana. 'How about it? We've got unfinished business after all.'

Ant's mouth snapped shut, and he attempted to articulate a response, but all that came out was a strangled gasp.

'I told you,' said Josie, 'he's so useless he can't even say it, but this is Ant we're talking about, he hasn't changed. No offence, Ant.'

'None taken,' said Ant, who seemed to have temporarily recovered the power of speech.

'You spoilt, spoilt little princess.' Josie had never seen Diana so enraged. 'You think the world revolves around you. Why can't I be happy too?'

'That's not what I'm saying –' Josie protested, but Diana was on a roll now and oblivious to anything her friend was saying.

'Why poor Harry still wants to marry you after the fuss you've made about this sodding wedding is anyone's guess,' she continued. 'All he wants to do is keep things simple, but no, *perfect* little Josie has to have her *perfect* wedding, sod what everyone else wants. He's put everything on hold for you, even his travel plans, but you don't care, do you? It's all about you. Christ, I didn't just create a bridezilla, I've created a wedding monster.'

Josie was flabbergasted. In all the years she'd known Di, she'd never been subjected to the full force of Diana's bitterness, though she'd often witnessed Di demolishing others. It was like sharp shards of glass falling on her from a great height, each more painful than the last.

'Di, that's a bit strong,' said Harry. Her hero. Why wasn't he standing up for her more? 'I think you should apologise.'

'I have nothing to apologise for,' said Diana, looking truculent and moody.

'You were out of order and should say sorry immediately,' Ant butted in.

Diana looked as if she'd been punched in the stomach.

'I might have known you'd take Miss Goody Two-Shoes' side,' said Diana bitterly. 'Three against one. Nice. I'm done here. I'm going back to the house, and tomorrow I'm going to make my own way home.'

'What about the contract?'

'What about it?' said Diana. 'I stayed till midnight; it's been an utter disaster. I'm out of here.'

'Diana –' Josie started to protest. Underneath the bravado, she could see that Di was struggling to hold it together.

'Find yourself another bridesmaid, Josie. That is, if you ever make it down the aisle, which somehow I doubt.' Getting up, Diana stormed off down the path, leaving the three of them stunned.

'And then there were three,' said Harry, trying to sound light-hearted.

'Oh, shut up, Harry,' Josie said. She was devastated. It looked as though she'd just lost her best friend.

Harry was stunned, first by Diana's declaration, and then by the bile that had spewed from her lips. He'd always seen her as Josie's feisty friend. Sure, she could be a bit sharp sometimes, but essentially she meant well. He'd had no idea that she had been harbouring such bitter thoughts against Josie. Nor that she still had feelings for Ant. She'd spent so much of the weekend on his case, it was the last thing he'd been expecting. But then again, maybe she'd been protesting too much.

'She'll get over it, Josie,' he said, putting a tentative arm round her shoulder. 'I'm sure in the morning she'll have calmed down and everything will be okay.'

'But it won't, though, will it?' said Josie, 'I only wanted Di as my bridesmaid. How can I have a bridesmaid who doesn't want to speak to me?'

'Fair point,' said Ant.

Josie flopped down on the grass, and started tearing clumps of grass out of the ground. She looked as if she was pondering something. Eventually she burst out with 'Do you think she's right about the wedding? Have I been a complete nightmare about it?'

Harry said nothing, staring into the darkness, chewing his lip and wondering what to tell her. The silence that followed was almost unbearable.

'I think she deserves an answer, mate,' Ant said quietly, and Harry felt like thumping him. Since when did Ant have the monopoly on relationship advice?

'Well?' Josie looked at him. 'You do still want to get married, don't you?'

Oh God. He wasn't ready for this.

'Look, Josie, I love you, you know I do,' said Harry. 'Earlier, when I thought you'd walked out on me, I felt as if my whole world had collapsed . . .'

'You haven't answered my question,' Josie fixed him with those piercing blue eyes. He felt like a rabbit caught in the headlights.

'Josie, I want to spend the rest of my life with you,' he began.

'I sense a *but* here,' Josie replied.

'But it's too soon,' Harry said miserably. 'I'm not ready for marriage, there are too many things I want to do . . .'

'I see,' said Josie, tight-lipped, but it was clear she didn't.

'And I want to do them with you,' said Harry helplessly.

'But not *married* to me,' said Josie. 'I can be forever dangling at your side, but you will never commit, will you? I'm sorry, Harry. I'm an all-or-nothing kind of girl. I just can't do that.'

They stared at one another in dismay, until Josie finally looked away.

'It's very late,' she said. 'Di's right. We should go home. But at the moment I can't be around you. Can you just go away, please?'

'Do you want me to stay with you?' Why was Ant being so solicitous to Josie? It was really annoying.

'Kind offer, Ant, but I really want to be on my own,' said Josie.

'Yes, of course,' said Ant. 'Maybe we should go and see if Di's okay.'

'I don't really care,' said Josie, 'so long as you don't involve me.'

'Josie,' said Harry. 'Please, you can't mean it?'

'Just go,' she said. 'If you really loved me, you'd let me be.'

Feeling dejected and miserable, and not knowing quite what to do, Harry got up to go. It had been a disastrous evening and he wasn't sure if there was a way back from it.

Diana was furious with herself. Why had she acted on impulse like that? It was completely unlike her. Those things she'd said to Josie. She hadn't even realised she felt like that until she'd said them. And she'd made a total tit of herself in front of Ant. He wasn't interested in her anymore, and who could blame him. She'd been on his case ever since she got here. He probably thought she was winding him up. Bugger, bugger, bugger. If only she had a car, she'd drive off to find a hotel; she doubted that any of the little B&Bs in the village would open their doors to her at this time of night.

'What a sodding nightmare,' she said. Her fury had propelled her so far, but now she was slumped down and leaned against a tree, feeling utterly bereft. Her whole life seemed to be leading up to this moment: the disappointment of her parents, all the failed relationships, the loneliness – it all went back to that day in the hospital, when Ant had let her down.

Tears rolled down her cheeks. The baby. She'd made a point of never letting herself think about it. But tonight, after that conversation with Ant and everything that had happened since, she couldn't box it away anymore. Huge sobs overwhelmed her. She was hugging her knees and feeling pathetically sorry for herself, and still the tears came.

'Oh, dear, are you all right?' Auberon Fanshawe was standing before her. 'I was just going back to the theatre to meet Freddie and Will,' he said, 'and I couldn't help noticing you were a bit upset.'

Mortified, Diana tried frantically to wipe away her tears.

'It's okay,' said Auberon, 'I'm an actor, I'm used to women crying. Hell, most of the time, it's my fault they're crying. May I?'

He pointed to a patch of ground next to her, and when she nodded sat down beside her.

'Fancy telling me what a nice girl like you is doing all alone in the woods bawling your eyes out?'

'An old trouble,' said Diana. 'One I thought I'd put behind me. Stupid really.'

'The worst kind,' said Auberon, looking rather sad. 'They have a habit of biting you on the bum.'

'You and Tatiana?' guessed Diana.

'You and . . .?'

'Ant,' said Diana. 'I thought he was the love of my life once, a long time ago. But he let me down really badly. And tonight I thought maybe I should let him back into my life again. But he's not interested, he's let me down again.'

'We men can be good at that,' said Auberon with a rueful sigh. 'I made a big mistake once. I've regretted it forever. You never know, your Ant may have done the same.'

'Maybe,' said Diana. 'But I doubt it.'

Ant followed Harry down the hill, feeling a mixture of emotions. Despite himself, he still felt the need to sort everything out; still felt responsible, and he felt really guilty about Diana. That had come as a bolt from the blue. What was he going to do about that? And more importantly, what about Harry and Josie? At the moment, he felt like thumping Harry. The look on Josie's face when they'd left had nearly cut him in two. She'd looked so lost and lonely.

'Why did you ask Josie to marry you if you didn't want to get married?' said Ant. 'I told you it was a bad idea.'

'I thought I did,' said Harry. 'I think I still do. But not now. Not yet. And not like this. All this wedding business. It's been like living with a demented hen for the last few months. It's all she ever talks about, and it's driving me nuts. I hadn't realised quite how bad it was till we got here and her mum ratcheted it up even more. Do you know Josie was looking up fire-eaters on the internet yesterday to have as evening entertainment? I tell you, it's insane.'

'So have a small wedding,' said Ant.

'But Josie set her heart on it being like this,' said Harry. 'I didn't want to let her down.'

'Too late for that, mate,' said Ant. 'I think you already have.'

'Thanks for the vote of confidence,' said Harry.

'So lie, then,' said Ant. 'That's what I'd do.'

'Yeah, and we all know how that goes,' said Harry.

'Meaning?' Ant bristled.

'Meaning you've never had a meaningful relationship in your life, partly because you lie. I want my relationship with Josie to be honest.'

'Then more fool you,' said Ant angrily. 'And that's not quite true. Di and I had something special once.'

'The emphasis there being on "had",' said Harry. 'You can't tell me anything about relationships.'

'I can tell you you're a bloody idiot. You have a gorgeous girlfriend and you are in serious danger of losing her.'

'Butt out of this, Ant,' said Harry. 'You know nothing about love. You're incapable of it. You've even managed, God knows how, to get Diana falling at your feet again, and you can't deal with that. You have no right to talk.'

Harry walked off into the darkness, leaving Ant fuming.

The two conflicting emotions, his loyalty to Harry and the way he was feeling about Josie, struggled to overcome one another, intertwined with a sense of responsibility towards Diana. But he realised if he went and found her now, he'd just make things worse. Bugger it, he'd tried. Harry didn't deserve her. Ant turned round and went back to search for Josie.

Chapter Twenty-Four

Harry strode on down the path, furious with bloody Ant. How dare he give him advice about his love life? How bloody dare he? As if Ant had ever really been in love. Apart from possibly whatever had gone on between him and Di, and look how that turned out. Ant had been down on the idea of him and Josie being together right from the start. He just couldn't stand for his friend to be happy.

But how happy was he, really?

Harry paused, and finding a convenient rock, sat down on it. He shivered and zipped up his fleece, glad Josie had made him wear it now. The night was colder now, and the last of the mist was dissipating. He could see the stars twinkling in the distance. It should have been a magical evening, spent in the company of the woman he loved and his best friends. Now none of them were speaking to one another. How could it have gone so badly wrong? And what did he really feel about the wedding?

Thinking back, this was his fault, Harry realised miserably. He should never have proposed when he did. He'd been thrilled to move in with Josie, and it had been enough for him. If it hadn't been for all that Halloween nonsense that Di had started, the thought of marriage wouldn't have entered his head. And he might have spent the last six months persuading Josie to come travelling with him, instead of feeling all his options were being shut down in the inexorable march to the Wedding Day. Had he not rushed things, he might have been able to explain to Josie how much he wanted to change his life, how he wanted to shake off his rut, and how much a part of that she could be.

Instead, he felt he was condemning himself to a life of stability and sensible behaviour. There was no reason why getting married shouldn't stop them travelling, but to Josie, it seemed to signal that the adventurous part of their life was over; whereas for Harry, he felt it had only just begun.

This was ridiculous. Sitting here thinking to himself wasn't going to alter anything. He just needed to go back, find Josie and have a sensible chat with her about what he really wanted. Harry felt sure if she could just give him the opportunity to explain, everything would be all right. He'd be happy enough to go along with the wedding plans if it meant that they could go travelling afterwards. Hell, if the only good thing that came out of this ridiculous hypnosis experiment was him persuading Josie to see the world with him, then it had been worth doing. Josie would surely see that too, once she'd had a chance to think about it.

With that, Harry got up and returned the way he'd come. There was only one way of finding out what Josie thought; he simply had to ask her.

'So what's the story with you and Tatiana?' said Diana, mildly amazed that she was sitting down in a wood discussing the love life of someone she'd grown up watching on TV.

'Same as you, I guess,' sighed Auberon. 'We were in love. It was all going well. She'd been pushing for an equal share on the show – it was before we were on TV, and Tati wanted her cut. Which was fair enough, but Freddie . . . well Freddie felt differently. He saw Tati as a nuisance. "There are plenty more fish in the sea," he used to say, "pretty assistants are replaceable." Except Tati, Tati wasn't.'

Bron sighed again.

'I never let her see how I felt, like an idiot, and she thought I agreed with Freddie. So when she fell pregnant, she booked herself into a clinic. She got rid of our baby and never said a word to me till afterwards. When I found out, she said it wasn't my decision, it was her body.'

'She was right, wasn't she?' said Diana. 'What would have happened to her career if she'd got pregnant then?'

'To my shame, I'd probably have let her go. I didn't really think of it from her point of view. Just that the show didn't need a pregnant assistant. I was wrong, of course.'

He looked into the distance, and sighed. 'I still think about that baby, you know. I always pictured it as a she, a little clone of my Tati. She'd have been thirty by now.'

Diana sat staring into the darkness. It felt like a warm cloak around her, and she found herself finding it remarkably easy to open up to Auberon, with whom she felt a natural affinity. Hearing his story emboldened her to tell him hers.

'I lost a baby too,' she said eventually. 'And until tonight, I've spent every day of the last eight years pretending it didn't exist.'

'Was it Ant's?'

'Yes, but he didn't know, till it was too late. I hadn't got round to telling him, and then it was gone. I was barely pregnant at all.'

'So what did Ant do?'

'That's it,' said Diana. 'Nothing. I called him from the

245

hospital, and he never came. And when I came out, I found him in the arms of my best friend. It broke my heart.'

'You never know,' said Auberon, patting her hand, 'he might regret that now. Lord alone knows I do.'

'He says he never got my messages,' said Diana, 'but I don't know whether or not I believe him.'

'Give him a chance,' said Auberon: 'Before you ruin your life with bitter regrets, like I've done.'

Give Ant a chance? It was still a strange thought, after she'd spent so many years hating him, but Auberon was right, it was time she put her past behind her.

'I'd love to,' she said sadly, 'but he's made it abundantly clear he doesn't want me.'

Ant walked back to the place where they'd left Josie, but she was no longer there. Where on earth could she have gone? Why couldn't the wretched girl stay in one place? It was infuriating.

Perhaps she'd gone back to the theatre. Harry had mentioned it earlier as the place where they'd been on their first date. Maybe if she were still feeling upset about Harry, she'd want to go there and remember a happier time.

Bloody Harry. Stealing a march on him. He'd seen Josie first, in the bar at uni. He'd been the one who got to know her; inveigled himself into her crowd, turned up at her parties, and eventually wangled an invitation down here. They'd always got on well, and Ant had intended to ask Josie out, but then Kerry or Kelly got under his skin and he'd been distracted. By the time he realised his mistake, Harry had snuck Josie out from under his nose.

At the time it had been utterly baffling. Harry was a good mate, but so quiet and retiring compared to Ant. What had Josie seen in him, that she hadn't seen in Ant? After all, she had flirted with Ant quite a lot, and never paid any attention to Harry before that week. Ant wasn't surprised it hadn't lasted after they left university and all went their separate ways. It was clearly never meant to be. Like an idiot, he hadn't kept in touch with Josie, and he was stunned when Harry had emailed him out of the blue to say they were an item again.

Ant still didn't get why Josie had chosen Harry to share her life with. He was so modest and unambitious. Surely a girl like Josie deserved someone with more get up and go? Ant had more money and prospects, was better looking, drove a faster car. Hell, even her dad liked him better than he liked Harry. The more Ant thought about it, the more furious he became. He was going to go and show her what was what. How a real man behaved. Show her just how masterfully he could sweep her off her feet. Show her what she'd been missing.

What about Harry? The responsible pricking of his conscience kept butting in. Ant ruthlessly repressed it. He hadn't got as far as this in life paying too much attention to his conscience. What *about* Harry? He'd had his chance with Josie and blown it. Now it was Ant's turn.

Josie sat for a while staring out to sea, where a pale moon was just visible through the swirling clouds. So much for the exciting magical evening Freddie had promised. She was cross with everyone: Harry for being so frustrating, Di for the things she'd said, and Ant for, well, being Ant. God knows why he'd appointed himself relationship guru for the weekend, but he'd made a dreadful fist of it. She decided she'd preferred it when he was just playing the field.

After a little while she got up. It was no good; she couldn't stay here all night. Time to get home. Even if she ended up leaving them all in the annexe, and sleeping in her own bed. Thank God Mum and Dad had gone away for the night, she wouldn't have any explaining to do. Time to sort everything out tomorrow.

She was halfway down the path which led to the back of the theatre, when she saw torches dancing among the bushes.

'Hello,' called a quavering voice, sounding as if it was about to jump out of its skin any moment. 'Is anyone there? Only we're terribly lost.'

'Where on earth are you trying to get to?' Josie could make out three huddled figures in the gloom. On closer inspection she realised it was Tatiana's retinue. What on earth where they doing out here at this time of night?

'We're looking for the theatre. Tati went out hours ago, and we don't know what's happened to her. We think that that Slowbotham fellow might have done something to her.'

'He hadn't last time I saw,' said Josie with a grin. 'She was auditioning for *A Midsummer Night's Dream*.'

'Oh, thank goodness,' cried M'stard with relief. 'I've been *so* worried. My auras just don't feel right. I couldn't imagine what I was going to say to her agent.'

'Come with me,' said Josie, 'you're not too far away. I'll show you the way.'

2007: Tatiana

'Look can you book me in on Wednesday or not?' Tatiana said in exasperation.

'We're pretty busy,' the girl on the other end sounded both bored and vague. 'I'll ring you if there's a cancellation.'

'You do that,' said Tatiana crisply, and tried to turn her phone off. It promptly came back to life. Damned thing. She swore her new mobile required more fingers than she had.

Time was when people would have bent over backwards to have her in their salon. But these days most people didn't even recognise her. Tatiana who? To her humiliation *The Sun* had recently run a *Where Are they Now?* feature and she hadn't even been in it. Bron had. There'd been a big piece on him and Freddie and the whole *Illusions* phenomenon. The article had even mentioned they might be making a comeback. It didn't seem fair that people still remembered Bron, whereas their eyes would glaze over politely when she introduced herself, shrugging their shoulders and muttering about people being past it when they thought she wasn't listening. It was galling to think that despite everything she'd achieved, she might have been better known as Bron's Debbie McGee after all. It was so hurtful. And unfair.

Bron was still in vogue, popping up on the occasional chat show, his and Freddie's company going from strength to strength, thanks to some shrewd investment in several successful movies. And Bron had started directing Shakespeare too. She'd always wanted to do Shakespeare. But these days, she was even lucky to get a panto. Thank God for UK Gold and repeat fees.

'What am I to do?' she said. 'They can't fit me in till God knows when. My roots are showing. It's a disaster!'

'Darling, we'll just get you booked into Anthony's,' said Gray M'stard, her new stylist. 'Everyone's going there.'

'I need more than a new hair style,' said Tatiana, with a sigh. 'I need to get my profile raised. Get back on to Susan as quickly as you can. The sooner we start, the better.'

Chapter Twenty-Five

Josie led them through the theatre, to where Tatiana was lying prone on the stage, with Mike hovering awkwardly around her.

Tatiana sat up, stretching languorously.

'What angel wakes me from my flow'ry bed?' she declaimed.

'The finch, the sparrow and the lark,' warbled Mike, woefully out of tune. 'Who would set his wit to what?' He paused, 'sorry, just lost my place, ah yes, let me see . . .'

'And thy fair virtue's force perforce doth move . . .'

'Methinks mistress . . .'

'No, no, no! Darling,' Tatiana held up her hand. 'You need to wait for me to finish the line. Your cue is "To swear I love thee".'

'Which of course, dear lady, I do,' said Mike, bowing ingratiatingly.

Tatiana waved him away as if swatting a gnat, 'Now carry on . . .'

Josie was in pieces. Mike's attempts to prove his actor credentials hadn't improved as the night wore on; he was appalling. He was trying to make Bottom seem a romantic lead, but was channelling his inner buffoon. Plus he was so loud he kept drowning out Tatiana's lines, and Josie could see Tatiana was getting very fed up with it.

When Mike got to the line 'if I had wit enough to get out of this wood', it was all Josie could do not to burst out laughing at the look on Tatiana's face. She was probably hoping he'd do just that. Josie found herself wishing Harry was sitting here with her watching it together, laughing at Mike, rather than with Tatiana's bunch of lunatics, who kept standing up, applauding every line she delivered. She was good, though maybe not deserving of a standing ovation after delivering three lines.

Could you break off an engagement and still stay together? Josie wondered. That's what Harry seemed to be suggesting, and she wasn't sure how she felt about it. She didn't want to lose him, but how could they carry on after that?

'. . . And when she weeps, weeps every little flower,

Lamenting some enforced chastity.

Tie up my lover's tongue, bring him silently.' Tatiana finished triumphantly.

'Oh, bravo, Tati, Bravo!' M'stard stood up clapping loudly. 'Isn't she good,' he said enthusiastically, 'I say, isn't she good?'

'Marvellous, darling. Marvellous,' said Gypsy.

'You were magnificent,' said Ariadne, 'simply magnificent.'

'Thank you, darlings,' said Tatiana gracefully. 'One does one's best.'

Josie had to suppress another snigger. Poor Tatiana. Everyone around her was so unctuous and self-serving, she probably never had a true word spoken to her in her life. Or certainly not for years. Josie felt sorry for her in a way. All that fame and fortune, to end up surrounded by arse lickers and having to butter up the likes of Mike Slowbotham, who she noticed with amusement was being very touchy-feely with Tatiana.

Tatiana seemed to be responding, but Josie couldn't be

sure if she was just acting. Surely she couldn't find a creep like Mike attractive, could she? However desperate she was.

'Let's run through that again,' said Tatiana, lying back down on the ground. 'Now, from the top . . .'

'Oh well,' thought Josie, repressing a yawn. 'I may as well stay here.'

For all she knew, the others might have all gone back to the house by now, Harry had a spare set of keys. She didn't want to go home and face whatever was there. Much better to stay put. At least she'd have a laugh.

Ant was determined to find Josie before Harry got it into his head that he needed to sort things out. Maybe if Ant got there first, she'd be prepared to listen to him. For a moment he indulged in a fantasy that he and Josie were alone on a desert island and she had agreed that he was the only man for her . . .

But where had she gone? He made his way down the cliff path and was nearly back in the village when he ran into Freddie, who said, 'How's it going?'

'How do you think?' said Ant. 'Can't you get anything right? Josie is over Di, but has fallen out with Harry, Di is in love with me, and I apparently am in love with Josie. What have you done to us?'

'I'll sort it, I promise,' said Freddie.

'Why not sort it this time that Josie falls for me, eh?' said Ant. 'That's what I'd call a result.'

'Hmm,' said Freddie. 'Look, I haven't seen any of the others coming this way, but I think Josie might have been heading for the theatre.'

'Right, I'm off, then,' said Ant, and he went haring back up the path. He ran and ran as if his life was depending on it. He had to get to Josie before Harry did. Soon he was puffed out and exhausted. Maybe it was time to knock the fags on the head. He was sweating profusely by the time he got back to the theatre, but there was no sign of Harry, so that was something.

He found Josie sitting among Tatiana's retinue, trying not to giggle as they fell over each other in their bids to get her attention. Tatiana was looking as if she was finding Mike's attentions a bit too much. He appeared to have developed into a very amorous Bottom . . .

'You okay?' Ant sat down next to Josie. He wanted to play this carefully, didn't want to frighten her off.

'Not sure yet,' said Josie. 'I'm trying not to think about it.'

'Well, if you need me, I'm here,' said Ant. And for once it wasn't a corny come-on. He actually meant it.

'You're not so bad under all that bravado, are you?' said Josie, smiling. 'I've seen a different side to you tonight.'

'Shh, don't tell anyone,' said Ant, 'it would ruin my reputation.'

He could do it, make her fall for him, he knew he could. She was vulnerable and upset. He was the obvious shoulder to cry on. He'd done it dozens of times in the past, so what was making him hesitate? Why did he feel so different?

Because she's in love with your best mate, you cretin. He could almost feel Freddie's words splintering in his head. Damn. This responsibility shit was still sticking. Sod, sod, and double sod.

Diana was feeling much better after her chat with Auberon, who'd insisted she call him Bron. He seemed to completely understand what had happened to her. No one had done that before. Not even Josie, she realised. Josie was a good listener, and was always sweetly sympathetic, but she hadn't ever been through any of the things that Di had, and her charmed life hadn't prepared her for the kind of pain Di had experienced. It meant there was a gap in empathy sometimes, and Di could see now that she hadn't really understood.

'You've been very sweet,' she said. 'I've never told anyone else the whole story.'

'Curse of old age, my dear,' he said. 'You finally learn empathy when it's far too late.'

'You're not that old,' said Diana. 'And anyway, maybe it's not too late. Have you tried talking to Tatiana since you've been here?'

'No,' admitted Bron, 'but I don't think she'll want to talk to me, particularly with Freddie around. She can't stand him. And anyway . . . it's probably too late now.'

'Why?'

'Like an idiot I let Freddie persuade me it would be fun to take Tati down a peg or two. It was after the scene in the pub the other night. I was really cross with her, so I told Freddie I wanted revenge.'

'And?'

'Freddie's hypnotised Mike Slowbotham to think she's in love with him. She thinks he's genuinely offering her a part when he hasn't even got proper funding, and all he really wants to do is get inside her knickers.'

'I gathered that,' said Diana drily. 'Do you always go to Freddie for your relationship advice? Because quite frankly that's the worst idea I've ever heard . . .'

'Freddie can be very persuasive,' said Bron. 'It used to drive Tati nuts.'

'I'm not surprised,' said Diana. 'If I were you I'd get myself another mate. And stop Freddie before it's too late. What you're doing to Tatiana is monstrous. The poor woman thinks she's in with a chance of a leading role.'

'Oh,' said Bron, looking mournful. 'It did seem funnier in the pub when I was in my cups. Freddie can be very cruel. Speak of the devil.'

Freddie came puffing up the hill.

'Why you lot can't stay in one place, I don't know,' he complained. 'Diana, can you possibly stay here, and I'll get you all together again, and see if we can finally get this to work. Have you seen Harry?'

'Someone mention my name?' said Harry.

'Where did you spring from?' said Diana in surprise.

'I just came through those bushes,' said Harry, 'and here you all were. I was looking for Josie. Have you seen her?'

'What do you think?' said Diana. 'I'm the last person she wants to see at the moment.'

She felt like kicking herself. She'd been a horrible cow to Josie tonight.

'I'm sorry about earlier,' she said to Harry.

'No worries,' he said. 'It's been a funny old night.'

'You can say that again,' said Diana with feeling.

Despite everything that had happened, Harry felt sorry for Diana, it was clear she'd been crying, and she obviously regretted what she'd said to Josie earlier. He'd have to make sure Josie was prepared to forgive her when they caught up with one another.

'As you're both here,' said Freddie, interrupting his thoughts, 'can we get some of your response to this evening on camera?'

'I don't think you'd like what I've got to say,' said Harry, spotting that Will was hovering behind Freddie, camera in hand. Bloody hell, they never stopped.

'Nor me,' said Diana. 'Disastrous doesn't cover it.'

'All you've done is bugger things up,' said Harry. 'So far I don't think your experiment has been a success.'

'The night is still young,' said Freddie, 'plenty of time to put things right before morning.'

'You're enjoying this, aren't you?' Diana accused Freddie.

'No, of course I'm not,' said Freddie, 'but hypnotism isn't an exact science; things sometimes take an unexpected turn. Everything will work out in the end, I'm sure. And the money will make it all worthwhile.'

The money. That was the main reason Harry was doing this, so he could show Josie how much he loved her when they got married – if they got married. But what was the point in that, if Josie wasn't going to come with him?

Suddenly feeling tired, defeated and very sorry for himself, Harry sat down with a thump.

'Three, two, one,' he heard Freddie say.

Bloody hell. Not again.

Harry was out like a light, dreaming of being rooted to the spot while Josie endlessly danced in among the moonbeams. When he went to reach her she ran away laughing . . .

Chapter Twenty-Six

Ant was trying to do the decent thing, and had been planning to tell Josie she should go and talk to Harry, when he was suddenly aware that she was weeping silently beside him. Suddenly his resolve to do the right thing was sorely tempted, it would be all too easy to take advantage of her vulnerability.

'Here Josie, don't cry,' he said awkwardly patting her arm. He desperately wanted to put his arm round her, but didn't want to appear too pushy.

'Here, have a tissue,' he felt in his pockets and pulled out his fags, 'no sorry, here, I do have one.'

Gently, he wiped her eyes.

'He's an idiot, you know,' said Ant. 'If you were mine, I'd never let you go.'

'But I'm not, am I?' said Josie. 'I just can't believe he'd do this to me. I thought he really wanted to marry me. But now . . .'

This could be his moment, and in the past would have been, but the damned sense of responsibility was hovering over him with a vengeance.

'Maybe you rushed things,' he found himself saying. 'Maybe he needs more time.'

'He's had six months,' said Josie.

'Well, if it were me, I'd need at least two years, probably five,' said Ant with a grin. 'And I certainly couldn't handle all that chat about dresses and flowers. You've talked about nothing else since we got here.'

'You think I've become a bit obsessed?' Josie looked appalled.

'Just a smidgeon,' said Ant. 'What do I know? I've never been engaged. But I think the circus acts may have been a tipping point.'

'Oh, God, I've turned into a bridezilla, haven't I?' Josie groaned. 'Why did no one tell me?'

'You can be quite hard to resist,' said Ant, 'and to be honest I don't think anyone wanted to upset you.'

'Really?' Josie looked stricken. 'Am I really that bad?'

'No,' said Ant, cursing himself for his clumsiness. 'I think it might have been a bit overwhelming for Harry, that's all.'

'Maybe 250 guests *is* too many,' said Josie slowly. 'Harry did mention it, but I ignored him.'

She looked as if something was dawning on her.

'Perhaps it's my fault,' she said, 'perhaps I've been ignoring Harry too much.'

'No, no, no,' said Ant, 'I think you've just got a bit more involved than him. It's natural, I'm sure.'

'All I wanted was for things to be perfect,' said Josie rather sadly. 'I didn't want to put Harry off.'

'And you probably haven't,' said Ant. 'Maybe you need to talk to him about it.'

'Maybe I do,' said Josie. 'Thinking about the sort of people my mum and dad want to invite, I can understand Harry being intimidated. I never meant to upset him, I got a bit carried away.'

'Maybe just a little bit,' said Ant. 'Come on, let's go and

see where Harry's got to. Maybe we can try and work this out.'

Still not quite believing he could be so noble, Ant took Josie by the hand and led her out of the theatre.

Diana sat watching Harry sleeping, wishing it was Ant lying there. Freddie, Bron and Will had wandered off to see what was happening at the theatre and, nervous of the reaction she would get when she saw Ant again, she'd elected to stay put. What was she going to do? She was overcome with the strength of her feelings for Ant. They'd come like a bolt from the blue, a real *coup de foudre*. Only, maybe it hadn't been that sudden. Talking to Bron had made her remember how much she'd loved him. In her hurt and bitterness she'd forgotten that. But maybe it was time to let that hurt and bitterness go. At least he'd been prepared to talk to her tonight, and thinking again about the whole situation with Sian, perhaps she had misjudged him.

Maybe he was being so standoffish with her because he was still hurting too. Perhaps all she needed to do was come clean, say sorry, and say what was going on her head. She can't have imagined what they'd had between them. It had been special. She knew he'd felt it too. If only she could remind him of how they used to be, everything would be all right again and they could put the past behind them . . .

It was a nice dream. But a foolish one. This story wasn't going to end the way she wanted. They never did. Diana should be used to it by now. She was coming to the conclusion that she was never going to find someone to live happily ever after with.

Still, a girl could fantasise . . . It was getting a little chilly and Harry looked cosy and warm. There could be no harm in snuggling up to him . . .

She lay down next to him, and Harry rolled over and put his arms round her. For a moment, she lay in blissful happiness, imagining that she was lying next to Ant, before he ruined it entirely, by saying 'Josie' really loudly.

She knew she was kidding herself, Ant was never going to fall for her again. But she was tired, and if she just shut her eyes, in her dreams he could be hers . . .

Harry was having a lovely dream about Josie, about when they'd first met. She was coming towards him in a pretty floral dress, her long fair curls flapping in the breeze, saying shyly, 'It's Harry isn't it?'

He could still remember the thrill when he closed his hand over hers, and said 'yes,' and they'd walked off together, as they went to the theatre as if it was the most natural thing in the world to do. Things like that never happened to Harry. They happened to Ant all the time, but not to Harry. It had been such a sweet moment, he recalled, as he woke up slowly and found himself cuddling her. How lovely. This whole mad night had been a bad dream. Here was Josie in bed beside him, and everything was going to be okay.

Except . . . something wasn't quite right. He was lying on something hard and stony. A bush was poking in his back. And as the person lying beside him rolled round and stared at him, he groaned in dismay.

'Diana?' he said, incredulous. What was she doing here?

At that moment, he heard voices coming down the path towards them, and the next thing he knew . . .

'Harry, you bastard, you bloody bastard!' Josie was standing over him, looking shattered.

'Josie, this isn't how it looks,' Harry got up to try and remonstrate.

'I trusted you!' said Josie, delivering a stinging slap around his cheeks, before running into the darkness.

'What's going on?' Diana was sitting up, looking really confused.

'I have no idea,' said Harry. 'But thanks for nothing!'

He shot off in the darkness to find Josie. He had to make her understand that nothing had happened, or they really *were* finished.

Chapter Twenty-Seven

Ant was flabbergasted. Of all the things he'd expected to see, it hadn't been that. Maybe despite his denials, Harry did have a thing going on with Diana, although it didn't seem likely. He'd looked so distraught when Josie had slapped him. Ant was at a loss as to what to do now. They seemed locked in a nightmarish situation, which looked like never getting resolved.

But maybe you've got more chance with Josie now, said a whispering voice in his head. Maybe. Or maybe she'll be blaming you for setting the whole thing up . . .

'Oh, God, oh, God, I'm such a fool.'

Ant had almost forgotten Di. What was going on there? Had she changed her mind about him, and transferred her attentions to Harry? She was rocking herself backwards and forwards, crying. Awkwardly, Ant sat down next to her. Another crying woman. What had he done to deserve this? He'd never spent so much time comforting crying women without some kind of reward. It was an odd feeling.

'Hey, it's not as bad as that,' he said. 'I can see you're a bit confused this evening, but how do you know what you or any of us think we're feeling is real? Freddie's messed with our minds good and proper.'

That applied to the way he felt about Josie, he realised with a jolt. Could he be sure those emotions were real? They certainly *felt* real.

'I don't know,' said Diana. 'I'm not just upset about screwing things up for Harry and Josie. It's life in general. I'm single, jobless, talentless. I've worked so hard to get where I am, and now I've lost it all. My dad will feel completely vindicated when I tell him. He never thought I should go into the travel business.'

'Now that is ridiculous,' said Ant. 'From what I recall, your dad never understood how talented you are. Talented and gorgeous.'

He surprised himself by saying it, but he'd suddenly remembered how insecure Di had always been, and how little support her parents had given her. Somehow he felt he wanted to cheer her up . . .

'Do you really think so?' said Di, looking shy. 'But look at me. I'm unemployed, don't even own my own flat, *and* single.'

'Cheer up, worse things happen at sea,' said Ant.

'I doubt that somehow,' said Diana.

'Don't be too hard on yourself,' said Ant, putting his arms round her and giving her a hug. 'It's been a weird night, and quite frankly the way Josie's been banging on about the wedding, I'm not surprised Harry's been having second thoughts. That's not your fault.'

'She has been a bit hideous hasn't she?' Diana laughed.

They sat for a few moments, feeling the wind on their cheeks, and Ant felt something harmonious pass between them. Not that he wanted to get back together, or anything, but at least it was a start to being friends again.

Night was passing and the moon was getting low in the sky.

'I'd almost forgotten you could be like this,' said Diana.
'Like what?'

'Nice,' said Diana, looking dreamy. 'Kind. You hide it well, but it's still there.'

'Thanks,' said Ant, 'you're not so bad yourself.'

He gave her a squeeze.

'Friends?' he said.

'Friends,' said Diana.

Friends. So much better than enemies.

Diana felt as if her heart was going to explode sitting next to Ant. It was as though the man she'd once known was just re-emerging; maybe he would reconnect with her, remember too what they'd had.

'Why did you stop being kind to people?' said Diana. 'Was it my fault?'

Ant didn't say anything, but continued to stare out to sea.

'Why didn't you give me a chance to explain?' he said.

The question hung between them. It was a fair point, and Di suddenly realised she'd been carrying her bitterness around with her for so long, it had never occurred to her she could have asked him his side of the story.

'What were you going to say that would have made a difference?' she said. 'I'd have thought it was obvious.'

'Not to me it wasn't,' said Ant. 'You spent weeks avoiding me, and then you disappeared one evening. I was frantic. I looked everywhere for you and no one knew where you'd gone.'

'Yeah, it looked like it,' said Diana, remembering the churning uncertainty of that night. 'I came back from hospital and you were in the bar all over Sian like a rash.'

'Sian was comforting me,' said Ant.

'Is that what you call it?' Old habits die hard, and she felt angry all over again.

'Yes,' said Ant. 'Di, listen, please.'

Something about the urgency in the way he spoke made her pause. It was time she heard him out.

'I genuinely thought you'd gone off me. You were always working shifts when I was free. Sian kept hinting that you were doing it deliberately, and even that you'd found someone else,' he said. 'I was worrying you were cheating on me.'

'Oh,' Diana wasn't sure whether to believe him. 'Did you believe her?'

'I didn't know what to think,' said Ant. 'I wanted to ask you but I didn't have the nerve, in case you told me we were finished. And then you ditched me in front of everyone.'

'But Sian *knew*,' said Diana. 'I told her about the miscarriage before I went to hospital. She was meant to tell you. Are you telling me she never did?'

'She never breathed a word,' said Ant. 'I know I'm a lot of things, but I would never have left you to go through that on your own. I am so sorry.'

Diana took a sharp intake of breath and blinked away the tears.

'All these years,' she said, 'and I blamed you. It's me who should be sorry.'

'I was a bit of a shit to you afterwards,' said Ant. 'I thought you didn't love me anymore. Sian was meant to be my consolation prize. God, she was a piece of work.'

'Wasn't she just?' said Diana.

'Why didn't you tell me you were pregnant?'

'I nearly did,' said Diana. 'It never felt like the right

moment, and then I lost the baby, and you . . . We were so young, and I was frightened you wouldn't support me, and then it looked as if you wouldn't.'

'And I let you down,' said Ant. 'For what it's worth, I was devastated when I found out about the baby from the message on my answerphone. I wanted to go after you, but Sian said to leave it. I can't believe I was daft enough to listen. I'm sorry, Di. You deserved better. Much better.'

To her astonishment, there were tears in his eyes.

She stared into his eyes. This was her moment, it had to be.

Leaning forward, she kissed him on the lips.

Ant leapt back as if he'd been scalded.

'Di, I'm sorry, I didn't mean . . .' He let go of her hand, and got up. 'I'm sorry, Di, it's not you, it's me.'

And with that, he stumbled off into the dark, leaving Diana alone with her broken heart.

Harry stumbled through the darkness, calling Josie's name. Where had she gone now? He had a feeling she wasn't going back home.

He felt wrecked from this evening. Utterly wrecked. He wished he'd never set eyes on bloody Diana for a start, or let himself get pushed into the whole engagement thing. He knew he wanted to spend the rest of his life with Josie, but the rest of his life was a long time. Marriage could wait. He wanted to have adventures with Josie, see the world before they settled down. If he hadn't been such an idiot and proposed when he had, they could be living happily together right now, without any of this pressure. Standing on this cliffedge looking out to sea, thinking about all the adventurers who'd left these shores in olden days, made him feel suddenly confined and restricted. He'd always played safe, been Mr Dependable. Now it was time to do something different, be someone different. And if Josie didn't want that person, so be it.

He found her on a small beach which led away from the cliff, to one side of the theatre. He remembered them picnicking here once. It had been a happy, relaxed day, early in their courtship. Maybe the fact that she was here was a good sign . . .

'Josie,' he said. She was sitting still on a rock, looking ghostly white in the pale moonlight, for all the world like an enchantress who'd just come out of the sea. She didn't say anything, so he hunkered down next to her.

'Look, I'm not going to beg, and I'm not going to plead, but hear me out, will you? I know things have gone wrong between us this weekend, but you have to believe me. I love you more than anything else in the world, and I would never hurt you.'

'But not enough to marry me,' said Josie. 'And not enough not to cheat with my best friend.'

'I fell asleep and woke up to find Di beside me,' said Harry. 'I'm not remotely interested in Diana. You can believe that or not, but it's the truth. When have I ever lied to you?'

'When you asked me to marry you?' said Josie.

'Oh, that,' said Harry.

'Yes, *that*,' said Josie, looking angry.

'I do want to marry you,' said Harry. 'But not yet. I think we've rushed things. I know it's my fault, but there's a whole world out there. Come and see it with me, please. I want to travel, but not alone.'

Josie said nothing.

'That's it,' said Harry. 'That's all I have to say. I'm going back now. And in the morning I'm going home. Then I'm going to plan a world tour. I hope you'll be with me, but if not, I'm going anyway.'

Josie still didn't say anything, twisting her finger round and round, till eventually he realised what she was doing.

'No, Josie,' he said, tears choking him, 'no, please don't do this.'

'Sorry,' she said, crying too, as she handed him the ring, 'it's over.'

Harry took the ring without another word, and turned round to leave. There was nothing more to be said.

Josie sat back down on a rock after he'd gone, staring out to sea. Her thoughts were a mixed jumble. She'd been so excited about this weekend, excited to be marrying Harry, how could it all have gone so wrong?

He'd never said anything serious before about wanting adventures. Harry had on occasion mentioned going travelling, but in such a jokey way, Josie never thought he meant it. Why did he suddenly want to go travelling now? Unless it was another nonsensical thing that Freddie had put in his head.

What a night. What a bloody night.

She heard a shout from above, and then heard someone frantically scrambling down the path. It was Tatiana, looking somewhat dishevelled.

'Are you all right?' said Josie.

'All right? All right?' said Tatiana, spitting feathers. 'The man's gone completely mad.'

'Which man?'

'Mike,' said Tatiana. 'He tried – he tried to kiss me!'

She looked so indignant, Josie had to stifle a grin.

'I can't believe it. We were *acting*, and then he tried to

kiss my arm. It was revolting. He called me – his little flower. Oh, God. Now I've probably lost the only chance of ever playing Titania. Why is life so unfair?'

'Where is he now?' asked Josie.

'I don't know,' moaned Tatiana, 'I pushed him over and ran down here.'

A tinkling of stones on the path above led to a panicked look on Tatiana's face.

'Hide me, please!' she said.

'There's a cave just there in the corner,' said Josie. 'Don't go too far in, it connects with the cove next door, and it's easy to get trapped by the sea. You have to know it's there. He won't find you, I promise.'

'You're an angel,' said Tatiana, and stumbled off towards the cave.

The sound of footsteps came nearer, and suddenly someone burst onto the beach.

Oh, shit now what should she do? Memories of Mike being very intense with every girlfriend he'd ever had, meant she knew how unlikely it was he was going to let Tatiana out of his sight.

But it wasn't Mike, it was Ant.

'Josie,' he said, 'are you okay? I just saw Harry. He said you'd given your ring back.'

'It was the right thing to do,' said Josie.

'And you're okay?' he said, 'you're really okay?'

'I will be,' said Josie, surprised. 'Since when did you care?'

In answer, Ant enveloped her in a big hug. It felt warm and comforting and secure.

'Oh, I've always cared,' said Ant. 'I just didn't realise how much, until tonight.'

Josie looked up into his eyes and suddenly everything

made sense, the moon, and the stars, the lapping of the waves. She remembered how she'd felt as a student, when she'd longed and longed to know what it would feel like for Ant to kiss her.

2012: Tatiana

'Darling, Susan here. How are you?' Tatiana sighed. What did she want? It wouldn't be anything worth hearing. These days Susan rang rarely, and then it was mainly to remind her about tax issues.

'Fine,' said Tatiana. 'I know, I know, my tax return is due.'

'No, it's not that, darling,' said Susan. 'I have a possible opening.'

'Not Bournemouth Pier again?' said Tatiana. 'I think I'd rather starve.'

Particularly as she'd just read in the papers that Bron and Freddie were in talks about a new TV show. Something to do with hypnotism and English myths, she thought. Sounded like Freddie's usual bullshit. It made her a little sad to think Bron was still falling for it.

'No, no. It's a little more thrilling,' said Susan. 'It's Shakespeare. You've always wanted to do Shakespeare, haven't you, darling?'

'Oh my,' Tatiana could feel the excitement growing. 'Where? Is it rep, will it be going to the West End? What?'

'Calm down, darling, it's not that grand.' Susan instantly put a downer on it. 'It's a funny little place in Cornwall. A local theatre, trying to revive its fortunes. The producer is, er, let me look at my notes – a Mike Slowbotham, would you believe.'

'Cornwall? I'm not sure,' said Tatiana. 'Sounds muddy.'

'I'm sure it will be wonderful. There are opportunities for glamping. You can stay in a yurt. It's by the sea. The theatre's on a clifftop. It sounds heavenly. Darling, I'm sure you'd love it.'

'And the name of this idyll?'

'Tresgothen.'

Part Four

And All is Mended

'I will undo
This hateful imperfection of her eyes.
And, gentle Puck, take this transformed scalp
From off the head of this Athenian swain,
That he awaking when the other do,
May all to Athens back again repair,
And think no more of this night's accidents,
But as the fierce vexation of a dream.'

A Midsummer Night's Dream: Act IV, Scene 1

'Oh, go on then. Yes, I get a bit of a kick out of it. Having
people in the palm of my hand, persuading them to do
silly things. But no, I don't take advantage of gullible
people. That wouldn't be ethical. And believe it or not,
Piers, I do have a moral compass.'

Freddie Puck on *Piers Morgan's Life Stories*

Chapter Twenty-Eight

Diana had climbed back towards the Standing Stones. She didn't feel like going back to Josie's now. She couldn't face any of them: Josie, Harry, Ant. She'd never made such a spectacular fool of herself in her life. Oh, God. Even after their mutual soul-bearing, Ant had still rejected her. The look on his face had been horrendous to witness. He'd looked appalled. She felt sick to her stomach. The best thing she could do was keep out of everyone's way, Diana thought, so she might as well stay here till the sun rose. Then she would sneak back to the house, get her things and go and find a train. She had a feeling there might not be a train station in Tresgothen, but come hell or high water she was going to make her way home on her own. She had too much pride to go with Harry and Josie, and she certainly couldn't cope with Ant for four hours in a car in this raw state.

Looking over the sea, she became aware that the sky was becoming a tad lighter, deep blue giving way to steely grey. She watched as seagulls dipped down among the waves, and the light started to spread softly across the sky. After the excitements of the night, she wasn't sure she wanted to face what this new dawn was going to bring. All she knew was that nothing was ever going to be the same, and she wasn't sure if any of them were going to be able to come to terms with the consequences of what had happened tonight.

Harry stumbled back up the path, feeling completely heartbroken. He'd tried and he'd failed. Josie had given him back her engagement ring. She didn't want him any longer. Meeting Ant on the way, he'd sent him down to comfort Josie and then, not knowing what else to do, wandered back to the theatre, where he found a huge commotion going on.

'Where is she?' Mike Slowbotham was wailing. 'Where is she?' while M'stard and the rest of Tatiana's gang were holding him back. M'stard turned out to be stronger than he looked.

'Who?' asked Harry, intrigued. Yet another weird happening on this very strange night.

'Tatiana, of course,' boomed Mike. 'I love her, and she loves me. The little minx is only teasing me.'

'She doesn't love you,' said Gypsy. 'It's called acting.'

'Oh, woe is me,' declaimed Mike soulfully, 'my true love loves me not.'

'You, me both,' said Harry.

'Look, she's not your true love, and she doesn't love you,' said M'stard. 'I think you need to get home. Someone's had a teensy bit too much to drink.'

'Or he's been Freddieised,' said Harry with a sudden realisation. 'Didn't Freddie Puck hypnotise you, yesterday?' he said to Mike.

'Erm, I don't think so,' said Mike, looking confused.

'You stay here,' said Harry. 'I'm going to go and get Freddie. He's done a lot of damage tonight, and he's got a lot of making up to do.'

He left them to it. Mike was trying to break free again, so M'stard solved the problem by sitting on him, while the other two pinned him down. That was one way of doing things.

Harry walked with a renewed sense of purpose. It was time to tell Freddie Puck this damned experiment was at an end. He felt in his pocket and curled his hand round Josie's engagement ring. 'It's not over till the fat lady sings,' he muttered. Well, she'd better put off singing a little while longer.

Josie took a sudden step back. She'd been overpowered briefly by the moment.

'Sorry, Ant – I shouldn't have – this is just too soon,' she broke away from him, feeling raw and confused. 'Please don't expect anything.'

'It was my fault too,' said Ant. 'I'm sorry, Josie, I couldn't help it. You looked so sad and lonely. And I remember how I felt about you all those years ago.'

'That was then, this is now,' said Josie. 'And Freddie Puck's been messing with our heads. I don't know what's real anymore.'

'I'll give you as much time as you need,' said Ant, lacing his fingers over hers.

'I never knew you had such a sensitive side,' said Josie with a wry smile.

'I didn't either till this weekend,' said Ant. 'I'm so sorry about all of this.'

'It's not your fault,' said Josie.

'It is. You were right, and I was wrong about the hypnotism,' said Ant. 'I got totally carried away with seeing Freddie Puck. I thought it would be a bit of a laugh. I had no idea it would end up like this.'

'Does it have to?' said Josie. 'Maybe we should just go back and ask to get back to where we all were at the start.'

'I'm not exactly sure I want to,' said Ant. 'I think I've been a better person tonight than I have in a long time. And then there's you . . .'

Josie didn't answer him. She no longer knew what she wanted. But she'd give anything for none of this to have happened. The trouble was, could things ever be the same again? Even if they went back to their default positions, she now knew that Harry didn't want to marry her. And she had a feeling that no amount of hypnotism could make her forget that . . .

Ant was feeling hyper-aware of his surroundings as he walked back up the cliff path with Josie. She hadn't said yes, but she hadn't said no either. Maybe after all this was over and the dust had settled, they could work something out. Maybe . . .

They arrived back at the theatre to hear a debate going on.

'Do you think we should have tied him up? Isn't that like assault?'

'It was for his own good,' said another voice. 'He would have run after Tati, and then where would we be?'

'Where is she do you think?' a third voice fretted. 'I do hope she's okay.'

'It's okay,' said Josie, pushing the theatre gate open, where she found Tatiana's three companions holding down a very defiant Mike. 'She's safe.'

'Where is she?' wailed Mike. 'She must love me, she must. Why would she have met me here at midnight if not for love?'

'To get a part in your play, you silly little man,' said

M'stard in exasperation. 'Why on earth would a goddess like Tati be interested in a mere mortal like you?'

'Why indeed?' whispered Ant, laughing. The one funny thing that had happened all night had been watching Mike Slowbotham getting carried away.

They heard more voices, and Auberon and Freddie appeared, Harry hard at their heels.

'This nonsense has gone on long enough,' said Bron, 'Poor Tati. What have we done?'

'I thought you wanted to punish her,' said Freddie.

'I did,' said Bron, 'but it turns out I didn't want to humiliate her after all. Where is she, by the way?'

'Down on the beach,' said Josie. 'I left her hiding in a cave.'

'Where? Can you show me?' said Bron.

'With pleasure,' Josie said, and took him down the cliff path, Ant following behind. The day was dawning, and white light was poking under grey clouds, so they got a clear view of the beach as they scrambled towards it. Ant suddenly realised the beach was much smaller than when they'd left.

'Hang on,' he said. 'What's happening? Is the tide coming in?'

'Oh no!' said Josie.

'What's the matter?' asked Bron.

'I forgot about the tide,' said Josie in a whisper; she'd gone deathly pale. 'It's going to block off the entrance to the cave and Tatiana's trapped inside.'

Chapter Twenty-Nine

Harry had only just about taken in the sight of Josie and Ant holding hands (it was so swift he thought he'd made it up) before they disappeared with Bron to show him where Tatiana had gone. He was going to ask Ant just what the hell he thought he was doing, but was stopped in his tracks by Josie bursting back up the track, shouting for help.

'What's going on?' said Harry, alert for an opportunity to redeem himself in Josie's eyes.

'It's Tatiana,' gasped Josie. 'She's stuck in a cave and the tide's coming in. Has anyone got a signal? We need to ring the coastguard.'

Several people tried and failed to get their phones working. Eventually Freddie managed to patch a call through, and was shouting rapid instructions to the person on the other end.

'Where are we again, Josie?'

'Tresgothen Cove,' she said, 'it's just beyond Torpoint.'

Freddie relayed the information. 'They said they know where to find us,' he said, putting his phone in his pocket.

'How long?' said Josie.

'Twenty minutes, they think,' said Freddie.

Josie looked anxious, gnawing her lip in a gesture Harry knew and loved.

'We may not have twenty minutes. We have to get Tatiana out of there. We need a rope, *now*.'

'What did you tie Mike up with?' said Harry with sudden inspiration.

'The belt from my kimono,' said M'stard. 'It's quite long and tough.'

He pointed at the obi belt Mike was tied up with, it was the kind Josie associated with sumo wrestlers and looked like it could do the job.

'You mean dressing gown,' said Freddie.

'It's better than nothing, and it's long enough,' said Harry. 'Untie Mike and give it to me.'

'What about Mike?'

Mike was huffing and puffing about the indignity of it all.

'Oh, leave it to me,' said Freddie, clicking his fingers, and instantly Mike fell into a deep snoring sleep.

Once the cord to the kimono – which luckily seemed quite strong – was removed, everyone hurried down to the beach where Bron was standing in a pool of water at the entrance of the cave, shouting encouragement to Tatiana. The sea was swirling dangerously round the entrance, and the beach was rapidly being eaten up. Tatiana's crew stood around helplessly wringing their hands.

'Right,' said Harry. 'It's not far to your yurt is it? One of you, go and get blankets, towels, a flask; anything that we might need. Someone needs to try and get into the cave and rescue Tatiana. If we tie the rope round that person's waist, and the rest of us form a human chain, we might be able to do it.'

'Me,' said Bron. 'I'll do it. Tati, darling, help is at hand. We'll have you out of there as soon as we can.'

*   *   *

Diana heard the shouting from the top of the cliff. She peered over the edge, and in the early morning gloom, could see a gaggle of people gathering on the beach. They seemed to be panicking. What on earth could be going on?

Curiosity pricked, Diana went back to the cliff path, and found her way down to the beach.

It was definitely getting lighter now. Diana glanced at her watch. Nearly 5a.m. The grey clouds were outweighing the black, the lightening of the sky heralding the arrival of the sun. It was still warm, but a light spray was coming off the sea as she scrambled down the rocky path to where everyone was standing.

'What's happening?' She spotted Josie looking worried.

'It's all my fault,' said Josie, wringing her hands. 'I told Tatiana to hide from Mike in the cave, but I forgot about the tide coming in, and now she's trapped. We've called the coastguard, but we're not sure when they're going to get here. Bron's insisting he's going in to get her.'

'Right.' Harry was at the cave's entrance, tying a knot in a rope around Bron's waist.

'Are you sure you want to do this?' he said.

'Bring it on,' said Bron. 'Are you sure this knot is secure?'

'It should be, I was a boy scout,' said Harry, testing it to be sure. 'I'll double it to make sure.'

Happy that it was fine, Harry turned to everyone else. 'I'll hold the rope, and everyone form a chain behind me. Bron can then swim into the cave, and he should be able to get Tati.'

'Shouldn't we wait for the coastguard?' asked Diana. This seemed immensely risky to her, and she liked Bron. She didn't want anything happening to him.

'No time,' said Harry.

'And I owe Tati,' said Bron. 'Wish me luck.'

He started to wade towards the cave, the water soon up to his shoulders. 'Tati, I'm coming to get you,' he shouted, before he was lost in the swirling waters of the cave.

'Do you think they're going to be okay?' said Diana.

'I hope so.' Josie was looking sick. 'People have drowned in that cave before now.'

Harry was beginning to strain on the rope. 'Come on, I need a hand here,' he shouted.

Ant ran forward, and then Freddie, and one by one they formed a human chain. The sea was pounding hard at their heels now, and faintly from the cave Diana could make out a voice calling, 'Tati, Tati, I'm coming for you.'

She just hoped it wasn't too late.

Ant took his place in the line behind Harry, feeling tense. God, they might both drown and he and Josie would be partly to blame. Josie had mentioned she was there, but they'd been so caught up in the moment, they'd completely forgotten about Tatiana. And now she was trapped.

'This is harder than it looks in the movies,' muttered Harry. 'I had no idea Bron would be this heavy.'

'Can you see anything?'

They peered into the darkness, and could just about make out Bron's head bouncing in the waves.

'Everything okay?' Harry called.

'I can see her . . .' said Bron.

'Keep going,' shouted Ant, 'you can do it!'

They felt the rope pull away from them and heard Bron shout, 'I've got her.'

'Brilliant,' said Harry. The rope went slack as Bron climbed up to the ledge where Tatiana was sheltering.

'Phew,' said Ant, 'thank God she's okay, I was beginning to feel guilty there.'

'Anything else you should be feeling guilty about, mate?' said Harry, with an emphasis on the *mate*.

'Sorry?' Ant didn't think he'd given anything away.

'You and Josie, you looked very cosy up there at the theatre.'

'I'm not sure I know what you mean,' bluffed Ant.

'Aren't you?' said Harry.

Ant was saved from having to answer by a tug of the rope.

'I've got her,' shouted Bron. 'I'm coming out.'

Josie was at the back of the line, not sure what was happening till she heard Ant yell, 'He's got her!'

Tatiana's entourage burst into a round of spontaneous applause.

'I was so worried,' said M'stard, to no one in particular.

'We've still got to get them out,' Josie pointed out. 'The boys need all the help they can get.'

Harry and Ant had the rope now and were straining to pull it backwards.

'A bit of help here, please,' shouted Ant, and everyone resumed their positions. But this time, even at the end of the line, Josie could feel how much harder it was; everyone was stumbling and slipping on the pebbles. There were two people to get out of that cave and the waves were getting higher and stronger.

'Come on,' roared Harry, 'we can do this!'

Everyone pulled as hard as they could.

'I feel like that nursery story about the old man and the turnip,' muttered Josie, panting as she too felt the strain.

They tugged and pulled and the waves dragged the rope back and forth.

Then an excited, 'I can see them!' came from Harry, and

they made one last pull, which caused them all to fall on top of each other higgledy-piggledy.

Harry was the first to stand up. He looked dazed, still holding onto one end of the rope. He pulled the other end, and it flew through the water into his hands.

'So much for scouts' knots,' muttered Ant.

The rope had come undone – and there was no sign of Tatiana and Bron.

Chapter Thirty

'Someone do something!' Harry heard Josie shout, and without thinking, he ripped off his shirt, kicked off his shoes and hurled himself into the water. It was freezing and the waves were crashing violently against the cave wall. But Harry was a strong swimmer and he confidently ploughed his way into the middle of the cave. Seconds later, he was aware that Ant was beside him.

'Can you see them?' shouted Ant above the waves.

He was going to reply in the negative, but then he caught sight of Bron, frantically bobbing about, trying to keep Tatiana's head out of the water.

'There!' he said, and swam towards them. It was confusing and dark in the cave and waves were coming in from the other side, which was making him disorientated. For every stroke forward, it felt as if he was being pushed two strokes back. But the adrenaline was pumping and kept him going.

Eventually he reached Bron and shouted, 'Here, let me help. I'll take Tatiana, and Ant will help you,' before realising that they were both stuck on a ridge, clinging to it for dear life.

'Tati's frightened,' said Bron, who looked worn out. 'I can't persuade her to come.'

'I can't swim,' wailed Tatiana.

'It's okay,' said Harry, 'I'm a trained lifeguard. Come, on I can help. We don't have much time.'

The waves were buffeting the rocks faster than ever, and water was pouring in from the other end of the cave at an alarming rate, making a broiling mass of wave, rock and seaweed.

'I can't!' screamed Tatiana.

'You can, or we're all going to bloody well drown,' said Harry with a decisiveness which took him by surprise. Taking her gently from Bron, and unpicking her fingers from where they were pinned against his shoulders, Harry got hold of her head, and began the slow swim on his back towards the mouth of the cave. It was hard going. The waves slapped in his face, and he was very aware of the ever-present threat of the rocks. But the first gleams of the sunrise were beginning to peek their way through and the cave entrance gradually grew nearer. Behind him, he could hear Ant muttering words of encouragement to Bron. They could and would do this, and Josie would be so proud.

'Oh my God, what has he done?' Josie pushed her way through the shocked throng, as she saw Harry dive into the thrashing water. It was bad enough Bron going in, but now Harry – and Ant, who followed in rapid succession. It was so stupid. They were all risking their lives. They were going to drown, and it was her fault. At this rate, by the time the coastguard arrived they'd be pulling four bodies out of the cave.

'They'll be okay,' said Diana, coming up to her and clutching her arm, 'they have to be.'

'I don't even know how well Harry can swim,' said Josie helplessly, 'he never shows much interest in the sea when we come down here.'

The sun was beginning to rise in earnest now, pink fingers spreading across the sky, making the sea appear both benign and friendly, and not the watery grave it threatened to be.

'The sea here can be so treacherous,' said Josie. 'Oh, why did I suggest Tatiana hide in the cave? I could kick myself.'

'Look, help's at hand.' Diana pointed as a boat rounded the cove and came speeding in their direction.

Thank God. Josie peered into the gloomy darkness of the cave; it was hard to see, but she thought she could make out figures battling their way through the water.

'Here! Over here!' She jumped up and down, waving to the coastguard. The boat was just puttering up to the cave entrance when Harry ploughed backwards through it, holding Tatiana. He looked magnificent, strong and brave, and Josie's heart leapt. He was okay. He was okay.

The men in the boat threw him a line, and picked Tatiana out of the water while Harry swam to shore. He was shivering, and Gypsy, who turned out to be surprisingly efficient, immediately threw the towels and blankets she'd brought back from the yurt over him. 'Here, darling, you need to get as warm as possible,' she said.

'Have this,' said Freddie, giving him a nip of brandy. 'I brought it with me tonight to keep me going, didn't realise it was going to come in so handy.'

Tatiana was being given the once over by the men on the boat, who had wrapped her up in blankets, and seemed to be checking for hypothermia. By the sound of her loud complaining, she was recovering well, but there was still no sign of Ant or Bron.

'There!' Josie suddenly spotted them at the entrance of the cave. But then a wave went over their heads and they were lost from view.

*   *   *

'This was a bloody stupid idea,' had been Ant's first thought as he followed Harry into the water, but then there was no time for thought as he battled with spray, wind, waves and the cold. Time and time again the current dragged him towards the side of the cave, and he forced himself back on track. By the time he reached Bron, Harry was halfway back with Tatiana.

'Fancy a lift?' Ant said. 'Only you look a bit knackered.'

Bron was looking very cold, shivering violently.

'Come on, let's get you out of here,' said Ant.

Ant was strong, but he wasn't the greatest of swimmers. It took all his brute strength to get to the middle of the cave. The dark and the pounding of the waves disorientated him, and he had several panicky moments when he thought they might not make it. Then he became dimly aware that the entrance of the cave might not be too far away, and forced himself to power on. Bron seemed too worn out now to help, barely even kicking. It was like having a lead weight in his arms, and Ant was struggling to get him to the entrance, which was tantalisingly close. He tried not to think about the effect that age, and the water, would be having on Auberon's body. If he was finding it tough, Bron must be really struggling. Don't think about that, Ant admonished himself, otherwise we're both lost. One stroke at a time, he told himself, one stroke at a time. Then just as he was nearly there, a huge wave smashed over his head, and Bron moved suddenly out of his grasp. And then Bron was gone, and Ant was alone with the waves and the wind, in the darkness.

Seeing that Josie was still perched anxiously at the side of the cave, Diana went up to Harry.

'You okay?' she said.

'Fine,' said Harry. 'Bit chilly.'

'Have another blanket then,' she said. 'You need to keep huddled up, to avoid hypothermia.'

'She's right,' said M'stard, throwing another blanket over him. 'And here, have another nip of whisky.'

'I'm going to be paralytic if you're not careful,' said Harry. He stared nervously at the cave. 'Has anyone seen Ant yet? He's taking a long time.'

'Too long,' said Diana. She looked really worried. She followed Josie to the edge of the cave, where they both watched in silent horror as the coastguard's boat shone torches in the water, to see if they could spot anyone.

Diana felt a chill go down her spine. Ant. Not Ant. Whether he wanted her or not, now she'd met up with him again, she couldn't imagine a world without his big brash presence in it. Didn't want to.

She strained to see in the gloom of the cave. It was easy to detect movements that weren't there, but . . .

'Jose – can you see?' She clutched at Josie's arm as she saw a body moving in the water, no, two bodies, swimming side by side. The men in the boat saw them at the same time, and shouted rapid orders. Ropes flew into the water, and first Bron, and then Ant, were hauled to safety.

'Thank God,' said Josie, tears in her eyes, 'I thought I'd lost him.'

'Sorry?' said Diana.

'Ant,' said Josie, her eyes shining. 'I've been so blind. I'm in love with Ant.'

Now: Bron

He'd felt he was going to be a hero, seeing Tati like that, frightened and trapped in the cave. But he'd messed up and managed to lose the rope. He'd needed rescuing himself, and then had to be ignominiously hauled into the boat. Not only that, he'd spent the coldest, wettest, most terrifying hour of his life, only to end up looking like a prize idiot. Tati would laugh at him more than ever.

She was sitting, hair bedraggled, wrapped in blankets, holding court with the coastguards, most of whom appeared to be completely under her spell. Even soaking wet and blue with cold, she was beautiful to him. Not just beautiful, Tati looked magnificent, like a mermaid straight from the ocean. Whereas he . . .

Bron allowed himself to be examined by the experts, who checked his vital signs and insisted on making him drink some weak hot tea. He'd rather have had whisky, but it did make him feel better rapidly. True he'd got quite cold in the water, but surrounded by blankets he'd warmed up quickly. But he must look a right state. Unlike Ant, who was a vision of glowing young manhood. Bron felt quite jealous of the admiring looks Tatiana was casting him. She was barely sending any looks in his direction. Bron sighed heavily. He'd wanted to prove something to Tati today, and had only succeeded in looking like a fool. A stupid romantic old fool.

Chapter Thirty-One

'You love Ant?' her friend's shock was palpable. 'What about Harry? What about *me*?'

Oh God. In her moment of clarity, Josie had forgotten all about Diana's declaration of love to Ant.

'I'm sorry, Di,' said Josie, 'but it's just the way I feel. I can't help it.'

She walked away feeling she should care more, but somehow she didn't. She'd spent the whole night in turmoil. But now the sun was rising, and a new day was dawning and everything had become crystal clear. Harry was her past. Ant was her future and she'd nearly lost him. The sight of Ant fearlessly ploughing through the water was one she wouldn't forget in a while. Harry was heroic too, a little voice in her head said, but she ignored it. She was done with confusion and misery. Now she knew what she had to do.

'Do you think they're going to be all right?' Josie said, anxiously scanning the boat where Ant and the others were being checked over. She felt so responsible for what had happened. She should have remembered the danger of getting cut off in the cave. It was something that had happened to her several times in her teenage years, but never so dramatically as this.

After what seemed like forever, the boat putt-putted slowly to the shore, and the coastguards let everyone climb out.

'You've all been very lucky,' the captain said. 'Nothing worse than a dousing. But that was incredibly dangerous. You should never have attempted a rescue like that.'

'Sorry,' said Harry, 'that was my fault. We were worried you wouldn't get here in time.'

'As it happens, you got away with it,' the coastguard said, less sternly. 'Besides,' he added with a twinkle, 'it's not every day we get to rescue celebrities. But don't do it again. That cave is notorious. Like I said, you were very lucky.'

Tatiana was looking slightly stunned, and her cavalcade rushed forward, making soothing noises, plying her with drinks, wrapping her up in so many layers she looked like a mummy, and generally behaving in the over-the-top manner Josie had come to expect.

'I'm so sorry, Tatiana,' said Josie, 'I was only trying to help. I'd completely forgotten the tide was coming in. It's all my fault.'

'Nonsense,' said Bron, briskly. 'If anyone's to blame it's me, for letting Freddie persuade me to go along with this hypnotism nonsense. It got out of hand, and we should have put a stop to it hours ago.'

'You?' Tatiana said. 'You had something to do with that – that idiot pursuing me?'

'Yes, and I'm sorry,' said Bron, 'but I can explain . . .'

'Forget it,' said Tatiana, delivering a ringing slap round his face. 'You and Freddie, same old, same old. And there I was, feeling grateful that you tried to rescue me. Come on, we're going back to the yurt.'

And with that, she and her cronies stormed off.

'I guess I deserved that,' said Bron with a sigh.

*   *   *

'Talking of Freddie,' Ant looked around, 'where is he?'

He'd been there when Harry and Ant had dived into the water, but he seemed conspicuously absent now. Having caused all this mayhem, he seemed to have done a runner with Will, who'd been filming the rescue. Light blue touch paper and retire . . .

'He might have gone back to the theatre to deal with Mike,' said Bron. 'If I know Freddie, he'll be getting him to sign all kinds of disclaimers.'

'Why are you still friends with him?' asked Ant curiously.

'Why is anyone friends with anyone?' said Bron. 'Habit, years of rubbing along together. Despite everything, we do make a good team.'

'Except when he ruins your love life,' said Ant.

'There is that,' said Bron.

Ant glanced at Harry, who was talking to the girls. He hadn't spoken to any of them since getting out of the water. He didn't like to go near Josie, because of what Harry had said earlier. He still wanted to be the decent friend. But something in what Bron said stirred up forgotten memories. Harry only knew Josie because of him. They'd come down here when they were at uni and he'd thought he was in with a chance, and then Harry, his mate, had stolen Josie from under his nose. Ant's indignation completely overrode his memories of having been distracted with Kerry – Kelly? He'd taken his eye off the prize and Harry had claimed it. And now Josie had chosen him again, and Harry had lost. It was the way of the world, and all was fair in love and war. He'd just nearly drowned. Life was too short to be noble; he wasn't going to pass up this opportunity. It might never come his way again.

*   *   *

297

Diana stood feeling miserable, trying to ignore the fact that Ant was making puppy dog eyes at Josie, who was clearly itching to be alone with him. But Harry had cornered her, and was talking earnestly to her, so when Bron and Ant decided it was time to leave, Josie had no choice but to stay. Diana decided to follow them though she didn't quite know why. Nothing was ever going to bring him back to her. The whole thing was a total mess, and she couldn't think how they could remain friends after this.

'That was brave,' she said, as she caught up with Bron.

'Brave or stupid?' said Bron. 'Tati wasn't impressed, and without Ant coming to my rescue, it could have been a very different story.'

'It was nothing,' said Ant. 'It was pretty stupid of all of us to have gone in. The things we do for love, eh?'

'So you only went in to help to show off to Josie?' said Diana, feeling worse than ever. 'Ant, you're unbelievable. And there was me thinking you had a vulnerable side.'

'It wasn't just that,' protested Ant.

'It's all right,' Bron patted him on the shoulder, 'I did the same. Even if I still gained nothing from it.'

'You don't think she's going to forgive you, then?' said Diana.

'You saw her face,' said Bron, with a sigh. 'I don't think she'll ever forgive me.'

Harry felt hopeful when Diana left with Bron and Ant. Josie was staring out to sea, ominously silent.

'Well?' he said in the end, unable to stand the silence.

'Well, what?' said Josie.

'What's happening with us?' said Harry.

He thought again of having seen Josie and Ant holding hands earlier, and how Ant hadn't acknowledged his comment about it. A short stab of jealousy shot through him.

'I thought we'd established there *is* no more us,' said Josie, her gaze unblinking from the horizon. 'I'm sorry, Harry. It's over.'

'This is about Ant, isn't it?' said Harry. 'Josie, he's my best friend.'

'And Di's mine,' Josie shot back, 'but that didn't stop you snogging her.'

'I didn't snog her,' said Harry. 'She threw her arms round me.'

'And I found you asleep with your arms wrapped round her,' said Josie.

'Again, not guilty,' said Harry. 'Diana curled up next to me when I was already asleep.'

'Ant told me the way he feels, and I wasn't sure,' said Josie, 'but now I am. It's him I want, not you.'

Without looking at him, she turned away and headed up the cliff.

'It's not what you really feel,' Harry shouted into the wind. 'It's just Freddie screwing with your mind. And I'm going to prove it.'

Chapter Thirty-Two

Ant, Bron and Diana reached the theatre and pushed their way in. Freddie was sitting with a dazed looking Mike, saying, 'When you awake, none of this will have happened. You never met Tatiana Okeby here, you never agreed to produce her in *A Midsummer Night's Dream*. You have just been on an early morning stroll and had a little doze. When I count to three, you will fall into a deep sleep, and when you wake up you will have forgotten everything, three, two, one . . .'

And Mike slumped down.

'Perfect,' said Freddie, to Will. 'I think we can use that.'

'Do you really think that's a good idea?' said Bron. 'I don't think Tati will be happy to be shown up on camera.'

'It was your idea,' said Freddie.

'And I've changed my mind,' said Bron. 'Come on, I thought it was going to be funny, but it hasn't turned out that way.'

'Maybe you're right,' said Freddie. 'I think the words *sue*, and *you* may have been uttered as she left.'

'And what about us?' said Ant, 'I don't think your experiment has been entirely successful.'

He'd kept a careful distance from Diana since getting out of the water. He had been so stunned when she'd tried to

300

kiss him earlier, he'd reacted instantly. He knew he'd been cruel, and felt bad about it, but Diana wasn't for him, not any more. Not now he'd found Josie again. He didn't want to hurt her any more than he had to.

'You can say that again,' said Diana. 'I think I can count this as one of the most traumatic, upsetting and humiliating experiences of my life. So I don't want you showing any footage of it at all, thank you very much.'

'Oh,' said Freddie, looking a little discomfited. 'Has it really been that bad?'

'Bad? It's been worse than bad.' She gave Ant a knowing look. 'I've fallen in love and been rejected, my best friend briefly chased me round this stage, and I've fallen out with all of the people I really care about. Tonight is the story of my life writ large. Everyone gets happy endings but me.'

'Do you really feel like that?' Ant was genuinely surprised. Despite her confidences in him earlier, Di had always seemed invulnerable to him, as if love didn't matter to her. He'd really thought the feelings she'd developed for him were skin-deep, brought about by the hypnotism; perhaps he'd been wrong.

'Not that you'd care,' snapped Diana. 'Because it looks like things have worked out for you.'

'What?' said Ant.

'She's coming up the path right now,' said Diana.

Ant turned as the gate creaked, and he saw Josie coming shyly towards him.

'I've made my decision,' she said shyly. 'And I choose you.'

And with that, she stood on tiptoes and kissed him on the cheek.

Diana felt sick to the pit of her stomach when she saw Josie kiss Ant. It didn't seem fair. She had both Ant and Harry lapping out of her hands, and Di had no one, even if it was the hypnotism that had addled their brains, they'd still both chosen Josie. Diana knew it was mean-spirited of her, but she wanted just for once for Josie to know how it was when life didn't go the way you wanted. Let her feel rejection and disillusionment.

'So you haven't managed to sort things out with Ant, then?' said Bron, putting a sympathetic arm round her shoulder.

'I thought maybe I had,' said Diana, 'but looks like I was wrong.'

She stared gloomily at Ant and Josie, who seemed oblivious to everyone else.

'You're still in love with Ant?' Bron said perceptively.

'I don't know – yes – no, maybe,' said Diana. 'I'm feeling extremely confused right now. I'm not sure which of my feelings are real anymore.'

'I think you'd know,' said Bron. 'Just as I do about Tati.'

'Do you think she'll get over what you did to her tonight?'

'Somehow, no,' said Bron sadly. 'I think I might have finally nailed the coffin on our relationship.'

'And I think I'm destined to be a bitter old spinster,' said Diana. 'Quite frankly it wouldn't matter who I was in love with, being friends with Josie means that no one looks at me. They all flood to her.'

Diana had never thought about this before, but suddenly realised it was true. It hadn't mattered so much when she and Josie were both playing the field, and nothing was serious. But since Josie had met Harry it mattered very much. Very much indeed.

*   *   *

302

Harry sat down after Josie was gone.

Josie had got muddled up tonight. They all had. She didn't know what she was doing. He'd have to remind her of how she really felt. Harry got up and strode off. He was going to find Freddie Puck and sort this out once and for all. Ant had had his chance with Josie all those years ago, and blown it. Faint heart never won fair lady. Harry was damned if he was going to let her go so easily now.

He set off back up the cliff path, not quite sure what he was going to do. As he reached the theatre, he saw Mike Slowbotham stumble out, looking sleepy.

'Hello old boy,' he said. 'Seems to be a bit of a party going on in there. I must have had a hell of a night. I can't remember a thing.'

Maybe Freddie had put one thing right, thought Harry. Time for him to get everything else right too.

Josie was sitting on a hillock, holding Ant's hand in a happy daze, completely oblivious to everyone else. She felt other-worldly. A morning mist was creeping over the theatre, casting strange shapes and making her feel quite ethereal. She knew Diana was angry with her, but she couldn't mind somehow – though a bit of her thought she should – because sitting here, leaning against Ant, was making her feel sublimely happy. Happier then she'd ever felt in her life before.

They hadn't said much, but Josie felt as if they didn't need to. They could communicate through their minds, their senses; everything was accentuated. The sound of the sea, the soft summer breeze, the brush of his cheek against hers. Never had she felt like this. Never had she felt this dizzying rush of love and sweet desire. She wanted the moment to go on and on for ever.

'Good. I thought I'd find you here.' Tatiana swept in, with M'stard rushing behind her saying, 'Please, Tati, I think you should get back to the yurt, I'm not sure this will help.'

'I want to know what you did to me tonight, Freddie, you bastard. And I want any footage you've got of this evening, destroyed, *capisce*?'

Bron got up. 'Tati. Look, this was my fault. I thought I wanted to get back at you, and let Freddie persuade me it was a good idea. I realise now it wasn't.'

Tatiana looked sad suddenly.

'That's the trouble with you, Bron, isn't it?' she said. 'You've always let Freddie dictate to you. Even when it comes to us. *Especially* when it comes to us.'

'I know, and I'm sorry,' said Bron. 'You're right. Freddie, mate, I think this hypnosis thing has gone far enough. You need to sort things out.'

'If you absolutely insist,' said Freddie, 'but you have to admit, it has been such fun.'

'Not for me, it hasn't.' Josie turned to see Harry glowering fiercely at Freddie. She'd never seen him look so angry before.

'Oi, Ant,' he said. 'Leave my fiancée alone.'

Ant stood up. 'I'm sure we can sort this out in a civilized fashion . . .' Ant began, before Harry launched himself at him.

'I'm not,' said Harry. Josie screamed as he struck Ant on the nose, and knocked him to the ground.

Chapter Thirty-Three

Diana leapt to her feet, hand over her mouth as she watched Harry tackle Ant to the ground. 'Harry, no!' she screamed as Harry sat on Ant's stomach and pummelled his face, followed by, 'Please don't hurt him.' Not that he looked in danger of doing so. Ant being the stronger, he soon recovered from the element of surprise, and managed to push Harry off him.

'Come on, mate,' he said, 'we'll never solve anything like this.' But Harry just threw another blow at him. Ant ducked and Harry nearly tripped over.

'You bastard, Ant,' he panted, arms flailing wildly. 'You're not going to get away with this.'

He was bright red in the face from the exertion, and made a most unlikely boxer.

'You're mad,' said Ant, 'but if you really have to do this then –'

He struck out and caught Harry a glancing blow on the cheek.

Harry appeared infuriated by this and charged Ant, who pushed him away easily. The pair tussled to and fro for an instant, neither gaining much advantage, Josie shrieking helplessly, 'Stop! The both of you. Please.'

'You're never satisfied, are you?' spat Harry, as Ant

managed to land another blow. 'You think you're so much better than everyone else, that you're entitled to take what you want. Well, you're not having Josie, do you hear?'

He hit out wildly, and managed a lucky blow in the stomach.

'Oof,' said Ant, before coming back at Harry with a huge shove, which made Harry fall over.

'It's not up to you, mate,' he said. 'Why don't you ask Josie?'

'What, so you can treat her like you did Di?' said Harry. 'Josie, you can't have forgotten that this is the man who left his girlfriend alone while she was having a miscarriage? Some romantic he is.'

'You bastard,' said Ant. 'It wasn't like that, and Di knows it.'

And with that, he was like a raging animal, raining blows down on Harry like a man possessed.

'Stop!' screamed Di. 'Both of you, please, just stop!'

Ant had never been so furious in his life. He couldn't think of anything but that he wanted to punish Harry, and pummel him half to death. How dare he say that about Diana? What did he bloody know about it?

Harry wasn't going to back down easily though. He might not be as strong as Ant, but he was good at ducking and diving, and hard as Ant tried, he wasn't connecting many punches. Ant was soon breathless from trying to keep up. He'd put on weight since he'd been home and Harry spent more time in the gym, which was giving him an advantage.

'And what about you?' he taunted. 'Some loyal fiancé you are. Not even prepared to follow through your promises. Josie's better off without you.'

'You!' Harry launched straight at him, forgetting to parry,

so Ant managed to catch him in the stomach. Not so much of an advantage then. Ant had evidently spent more of his youth scrapping than Harry.

'Ugh,' Harry staggered backwards, but he soon steadied himself, and like the Duracell Bunny, he kept coming back for more. It seemed as if nothing was going to stop him.

'Don't you dare talk about Josie,' Harry said and he was off again, darting round Ant, throwing punches when he could.

Ant was beginning to tire. It had been a very long night. He was vaguely aware the girls were yelling at them to stop, but he found himself unable to step back. Harry had started and Ant was buggered if he was going to back out now.

'Can't you do something?' said Josie in desperation to Freddie, who looked like he was enjoying himself. 'They're going to kill each other.'

'I doubt that,' said Freddie. 'It's not like either of them is much cop.'

It was true that neither of them had really managed to inflict that much damage on the other, which was something, Josie thought. But they were beginning to tire now and were staggering round the theatre. Ant had a cut on his lip, and Harry had a bruised cheek. Josie couldn't bear that either of them was being hurt. She felt the first smidgeon of doubt about her behaviour. Had she done the right thing, choosing Ant? Maybe she'd have been better off choosing neither of them.

'This is all your fault, Freddie,' she said. 'We were fine till we met you.'

'You all agreed to be hypnotised,' shrugged Freddie, 'and the subconscious is a strange thing. You all appear to have acted out secret desires tonight.'

'Yes, but we didn't expect this,' said Josie. 'Di's barely speaking to me, the boys are fighting, I've no idea what I feel about anyone. You have to stop it.'

'She's right,' Bron said. 'Freddie, this has gone too far. What we did to Tati was bad enough. But this – you're playing with people's lives. It's not fair.'

'And so the lion eventually roars,' said Tatiana, looking slightly admiring.

'You still got something to give?' Ant taunted Harry, panting wildly. 'Come on then, come and get me!'

'I could keep this going all day,' said Harry savagely, and launched another attack.

Two of them fighting over her. Some other woman might be thrilled about that, but not Josie.

'Freddie, Bron's right, you need to do something now!'

Harry could barely stand. His ribs were aching, he had a huge stitch, his shirt was torn and his fists felt bruised. He hadn't had a physical fight with anyone since he was eight, when he'd punched Adam Fellows on the nose for saying Katrina Jones was a cow. Katrina had been his girlfriend at the time. Which just went to show chivalry wasn't dead.

Despite how rough he was feeling, Harry had no intention of backing down. Ant had crossed a line, and he was going to have to pay for it.

'Gentleman, I think it's time to call it a day.' Harry was suddenly aware that Freddie Puck was standing in his way. 'This has gone far enough.'

Enraged that anyone would try to stop him now, and doubly enraged by all the trouble Freddie had wrought, Harry punched him on the nose.

'Ouch!' said Freddie, clutching his nose, which was pouring blood. 'There was no need for that!'

'Go, Harry,' said Tatiana. 'Team Harry for the win!'

'Not helping, Tati darling,' said Bron.

'Keep out of this,' said Harry to Freddie. 'It's my fight.'

He threw himself at Ant once more and soon they were rolling and scrapping on the grass like two street kids.

'Harry, stop it! You'll kill him!' He vaguely heard Josie's voice, which enraged him further. Harry fought like a madman, till he felt arms reaching from behind him and dragging him away from Ant. It was Bron.

'Enough, Harry, it's enough. This isn't going to solve anything.'

Harry stood panting, his heart hammering. The fury started to drain away. He looked down at himself. What a state. 'I suppose,' he said.

Ant got up, looking rather sheepish, the cut on his lip still bleeding.

'Did I do that?' Harry was quite proud of himself. He'd never really considered fighting one of his life skills.

'Right,' said Bron. 'Let's be civilised about this.'

'So long as Ant says sorry,' said Harry.

'Sorry? You started it,' said Ant.

'If you can't keep your hands to yourself,' glared Harry.

'She was up for it,' taunted Ant. 'Let's face it, you lost her.'

'You . . .!' Harry threw a final enraged punch at Ant, which, catching him by surprise, caught him bang on the nose.

'Oh,' said Ant in surprise. He wobbled a bit, and unlike a Weeble, fell down.

'Ant!' there was a shriek from the girls.

'Oh, Harry,' said Josie. 'What have you done?'

Now: Bron

'My my, quite the hero tonight, aren't we?' Tatiana said.

Bron had taken Harry to one side and calmed him down while the girls were tending to Ant. Harry was sitting, looking genuinely stunned.

'I didn't mean to hit him that hard,' he kept saying, 'really I didn't.'

'I know old chap,' said Bron, patting him on the back. 'Heat of the moment, passions flying, and all that. If this were on the stage, it would make a great tragedy.'

'Thanks,' said Harry, 'but my life isn't normally this dramatic, and quite frankly, I prefer it like that.'

Bron paused from what he was doing and looked up at Tati.

'No,' he said, 'you know I'm not. I've never been the hero you deserved.'

This was an improvement. At least Tati was talking to him.

'You could always change that,' she said, a little smile playing on her lips.

Hang on, this was Tati warmer than he'd seen her towards him for years.

'Erm, how exactly?' he said, wondering if this were some kind of trick.

'By following it through.'

'What?'

'The standing up to Freddie thing,' she said. 'I rather like it.'

'Well, then, I shall do it some more,' said Bron. He strode over to Freddie, who was still nursing his sore nose.

'It hurts,' he complained. 'I should sue.'

'Stop being such a baby,' said Bron. 'It serves you right. You need to sort all of this out, right now.'

'Why should I?' said Freddie sulkily. 'They signed contracts. I never promised them they'd fall in love with the right people. Just that they'd plight their troth at midnight. Which they've all done. It will make great telly.'

'Great telly, my arse!' roared Bron. 'You've muddled these lovely people up enough, they deserve to be back together with the ones they love. Got it?'

'Got it,' said Freddie, completely taken aback.

'Ooh,' cooed Tati, 'I do love a masterful man.'

And Bron glowed with pride.

Chapter Thirty-Four

Ant came to in a daze. He didn't know where he was for a moment, then had a sudden rush to the head. He was lying in snow, next to Diana, giggling his head off.

'Di,' he said as her face swam into view, but then another face was looking over him anxiously. 'Where's Diana?' he said. 'I want Di.'

'It's Josie, Ant,' the face said. 'You've had a bang on the head.'

Ant felt his nose, which really hurt, and his stomach was aching.

'Josie?' he said tentatively. He wasn't lying in snow. Diana wasn't beside him, he was lying in dew-soaked grass on top of a cliff in Cornwall. And everything seemed to hurt.

'Are you all right?' said Josie. 'I was so worried.'

Josie was worried about *him*?

'I think so,' said Ant. He tried to sit up, but felt a bit dizzy, and lay back down again. It was quite pleasant lying on the grass staring at the sky, relaxing. He had a feeling he had been under a lot of stress recently.

'Ant, Ant, talk to me,' Josie was rubbing his hands anxiously. Why was Josie rubbing his hands? Where was Diana?

'I'm fine really,' said Ant. 'Just give me a minute.'

'Yes, Josie, give him a minute,' he heard Diana say. 'Poor guy needs some air. Don't fuss so.'

'I'm not fussing,' said Josie.

'Here, this will help,' Diana produced something strong in a hip flask. 'It's brandy, I got it from Freddie.'

Ant took a sip and it nearly blew his head off.

Freddie? He felt more confused than ever. Then it all came flooding back. The hypnotism; the mix-ups, rescuing Tatiana, the fight.

He sat bolt upright, searching for Harry.

'You knocked me out,' Ant said indignantly.

Harry managed to look sheepish and defiant at the same time.

'You stole Josie from me.'

'You didn't want her,' said Ant.

'That's not true,' said Harry. 'I love Josie. I just don't want to get married . . . yet. Maybe one day, but not now.'

They stared at each other, and for a moment Ant thought Harry might be about to kick off again, but then Ant burst out laughing.

'I guess none of us has behaved brilliantly tonight,' he said. 'Look at the state of us.'

He was aware that his nose was bleeding and his shirt was caked in blood, while Harry's was ripped at the collar. They were both covered in bruises, Harry sporting a particularly fine one on his cheek.

'It's not funny,' scolded Josie, applying a hankie to his nose. 'Harry could have really hurt you.'

'Here, let me,' said Diana. 'He needs his head held right back if that bleeding's ever going to stop.'

'Who do you think you are?' said Josie, clearly feeling she had the right to take charge. 'His mother?'

'Ladies, ladies, I'm quite capable of holding my own

nose,' said Ant. 'Wonders will never cease. Two women fighting over me. I could get used to this.'

He pinched his nose, tipped his head back, got up and limped over to Harry.

'No hard feelings, mate,' he said proffering his hand.

'None,' said Harry. 'Sorry about your nose.'

'Sorry about your shirt.'

They stood awkwardly for a minute before Ant said, 'Come here you stupid sod,' and enveloped him in a bear hug.

'Now what?' said Harry.

'Now Freddie is going to put things right,' said Bron.

Josie was seething. Diana had pushed her way over to Ant, as soon as he'd gone down, and was acting as if he were her property. Diana, who hadn't done anything but sneer and snipe at Ant all weekend. Diana, who'd spent half the weekend chasing after Harry, and the other half chasing Ant.

'What is it with you and men,' hissed Josie. 'Do you always have to steal guys that belong to someone else?'

'Can't poor little Josie cope without her coterie of admirers?' sneered Diana. 'Are you going to add Freddie and Bron to the set? I bet Mike would happily join in too, given his recent disappointment.'

'What?' said Josie. 'I'm not the one who pursues other people's fiancés. Just because you can't get a man of your own doesn't mean you can steal mine.'

'You're the one who's spent the best part of the night pushing Harry away,' Diana said furiously. 'You know your trouble, Josie? You're spoilt rotten. With your big house, and your wealthy mummy and daddy who'll bail you out of the slightest crisis. You can't cope when things don't go your way. You're a spoilt little cow.'

'And you're a jealous bitch,' said Josie. 'I can't help it if you've had a crappy home life, you've lost your job, and screwed up your love life. You need to start taking responsibility for your own life. Not blaming other people for your mistakes.'

'You . . . you . . . You have no idea what it's been like for me!' Diana looked angrier than Josie had ever seen her. 'How dare you say that?' She slapped Josie round the face.

Josie clutched her face, stunned.

'Oh, God,' said Diana, 'I'm so sorry – I didn't mean to . . .'

'Josie, are you okay?' Ant and Harry both sprang up like knights in shining armour.

'Great,' said Diana slumping down, defeated. 'Always the bridesmaid, never the sodding bride.'

'Blimey, a catfight,' said Ant, trying to make light of things. 'Did you have to stop?'

'Shut up, Ant. Josie, are you okay?' Harry said, putting his arm round her.

'Fine,' said Josie, shaking his arm off. She was still glaring at Diana, who was sitting down on the ground, the wind completely out of her sails.

'Are you sure?' Ant was over in a trice, trying to find a gap in her defences no doubt. She was fed up with the lot of them. Men were just too much trouble.

'Absolutely,' said Josie. 'I'm tired, fed up and I just want to go home.'

Harry came over to her again.

'Come on, Josie,' he said gently. 'It's been a mad night. We can sort this out, I'm sure.'

'Can we?' said Josie. 'I think my whole life has just fallen apart in front of me, and no,' – she could see that Ant was taking that as an invitation – 'I made a mistake earlier on.

315

Being with you won't solve anything. I want to be alone, and this time I really mean it.'

And she got up and walked away.

Diana stood up too. 'I think I should go after her,' she said, her voice trailing off. 'I just said some unspeakable things.'

She felt sad and defeated. Josie was probably never going to speak to her again. Harry wasn't interested in her at all. The only thing she'd gained from this night was a truce with Ant.

'It might not do any good at the moment,' said Ant, squeezing her arm with surprising gentleness. 'I think we need to get back to where we were. Sorry I got us all into this. Truly I am.'

Ant saying sorry? Possibly the most surprising thing in a very surprising night? Diana raised a small smile.

'Since when did you start saying sorry?' she said.

'Since I realised what a pillock I was to you all those years ago, and how I've made it worse tonight,' said Ant. 'I can't be in love with Josie. It wouldn't work, and I'm sorry I hurt you by thinking I was. It's bad enough I hurt you before, I don't want to hurt you again.'

'I know,' said Diana, 'I'm not sure anything I've been feeling tonight is real. But I do know I've been carrying all that anger round with me for years. It hasn't done me much good. I can see now Sian had a lot to answer for; I should have given you the benefit of the doubt. I'm really sorry.'

'I'm glad we're friends,' said Ant. 'That's the only good thing that has come out of tonight.'

He kissed her on the cheek. Such a sweet tender kiss. And Diana felt something melt inside her. Ant. How very, very lovely he was. She wished he felt the same way about her.

'Come on, Freddie,' said Ant, 'time to get this show on the road.'

'You're all sure?' said Freddie.

'Absolutely,' said Diana. 'I'm fed up with feeling this miserable and confused. I'd rather wake up alone and never be in love again than feel like this.'

'And I just want Josie and me to be back the way we were,' said Harry.

'Ant, what about you?'

'Not to have to feel so responsible for everyone,' said Ant firmly. 'I prefer being a bastard. It's much less hassle.'

'In that case,' said Freddie, 'when I click my fingers, you will think you've been having a strange dream, but everything else will be back to normal.'

'And Josie?'

'I'll go after her,' said Bron, 'persuade her to come back.'

'Right,' said Freddie. 'I'm going to click my fingers, three, two, one, and you're asleep . . .'

Diana felt herself yawning, overcome with weariness. Sleep seemed so welcome. Vaguely she was aware that Freddie was saying something about the Standing Stones, and then she remembered nothing more. She was fast asleep.

Chapter Thirty-Five

Josie was sitting down by the beach. It must be nearly 7am by now. She didn't know what had drawn her back, but the solitude, and the pounding of the waves as the sun rose higher in the sky, were having a calming effect on her shattered nerves.

She didn't know what she felt anymore. Couldn't untangle in her head whether she wanted to be with anyone, but going straight from Harry to Ant seemed like the worst idea she'd ever had. What had possessed her? It must have been the hypnotism, that or madness and moonlight.

Josie felt ashamed of the things she'd said to Diana. Diana was right, she *could* be spoilt sometimes, and she didn't know how the other half lived. She knew Diana's life had been much harder than her own. It had been cruel of her to say so. Diana's tough exterior hid a heart of gold, and she'd been a good friend to Josie, always there when she needed her. And without Diana's prompting Harry would probably never have moved in with her in the first place, or asked her to marry him.

Maybe Josie had been at fault for letting herself get caught up in the moment. She'd rushed headlong into this marriage thing without thinking it through. And she had got carried away. She could see that now. No wonder poor Harry had freaked. Another stab of remorse went through her. She'd been tough on him over Diana, and then fallen straight into Ant's arms, without considering his feelings. The one constant of the night, she realised, had been Harry's dogged persistence that he loved her. Maybe she should give him another chance. Not that he deserved it . . .

'Josie.' She looked up to see Bron standing there. 'I know tonight's been a disaster, but I've just about stopped Freddie from meddling and he's put the others back to sleep. When they wake up none of this will have happened. What do you think?'

'I think that's the best idea I've heard all night,' said Josie.

Ant was dreaming. He was eighteen again, and he and Diana were dancing in a sun-filled meadow. Which couldn't be right, because he'd met Diana in Switzerland. But that didn't matter in the dream. She looked beautiful. Her eyes sparkled and shone, and her titian hair flowed and danced down her back. She wore a simple white flowing dress, bare feet and had flowers in her hair. Rays of sunshine danced in the dew at their feet.

'It's the summer solstice,' she said, laughing. 'A time for rebirth and new beginnings.'

He whirled her round and round, their dance growing wilder and more heady. He was caught up in a whirlwind of dizzying intoxicating love and felt almost as if he were flying. He remembered this feeling. He remembered it so clearly, he felt he could reach out and touch it. This was once him. This was once Diana. This was what they'd shared and lost. How stupid, stupid, he'd been to let this go. It felt so perfect and right . . .

And suddenly the dream was fading and it felt like he was coming down to land. No! he wanted to cry, let me stay here with her, where I know and feel love. But nearer, nearer, the earth approached and suddenly he had tumbled down to earth once more. He sat up, staring into a glaring morning sun.

Ant felt bereft. The dream that held him had seemed so real. Of course it was obvious now. It was Diana he loved; had never stopped loving her. He'd hidden it in the recesses of his mind. He hoped that she could remember too, what they'd had once, because despite what he'd been pretending for years, what they'd had, had been very special.

Then he took in his surroundings. He was by the Standing Stones. How had he got here? The last thing he remembered was being at the theatre. And then Ant saw her, curled up on a mound of grass, with flowers in her hair, looking for all the world like a sleeping angel.

Diana was dreaming that she was dancing across stepping stones. She was trying to reach someone. It was vital she found him. But the closer she came the further away he seemed. She ran lightly across the stones, barefoot, jumping from one to the other, yet not once did she slip and fall. The sound of the tinkling stream gave way to a louder sound and became a thundering roar, as she followed its path to a pool, where a waterfall gushed over the edge.

As she stared, a man emerged from the pool, a fine handsome figure with muscles to die for. He shook himself dry, and smiled at her, and her heart tumbled over itself as she remembered that she loved him, this man, whose name she had forgotten. Something had stopped them loving one another, but she couldn't think what. All she knew was that she longed for him now. So Diana ran as fast as she could towards him, her heart full of joy. But as she grew closer he faded away from her sight, until she woke up and found herself feeling a huge sense of regret and loss. The sun was getting quite bright in the sky. She shielded her eyes, as she became aware that someone was watching her.

She blushed as she realized who it was.

'Oh,' she blurted it out. 'I was just dreaming about you.'

'That's funny,' he said. 'I was dreaming about you too.'

There was a pause and Diana looked at him properly for the first time all weekend.

Suddenly she could see the young Ant, the Ant she'd fallen in love with.

'What was your dream about?' she said.

'We were dancing,' he said, 'and you were beautiful. You?'

Diana blushed again.

'You were swimming,' she said.

'And?'

'You were naked,' she admitted.

'Sounds like my kind of dream,' said Ant.

Diana blushed furiously.

'Come on, Di, don't be shy, it's not like we weren't close once' said Ant, and presenting her with a bunch of Pansies, he added mischievously, 'Maybe it's time we were that close again.'

'Maybe,' said Diana, 'it is.'

Harry couldn't get comfortable. Something was poking him in the back and his head was leaning on something hard. He was dreaming that he was in a forest ablaze with colour. Only suddenly he realised it wasn't flowers and leaves as he'd at first thought, but a genuine fire, and Josie was trapped on the other side of it. He had to get her. He had to walk through fire to be worthy of her love.

'Harry! Harry!' he could hear her frantic calling. The

flames looked fierce, but his love was stronger. Without a second thought he dived through them to reach her and was falling, falling, falling . . .

Harry woke up with a start. Pebbles were poking in his back and his head was perched awkwardly on a rock. But his arms were round a soft warm body. One he knew very well. His heart quickened with anticipation. What would she say when she knew it was him?

Josie turned round sleepily towards him.

'Oh, Harry,' she said. 'I was dreaming I'd lost you, but you were here all the time.'

'And I'll never go away again,' he said, kissing her softly on the lips, as the waves broke gently on the shore.

Chapter Thirty-Six

Ant couldn't believe it. He felt as if his eyes had been opened. As if he'd been washed clean and seen the world in a new light.

'Diana,' he said, hoping his voice was steadier than his unruly heart, which was beating at a rapid pace. 'I know this sounds mad, but I think I love you.'

Diana shook her head, and looked at him in a daze.

'It doesn't sound mad at all,' she said. 'In fact, I think it sounds perfect.'

'Are we sure this is real?' said Ant. 'It seems so sudden. The world feels so different.'

Diana pinched herself.

'Feels pretty real to me,' she said.

'But you hated me,' said Ant.

'And you hated *me*,' said Diana.

'I thought I did,' admitted Ant. 'But I was so gutted when you ditched me, I just turned against you. I didn't know about the baby. If I had known the truth, things would have been different. When I did find out, I thought you'd kept me away deliberately, and it made me even angrier.'

'I know,' said Diana. 'If I hadn't been so hurt and angry myself, I'd have stopped and thought it through. I knew you'd never have left me without a good reason. But at the time I thought you'd abandoned me.'

'I could never have done that,' said Ant. 'You're the one person who's ever given meaning to my life. All I ever wanted was to look after you.'

'Oh, Ant,' said Diana, 'I wish I'd known.'

Ant paused, and then said, 'Did you ever know what it was? Boy or girl?'

Diana shook her head and looked sad.

'No, it was too early to tell,' she said. 'If it had lived it would have been seven by now. What a mad thought.'

Ant took her hand and locked it in his.

'I wasn't there for you then,' he said, 'but I promise I always will be from now on. Come on. We've wasted enough time. Let's not waste any more.'

'Harry? Oh Harry!' Josie snuggled up to him. 'I've been having terrible dreams, and I thought you'd left me. It feels like I've been walking through the woods for hours. I kept nearly catching you, and then you'd skip away from me. But here you were all the time.'

'And here I'll always be,' said Harry. 'I love you, Josie, and always will. Without you my life would be meaningless.'

Josie felt her heart bursting with happiness. She felt as if she had been carrying around a great sadness, and now it was gone, to be replaced by a fizzing feeling of joy.

'I can barely remember anything about last night,' said Harry. 'Isn't that weird?'

'Me neither,' said Josie.

They lay watching the sea lap at the shore, feeling deeply content, and then Josie sat up suddenly.

'One thing I do remember,' she said urgently.

'Oh, what's that?' said Harry.

'Harry, do you truly in your heart of hearts want to marry me?' For some reason Josie knew she had to ask, even if she didn't like the answer.

Harry sat up too, and took her hand. He looked deep into her eyes, and kissed her.

'Josie, you have to know that I love you more than anything in the world. But I'm really sorry, I don't want to marry you – at least, not yet. I think, if I'm honest, we're rushing it.'

Josie took a deep breath.

'I think you're right,' she said simply. 'I got carried away with the ring and the big day. I'm sorry I've been such a nightmare about it. I didn't mean to be.'

'You were a bit,' said Harry, kissing her, 'but so long as I can still spend the rest of my life with you, I think I can forgive you.'

'So we are going to be together for ever?' said Josie, laughing.

'Most definitely,' said Harry. 'I couldn't imagine anyone else I'd rather be with.'

'Not even Diana?' said Josie.

'Especially not Diana,' he said kissing her on the lips.

'Come on,' said Josie, 'let's go home.'

Harry and Josie were coming down the path past the theatre, when they met Freddie and Bron.

'So how do you both feel?' said Freddie who looked unaccountably nervous.

'Great,' said Harry. 'I'm not sure if your hypnotism worked. Josie and I have been asleep all night.'

'Although I have been having some very weird dreams,' said Josie, 'and I can't work out how Harry's shirt got ripped, or he got that bruise on his cheek.'

'Maybe you elbowed him in your sleep,' said Bron.

'I'm sorry if we haven't given you any material to use,' said Harry.

'Oh, we got more than enough . . .' began Freddie, before Bron put in, 'I think we'll have to junk a lot of it, though. The quality wasn't that great.'

'Sorry it didn't work,' said Harry.

'Oh, I'm not sure about that,' said Freddie with a smile, looking past them. Harry and Josie turned round and to their astonishment, Diana and Ant were walking down the path wreathed in smiles, holding hands.

'What?' Harry and Josie both stood staring in disbelief.

'Guess what?' said Ant. 'The hypnotism worked. We've just plighted our troth to each other.'

'See, I told you,' said Freddie, smugly, 'I am the best.'

'Go on then,' said Ant, handing over twenty quid. 'Here's your money. You deserve it, mate.'

'You – really?' said Harry, gobsmacked. That was the last thing he'd been expecting. He was overcome with the urge to give his friend a huge bear hug. 'Well done, mate,' he said. 'What happened to your nose?'

'Don't know,' said Ant. 'I must have walked into one of those Stones in the dark. I've been having some very weird dreams.'

'So that's what I think I can call a success,' said Freddie. 'What about you two? Have you renewed your engagement?'

'Not exactly,' said Harry. 'We've decided to put off the wedding and go travelling for a bit. That is, as long as we still get our fee?'

Freddie was about to protest, but Bron nudged him, and he mumbled, 'Of course.'

'You two, travelling? Wow,' said Diana. 'That's amazing. Good luck with telling Josie's mum.'

'She can keep her hat for your wedding,' joshed Josie. 'I'm sure I can talk her round.'

'I do hope so,' said Harry, 'because I don't fancy having to kidnap you before our trip. Come on, let's go home, it's time to face the music.'

'Thanks,' said Diana to Freddie as they left. 'You've changed our lives for the better.'

Freddie bowed.

'Well, I'm glad to have been of service,' he said. 'I think the programme might need some fine tuning, but we can meet in the pub later and talk it all through.'

'What about you, Bron?' said Diana. 'What are you going to do?' She had a funny feeling she owed him a great deal.

He nodded in the direction of the theatre.

'Tati's asleep in there. But when she wakes up, I'm going to do something I should have done a very long time ago.'

'Best of luck,' said Di, and she kissed him on the cheek. 'I don't know why, but I think you deserve it.'

They set off down the path to Josie's house.

'I'm so happy for you, Di,' said Josie, giving her a hug.

Diana felt emotional as she hugged her friend back.

'Are you sure you're okay about not marrying Harry?' she said.

'Fine,' said Josie, 'we're going to have so many adventures together. I can't wait.'

'I could eat a horse,' said Ant, 'I can't believe how hungry I am.'

'I ache all over,' said Josie. 'It's strange but I feel like I've been running a lot. Which is weird, because I'm sure Harry and I spent the whole night on the beach.'

'That's funny,' said Diana. 'My calves are really aching too.'

'And I've got bruises everywhere,' said Ant.

'Harry, I've only just noticed,' said Josie, 'your shirt's ripped. How did that happen?'

Diana had a sudden flashback to running around in the dark, trying to look for someone.

'You don't suppose . . .' she said slowly.

'What?' asked Ant.

'That there's something Freddie's not telling us?' she said. 'How would we know if he'd hypnotised us and made us forget what happened?'

'That might explain why we're all aching so much,' said Josie.

'And why Ant and I have got bruises,' said Harry. 'If I didn't know any better, I'd think we'd been in a fight.'

'You two?' said Diana. 'Don't be so ridiculous.'

'Nah,' said Ant, shaking his head with conviction. 'That would be like us all having the same mad delusion. Don't believe it can be done.'

'Me neither,' said Josie. 'We must have strained ourselves from canoeing yesterday. Come on, race you home. If you're lucky, I might cook us eggs and bacon.'

And with that, the four friends ran laughing down the hill in the sunshine.

The world suddenly seemed a brighter, happier place.

As if by magic.

Now: Bron and Tatiana

'Tati, darling.' He'd been sitting looking at her as she slept. She had never looked more beautiful to him.

'Mmm,' she said sleepily. She stirred and stretched with a yawn. 'I've been having the strangest dreams. You actually stood up to Freddie for once.'

'That was no dream,' said Bron. 'I did. He deserved it. I should have done it a long, long time ago.'

'Yes,' said Tati, looking at him levelly. 'You should have.'

Bron took his courage in both hands. It was now or never.

'Look, Tati, I know I let you down, over the abortion. God knows I wanted to have a baby with you. But I thought Freddie would replace you in the act if he found out you were pregnant. And I couldn't stand it. It was the worst mistake of my life, and I've been paying for it ever since. Can you ever forgive me?'

'Oh, darling Bron,' she said. 'I forgave you a long time ago. But pride, jealousy and the few shreds of dignity I had left stopped me from saying so. And I treated you pretty shabbily too.'

'No more than I deserved,' said Bron.

Tati took his hand, 'Oh, you dear, dear man. It was cruel

and unkind of me to sell our story to the papers like that. Can *you* forgive *me*?'

Without hesitation, Bron leant over and kissed her.

'Nothing to forgive,' he said. 'Now, let's put the past behind us and get on with the rest of our lives.'

Epilogue: Three years later

'Now, until the break of day,
Through this house each fairy stray.
To the best bride-bed will we,
Which by us shall blessed be;
And the issue there create
Ever shall be fortunate.
So shall all the couples three
Ever true in loving be.'

                A Midsummer Night's Dream: Act V, Scene 1

'Dreams, Illusions, fancies. It's a bit of fun really. Some
mind trickery perhaps, but not to be taken too seriously.
I'm an entertainer, that's all. Mea culpa *if I've ever
offended you. But come on, have I . . . really?'*

                Freddie Puck: *The Art of Illusion*

'I'm so excited!' Diana was bouncing up and down like a two-year-old on speed. 'I can't wait to see them.'

'Me neither,' said Ant. 'Calm down. Their plane's only just landed. They'll be through soon.'

'I'll go and get us coffees,' said Diana. She went across to Costa Coffee. 'A latte and an Americano, please.'

'I don't believe it,' a familiar voice said behind her. 'Diana, is that you?'

'Bron!' said Diana. 'How fantastic to see you. What are you doing here?'

'Meeting Tati from New York,' he said. 'She's just been playing in *Cat on a Hot Tin Roof* on Broadway.'

'Oh yes, I saw that in the papers,' said Diana. 'So everything's going well, then?'

'Brilliant,' said Bron. 'You know we bought Tresgothen Manor, didn't you? You and Ant must come and see us.'

'That would be fantastic,' said Diana. 'I see Freddie has another series of *Let Me Hypnotise You* coming out.'

'He certainly does,' said Bron. 'It's amazing how successful that's been. People are starting to call for a revival of *Illusions*, so when Tati's had time to catch up, that's going to be our next project.'

'That's so brilliant,' said Diana. 'I'm really happy for you.'
'And you?'

'Ant and I are meeting Josie and Harry. They're finally coming home from their travels.'

'I can see congratulations are in order,' said Bron with a smile.

Diana blushed; it was hard to miss the enormous ring Ant had given her.

'Ant would insist on a rock,' she said. 'You and Tati should come to the wedding. Without you we might never have got together.'

'That would be lovely,' said Bron. He gave her a kiss. 'Tati's plane has just landed. I'd best be there or there'll be hell to pay.'

He slipped off out into the crowd, and Diana went back to find Ant.

'They're in baggage,' he said. 'Hopefully we don't need to wait much longer.'

'You'll never guess who I just met in Costa's,' said Di.

'Who?' said Ant.

'Only Bron,' said Diana.

'No! What's he doing here?' said Ant.

'Meeting Tati. You'll be pleased to know they're going to do a new series of *Illusions*.'

'Can't wait,' said Ant.

People had started to dribble through from customs. And they scoured the crowds, patiently until . . .

'There!' Ant pointed at Harry, who was pushing an enormous amount of luggage, with a fair-haired toddler sitting on the handlebars. Josie was following behind, pushing a six-month-old baby in a buggy.

Diana and Ant raced towards them, and soon they were all hugging and laughing together.

'Let's see the ring,' demanded Josie. 'Wow, that's a monster. Trust Ant to be so ostentatious.'

'And these must be Tony and Di!' Diana said, as the little boy hid behind Harry's legs and the baby burbled happily in the pushchair. 'I can't believe you named them after us.'

'I can't believe you've managed to get her knocked up, not once, but twice since you've been away,' said Ant, before Diana dug him in the ribs.

'How old are they again?' said Di.

'Tony's eighteen months and Di's six months,' said Josie.

Ant whistled, 'That's going it some,' he said, 'well done, Harry!'

'Oh do shut up,' said Di, 'I think it's perfectly lovely. Parenthood suits you, you both look fantastic.'

They did. The pair of them were tanned, and glowing, and relaxed with the children.

'Fine,' said Harry. 'I've got enough material from our travels for my new book, about going round the world with small children in tow.'

'And we've decided we're going to settle down in Cornwall,' said Josie. 'We got fed up of big cities on our travels.'

'Well, I'm glad you made it back in time to be my bridesmaid,' said Di. 'I couldn't have done it without you.'

'And to think it was meant to be the other way round,' laughed Josie.

'You still not made an honest woman of her yet?' said Ant.

'Ah,' said Harry, 'we did have a wedding ceremony in Thailand, just us and the children on the beach. But I think now we're back . . .'

'Mum's been emailing me every day, asking whether we've fixed a date yet,' sighed Josie. 'I suppose I have kept her waiting a long time.'

'You are not going to steal our thunder, I hope,' said Ant.

'No chance,' said Josie, 'I have no intention walking up the aisle pregnant.'

'You're never –?' said Diana.

'Seem to be,' said Josie. 'It's so hard to sort out contraception when you're travelling.'

'Harry, old man,' said Ant, 'nice to see you're firing on all cylinders.'

'Now I know I'm home,' said Harry. 'I so haven't missed Ant being rude to me.'

'And we're glad to have you back,' said Diana. 'Now I can start planning my wedding in earnest.'

'So long as you aren't thinking of having fire-eaters,' said Josie.

'I wouldn't dream of it,' said Diana. 'It's going to be a small wedding . . .'

'. . . With only 150 guests,' whispered Ant.

'Shh,' said Diana, thumping him. 'And now you two are back, I just know it's going to be perfect.'

'You want to know how it's done? I can't tell you that. Shh, or you'll spoil the magic.'

Freddie Puck: *The Art of Illusion*

Acknowledgements

This time around my first thanks have to be to the Bard, Ole Will himself, without whom I'd have never thought of – pinched – this idea. And also thanks to my parents Ann and Joseph Moffatt, who ignited my love of Shakespeare in the first place, and my two inspirational English teachers, Keith Ward and Sue Brown, who fanned the flames. Sue, I hope I've done justice to your favourite play!

At an early stage, I was inspired by the wonderful Pierces, whose song *You'll Be Mine* sends shivers up my spine and sparked an idea. I also delved deeply into Derren Brown's fascinating book *Tricks of the Mind* to get a proper understanding of how a real hypnotist works.

I am hugely grateful to the number of people on Twitter and Facebook who generously responded when I asked for experiences of hypnotism, and particularly to Clare Cody-Richardson, Rowan Coleman, Linda Green and Julie Mayhew, who generously shared their stories with me. And big thanks to my friend Rob Buckle for putting me right at the last minute on TV fees.

As ever, my thanks go to my wonderful agent Dot Lumley, who has always given me stonking support, and my editor Claire Bord and the brilliant team at Avon:

Caroline Ridding, Claire Power, Cleo Little, Helen Bolton, Sammia Rafique and Becke Parker.

And finally, thanks to the people who read this in its earliest form: my twin sister Virginia Moffatt who is always my greatest cheerleader; the wonderful Rachael Lucas whose life is similar to mine, only with more children and pets; Sue Brown whose talk of Cornwall is always inspirational, Iris Rooney whose insights were incredibly valuable; and my lovely Twitter friends: Susan Creamer who taught me that procrastination is really processing, and Sarah Williams – I hope your wedding plans work out somewhat better then Josie and Harry's!

And finally a very special thank you to a wonderful couple, Laura and Iwan Griffith for allowing me to share in their special day and giving me an insight into the joys of Welsh weddings!

Afterword

Ideas come from all over the place for writers. And like the greedy magpies we are, we hone in on their shiny brightness and grab every trinket we can get. Often they begin small and burgeon into something as time goes on, and such was the case for me writing this book.

All I knew at the beginning was that my editor, Claire, wanted me to write a summery book. And for a long time I was completely devoid of ideas. Then I heard a song on the radio, and a nugget of an idea began to form. (The song was called *You'll be Mine* by the Pierces, and if you go to my website www.juliawilliamsauthor.com and look in the About section; you will find a list of the soundtracks to my books, and you can listen to it there.)

Music is fantastically important to me when I'm writing, and often forms the inspiration for stories, scenes and characters. This time around the song, which I find very haunting, made me think of enchantments and spells and falling in love. Unusually for me (I have terrible trouble with titles normally), the idea of calling a book *Midsummer Magic* tumbled into my head. I thought immediately of Cornwall, (a place I find both mysterious and fascinating), Standing Stones, and magic. From there it wasn't too big a stretch to thinking about *A Midsummer Night's Dream*, and how I could write a modern take on it.

Initially, I thought this might be easy – after all, the plot's all there (thank you, Mr Shakespeare), but what works well in a play – an impish sprite dropping magical potion into people's eyes, seemed a bit more problematic in a novel. My first thought was to have my characters somehow take some hallucinogenic drugs, but that proved tricky, as it made my Puckish character seem rather sleazy, and Puck isn't a sleazy character . . .

In the end I hit on hypnotism as the key. I thought it could be a fun way of unlocking my characters' innermost desires in a way that perhaps they hadn't quite intended. I started to research the work of both Paul McKenna and Derren Brown for background and thus the characters of Freddie Puck, Auberon and Tatiana were born. I am indebted to Derren Brown's fascinating book, *Tricks of the Mind* for explaining the process of hypnotism to me and a lot else besides. If you're interested in mind games, it's well worth a read!

From then on in, I had my story, and though it has inevitably changed somewhat during the telling, the kernel of the original idea, which came from a simple song, remains. It's been a blast to write from start to finish. I hope you enjoyed reading it as much as I enjoyed writing it.

Amy Nicholson never expected to leave London for the Suffolk countryside. But she also never expected to be a 33-year-old widow, left alone with a young son. Fleeing her memories, she swaps her heels for wellies and embarks on a new rural life.

The big-hearted community of Nevermorewell welcome them with open arms. There's old Harry, offering pearls of advice (fuelled by whisky from his hip flask), Saffron, juggling motherhood with business (whilst searching for her lost libido), and Caroline, the scheming local vamp, who tramples over lives as easily as the allotments backing onto Amy's cottage.

But just when Amy thinks she's finally leaving the past behind, Ben Martin crashes into her life. Sexy and enigmatic, Ben is haunted by his own secrets. Will love blossom on the allotments? Or will it be once bitten, twice shy?

Curl up and smile through the tears with this warm and witty read, perfect for Jill Mansell and Fiona Walker fans.

Lawyer Emily promised her late father that she'd devote her life to good causes. So how come she spends her days defending Z-listers, desperate to prolong their 15 minutes of fame?

Katie is obsessed with being the perfect wife and mother - unlike her own one. In which case, why is husband Charlie permanently AWOL these days?

Dentist Mark is licking his wounds after his wife walked out on him and desperately missing his kids. Can he cope with becoming a singleton again – on top of a devastating legal case against him?

Meanwhile, happy-go-lucky Jack the Lad Rob is hiding a secret tragedy . . .

Isabella's dance class gives the four the perfect opportunity to forget their troubles and re-invent themselves. They can be whoever they want to be – they'll just let their feet do the talking.

Over the weeks, as they foxtrot, tango, waltz and cha-cha-cha their way into each other's lives, they discover the truth about each other – and themselves. But will they like what they learn?

**As children, Sarah, Dorrie, Beth and Caz were inseparable
and vowed to one day be each other's bridesmaids. But life got
complicated. Now they have one last chance to fulfil their promise.**

Dorrie is planning her ultimate Disney wedding to the delicious
Darren and is determined to have her friends back together for
the Big Day. But Dorrie's fairytale is not all that it seems . . .

Beth is desperate for a baby and is starting to resent her more fertile
friends. Is a mistake from her past about to destroy her future?

Caz's wild streak has tested her friendships over the years. One
by one she has let her friends down, not least when she commits
the ultimate betrayal to Susan. Can she change her ways and
more to the point, does she really want to?

Married to Steve, Sarah is plagued by doubts that she went down
the wrong path. Does Sarah have the strength to make a change
and will she ever be able to forgive Caz?

As Dorrie's big day dawns, all eyes are on whether the ultimate
act of friendship will be honoured and obeyed . . .

As summertime flourishes, it's time for new beginnings . . .

Lovelace Cottage is in desperate need of renovation. Its owner, widower Joel, is struggling to come to terms with life as a single dad. His plans to refurbish the house and garden suddenly seem like one burden too many.

Mum to twin girls, Lauren's life is a constant juggling act. When her ex, Troy, turns up she's determined to keep her distance while he gets to know his daughters. But it's a lot harder than she imagined . . .

Then erstwhile guerrilla gardener Kezzie bursts into their lives with her infectious enthusiasm to restore the gardens. But who is Kezzie? And what is she running away from?

As the warm days of summer draw closer, Lovelace Cottage and its beautiful love-knot garden are transformed. But will Joel, Kezzie and Lauren be able to restore their own hearts?

Kick off your sandals, enjoy a glass of rosé and escape into a gorgeous novel this summer with Julia Williams.